Praise for **Chop Chop**

'**Raucous and inventive**, peopled with technicolour characters and **savagely funny**, *Chop Chop* **announces Simon Wroe as both an heir to Martin Amis and an oven-fresh talent unto himself'** A D Miller

'Depicts the literal underworld of a restaurant kitchen with **wit, vigor,** and **gleeful, necessary profanity'**
New York Times

'**Dark, pungent, twisted, surprising and above all genuinely funny.** If you enjoy eating out, don't read this book' William Sutcliffe

'Perfectly baked [with] **a rich, gooey pool of dark comedy** hiding beneath the surface … Wroe's novel makes for **fresh, appetising reading'** *Independent*

'**Brutally funny …** Sometimes the truth is so strange it needs to be sautéed in a pan of fiction' Gary Shteyngart

'**Dave Eggers** channels **Anthony Bourdain'** *Kirkus*

'A complete page-turner. Reminiscent of *Kitchen Confidential* but with an **entirely fresh** voice that is **a pleasure to read**'   ✷   Thomasina Miers

'A greasy, **hilarious** tale of loyalty, revenge and dark appetites. A **gripping** look behind the kitchen wall'   ✷   *Shortlist*

'**Brace yourself** for this **lively, amusing and alarmingly informative novel**'   *Daily Mail*

'A great kitchen novel. From describing the battle-scarred hands of a chef to the overall rhythm that goes into making every plate of food, Wroe . . . **makes this ugly world delicious**'
Book of the Week, *Flavorwire*

'Lip-smacking . . . As **shocking and witty** as it is savage'
Vogue

HERE COMES TROUBLE

Simon Wroe is a freelance journalist and former chef.

He writes food and culture features for the *Guardian* and arts reviews for the *Economist*. His first book, *Chop Chop*, was shortlisted for the 2014 Costa First Novel Award, longlisted for the Desmond Elliott Prize and won a Betty Trask Award.

He was born in 1982 and lives in Camberwell, south London.

SIMON WROE

HERE
COMES
TROUBLE

W&N
WEIDENFELD & NICOLSON

First published in Great Britain in 2017
by Weidenfeld & Nicolson
an imprint of the Orion Publishing Group Ltd
Carmelite House, 50 Victoria Embankment
London EC4Y ODZ

An Hachette UK Company

1 3 5 7 9 10 8 6 4 2

A CIP catalogue record for this book is
available from the British Library.

ISBN (Hardback) 978 1 474 60495 6
ISBN (Export Trade Paperback) 978 1 474 60496 3
ISBN (eBook) 978 1 474 60498 7
ISBN (Audio) 978 1 409 16873 7

Typeset by Input Data Services Ltd, Bridgwater, Somerset

Printed in Great Britain by Clays Ltd, St Ives plc

www.orionbooks.co.uk

This novel owes a debt to two newspapers. First, the *New York Times*, which in a 2015 article accidentally invented the country of Kyrzbekistan where this story unfolds. A journalistic error created a fitting setting for the tale of an imperilled newspaper. But above all, a debt is owed to Kyrgyzstan's *kloop.kg*, a news site which holds power to account in a region where power is used to having things its way. I am extremely grateful to the dedicated and fearless *kloop* reporters for taking me out on their stories and letting me into their lives.

I   FIRST GLIMPSES   3

II   CUTS   109

III THESE WORDS ARE FORBIDDEN   217

HOWLS, hollers, thunk-thunk of bass. Torchlight catches the form of a swaying girl, eyes closed, pollution mask across her nose and mouth. The light careens to a boy, late teens, strutting to the beat bare-chested. He shouts a greeting or threat. Another face – skinhead, male – leers in to point out a couple tussling on a table. The floor around is awash with empty bottles and cigarette packets and little red and white flags, the cheap plastic sort given out at parades. A dog noses a birthday cake through the rubbish, nibbling at the frosting, head cocked like a thoughtful gourmet. It turns and cowers happily in the glare. It licks its whitened snout. Its eyes are beads of glass. It knows it has done wrong.

Glimpses of the room show columns and statues and a grand corniced ceiling high above. A monstrous writhing wall shadow is revealed as the conjuring of many dancers stomping and thrusting and shaping the air with automaton abandon. Now they see the light and pull the torchbearer in. The beam scans the forest of faces, turning from stare to stare, round and round, faster and faster, spinning or being spun as the crowd yells and blurs. Then a flash of movement – a punch? a stumble? – and the video cuts out.

Other footage from the Kyrzbekistan capital around that time: crowds running in panic, empty central streets, a blazing pyre, a hooded figure kneeling on a stage.

FIRST
GLIMPSES

'TELL ME . . . Explain it to me.'

'Ellis, tell your father.'

'You didn't mention any problems.'

'That's right. Not a word.'

'Then this?'

'Help us understand.'

His father had the letter in his hand. *We are writing to inform you. The decision not taken lightly. Given the circumstances what choice . . .*

Spare me, thought Ellis Dau. The letter's soothing words weren't for his parents or for him. They were for whoever had written them.

Here was the worst of it: the letter strongly recommended *he was supervised at all times.* He heard the locks sliding, the cell doors clanging. This was the scene in the movie where the prisoner shuffled into lockdown, the other convicts eyeballing him and licking their lips. What St Joseph's were saying was that he had not got away with it. If they were no longer his gaolers, gaolers he should still have.

'Is it drugs? The web?'

'Did you see something on the web? One of those chat forums?'

'Terrorists go on those things, you know. They brainwash people.'

And so on and so forth. He had betrayed them. He couldn't be trusted. The sentence was imprisonment without possibility of parole. Grounded for the rest of eternity. No visitors allowed – not even Vincent, especially Vincent. The parental eye was constantly on him, anxiously observing, the way old people stare at their mobile phones as though this thing may at any moment cause them grief.

The prisoner was consigned to the tower, the sixth-floor apartment known in better times as home.

The first morning, after his father left for work, he turned to the television and found it unresponsive.

'The TV isn't working,' he told his mother, Stella. She was typing at the kitchen table, transcribing interviews and minutes for far-away firms while she chewed her little rose sweets, undercutting the man in New York or London to the rhythmic crunch of her teeth.

'I'm sorry to hear that,' she said.

'How will I play the console?'

'It's a good question.'

'Maybe I could have my computer back?'

His mother was busy with her words and did not reply.

'At least my phone?'

She looked up and said, 'I think you already know the answer.'

'But what will I do?'

'Play with the parrot.'

'The parrot doesn't trust me.'

'He is a highly intelligent creature.'

'Really though, what will I look at?'

'People have been known to read books before now.'

'I'm serious.'

'So am I.'

'I mean what screen will I look at?'

'No screens.'

'This is child cruelty. I will call the child services.'

'You will probably need a telephone for that.'

'This is a gross injustice. I have rights.'

'Listen to him!' she said, half pleased. 'You have the right to remain silent, darling, and let your mother get on with some work.'

He was left to his own devices, without any actual devices. Mad with boredom, he examined and re-examined various knick-knacks and baubles: the picture of grazing horses cut from pieces of felt, the jaunty lake-side souvenirs, the ridiculous portrait of Uncle Joe. It was no good. Like those silly shop signs which get a laugh seen once but day after day raise only a scowl, these details merely confirmed how dull and predictable his life was. With the end of school he had expected more – he didn't know what, *just more*. A life without stabilisers. A fast track to freedom. But freedom proved a mirage; as he reached forward it shimmered and disappeared.

That was another thing: it was hot. In some places summer suggested a happy and desirable condition, here it was a word to whisper. Each day the heat crept higher, editing exchanges to their most basic components, bringing Mrs L. in 23 out to the tenement steps to sit with her lumpy potato feet in a saucepan of water. Bodies moved slowly as if in shock. The sense of being sullied by the heat was so great it became habitual – even in the relative cool of night or the first moments after bathing, people handled themselves as though they were sticky or unclean goods. Every summer a lunatic got hold of the thermostat, but usually Ellis could at least go outside, he could hop on the bike and create a little breeze. When he had to just lie there sweating and twisting up the sheets – oh, it was awful. Was he saying no teenager ever had it worse or was so hard done by? Was he saying he was the victim in all this? No, he was just floating these suggestions and asking for them to be considered. His suffering was so exquisite he almost feared it might be taken from him. Mr Anton, his former teacher, used to say a boy with nothing to kick against was a picture without a frame. But he didn't want to think about Mr Anton now.

The prisoner found solace at the window. He could hear the world grinding away out there, the traffic at all hours, the horns permanently applied until they became white noise, the megaphoned and monotoned woman who toured the neighbourhood proclaiming, 'I have carrots, I have cauliflowers, I have greens.' He heard the call to prayer and the revellers' return, for his country had both the muezzins who stood at the tip of dawn to sing towards the light and also enough grain spirit to put a person deep in the ground. Every evening he watched the setting sun move through the spectrum, lingering around the deep yellows, making shadow-theatre of the rusted satellite dishes and bent antennas before the plunge into night via darkest red. When it rained he smelled the salt in the air and watched the downpour pull a veil over the trees and tenements, raising cries as people ran for cover or home. Then he felt happy, or happier, because the rain was a great leveller and he and it were on the same page. On clear days he could spy the stretch of mountains to the north, white-topped all year round, peaked and jagged like the reading on a heart monitor. There were stories of how these mountains were giants who lay down to rest and slept so long that rocks and forests formed around them – the sort of yarns adults fed children. It was said one day the giants would wake and carry on their journey.

The window also brought pain. In the sounds of children playing, girls laughing, young lotharios showing off their wheels. He watched them in the courtyard, enjoying their freedom. That wasn't on. He hooted to attract attention, he threw toilet roll from the windows. In his heart he was still in the prison movie and hoping for a Hollywood payoff: a great breakout, a heartfelt protest, an eleventh-hour pardon. 'Free Ellis!' he hoped they would cry. Fat chance. It was almost like they didn't care.

Forget them, he could have fun too. Pacing his prison he sought a worthy pastime. A decent silhouette of Africa and a good slab of southern Europe were scratched out of the dining table's paintwork before his mother put a stop to it. Spitball after spitball was shot at the tin panels patching the neighbour's balcony. 'Is that the best use of your time?' Stella would ask, her tone somewhere in the area of concern but with a five-star view into the valley of despair. 'Don't you think you should act your age?' Answer: 'Yes' and 'Yes, I don't think.' This trick of using his age as a deterrent worked when he was younger, it cut deep – he hadn't known the rules of different ages and didn't know how other people knew. But that was when he was perhaps fifteen, when he knew nothing about anything. The hands spun fast on a teenage clock: last week was that regrettable previous decade, last month a lifetime ago, while the boy of earlier years was scarcely recognisable, a crude model of Neanderthal ancestor. He used to be *that*? Never!

His greatest innovation in those first weeks was the sport of body-bowling. A game of skill and precision, bravery and insight, it involved rolling up in the living room rug and unfurling himself as quickly as possible into the furniture. Hours of practice were devoted to this: he could knock over two chairs and a lamp with reasonable frequency, and sometimes got a picture to fall off the wall. If it was not happiness, it was the best way to be unhappy yet devised.

This creative thinking must have rubbed off on his mother, for at the end of the second week of imprisonment she gently but firmly prised open the carpet chrysalis (where he, the bowling ball and the butterfly, was psyching up for a full strike) to inform him she had a wonderful idea. From now on he would spend the days at work with his father.

The cell door swung open. Hello world! Hello secondary security gate because one can never be too sure about world. Hello shifty elevator, always in such a rush you start before the doors have fully closed. How happy Ellis was to see its chipped (gnawed?) buttons advertising the different floors, its hopeful flyers for IT tutors and *LEARN ENGLISH GOOD*, its wood-effect panelling, its graffiti which claimed it loved hip-hop. Could an elevator truly know what it was to love? This was a question for the ages. How happy also to see the dusty streets where he'd left them, as if waiting for him. Hi there! Hello! He was back, everyone. You may resume!

The prisoner drank it in. There was the Autolux car hire, its luxury fleet of Bentleys and Mercedes and Chryslers entirely white because white in this dust was absolutely the biggest bitch to maintain, impossible, and nothing said luxury like impossible. There was the small army of men who moved these cars from one spot to another seeking that elusive algorithm which would provoke their fellow countrymen who earned an average of one dollar an hour to suddenly rent a Bentley. Right next to them, further complicating a by-no-means-easy task, the puffy Russian hooker in leopard print who had marked the strip as her territory. Single-handedly, no matter the season, she performed a tip-top job of ensuring the luxury-hire guys got the minimum amount of business.

On the left, the derelict Savoy nightclub and casino. The hot place, it was said, before they outlawed gambling. Groups of men, perhaps in tribute to the building's past, played cards in the grass alongside. Sometimes they broke off their cries of 'Thief!' and 'I'm rich!' to call out to passers-by: 'Hey friend, want a seat at the table?' Only there was no table and their faces, though smiling, were lined with darker cares and it was not advisable to accept the offer.

Over on the right – guidebooks advise extra care crossing roads here, the traffic lights being more of a suggestion – the orange and lime-green flying saucer that was home to the national circus. Three years ago in this building Sergov Ivanov broke the world record for 'Greatest weight ever lifted with a beard'. Ivanov's winning weight was eighty-one point five kilos, the weight of a favourite chubby aunt. He was eighty-three years old at the time. Cue lights, fame, dollars. The holy Guinness Book brought tourists, sponsorship deals. The Kyrzbeks were always cool about it, in Ellis's opinion. Never made a big song and dance. Then the Uzbeks lifted a bigger weight with the beard and they wouldn't shut up about it. Every time he met an Uzbek it was, 'Oh, we have the stronger beard than you.' Really, Uzbeks? Again with the beard story? As a people they had no class.

On the subject of best and greatest: Kyrzbekistan also held the title of 'Most corrupt country 2011 and 2012', a regional accolade rather than a world record. Though, as many Kyrzbeks proudly pointed out, leading this region on that topic equated to the same thing. For this particular achievement there were no honours, corruption being its own reward.

Through Victory Square, where newly-weds and their primped and pouting guests posed beside the eternal flame. Past gardeners in big hats crouched among the flowers, and a large bronze sculpture of a typical family, child on father's shoulders, looking out towards the city centre. The father pointed in the direction of the still unfinished Exclusivo apartment complex as if to say, 'You see that, son? What a bunch of bums.'

And here was the *Chronicle* office Ellis walked into that first day, all 'What case needs solving, people?' To which the answer was silence. Not that there weren't stories to write and calls to make, just that he wasn't needed to do it. The staff talked over his head, looked straight through him. Photocopying was too much to ask. Coffee was way too serious a task. He was invisible – no, hold on, he had the comparison – he was the Russian hooker, relatively speaking, to their affairs. They *wished* he was invisible.

Perhaps they knew. His father wouldn't have told them, he was too mortified. Probably they knew because it was their business to know these things, they were nosy by profession, and if Ellis hadn't been the editor's son, Cornelius Dau's kid, they'd have swarmed him, snapping photos, throwing questions.

Had someone put him up to it?
Did he have a history of this sort of thing?
Was he sending a message?
Did he feel anything in the moment, or after?

He might have preferred that to being ignored. He did his

best to ignore them right back, though it wasn't easy. People were always running in or shouting at each other. Some story was always blowing up, some news always breaking. There was Miss Armitage (politics, education, health, you name it) striding to her desk, in such haste to file copy she didn't take the camera from her shoulder. Beside her, the news editor Mr Jonquil was on the phone, arguing joyfully with one disgruntled press officer after another. 'Is it inaccurate? Is it? Tell me it's inaccurate and we'll print a full retraction. I'll take you out to dinner at the Excelsior. Otherwise there's nothing else to say.' In the corner Mr Geffen (sports and gossip, a double-up that showed the paper's commitment to these subjects) was either shouting obscure commands at his aging terminal – *Use him wide! Play the man!* – or breathlessly wrangling confessions from the hands-free. 'You – are – kidding,' he'd say over and over. (The office theory, increasingly convincing the more of Geffen's column one read, was that his headset wasn't plugged in.) Above the bustle, Mr Urvin was trying to persuade Cornelius not to cut some detail in his crime report: a burnt teddy bear or a *tempers flared*. It was a cliché. It was a heart-tugger. Back and forth the two men went.

'Oh come on!' Urvin would cry. 'Are we trying to bore people to death? Are things not screwed? Let's flam it up!'

How anyone could work in this commotion Ellis did not know. He couldn't even do nothing properly in it.

Meanwhile, in the back room, Mr Kozlov attended to the matters of tech: the cameras and camcorders and microphones and tripods, the editing suites and Dictaphones and memory sticks. NO VALUES LEFT IN THIS OFFICE OVERNIGHT, a notice on the wall announced in thick black type. Next to that an angry red scrawl: *Hey asshole, don't just dump it –* RECHARGE IT. Pride of place in this set-up was a delicately cheap drone that Kozlov spent most of his time trying to coax into health. The robot laid out like a sickly child while anxious Kozlov applied the tonics and soothing balms. At the far end stood the clapped-out proofing press from olden times, too heavy to get rid of, beside boxes of old type and a nasty blackened bin Cornelius called a *hell box* for reasons not immediately clear. This room was where Ellis decided to sit. Kozlov was an antisocial man, attentive solely to the demands of his machines, but that was okay, Ellis cherished the quiet. Also he wanted to use the Internet without his father seeing.

Cornelius – pale skin, bony typist's fingers, a distracted air he carried with him like a scent. Not much of a talker. Sons are meant to be close to their fathers, but Ellis didn't think it was possible to be so close to his. (Example: when he fell off his bike wearing his father's hat, what were the first and second things the old man wanted to know were okay?) Every evening after dinner his father polished his shoes at the kitchen table. Every morning he stood on his head in the living room for exactly ten minutes, performing this exercise with such graveness it never once occurred to Ellis to find it funny. On weekends the old man sat in his armchair with a great stack of newspapers, reading for hours. Crazy – he worked in a newspaper, why did he need to read more? His thinking was a mystery to Ellis. Sometimes, when Cornelius wasn't home, Ellis would put on his father's spare town shoes and walk about, seeing if he could absorb the serious adult power he imagined lay within.

But in the office Ellis saw a different man. The dry riverbed of conversation became a raging torrent. He was constantly on the telephone or talking with the other reporters, questioning, clarifying, arguing about how a story should be covered, chasing pieces not yet filed, explaining what was needed. Sometimes he made little cynical comments that drew laughs from the other hacks – usually a reference Ellis couldn't follow to some local politician or previous story. Then he'd raise his eyebrows and twist his thin lips, not laughing but acknowledging a joke had been made. Even when silent he was rattling off emails or bashing out copy as if the river of words had not run dry, merely gone underground.

Two news stories were all the talk that first day, as they would be until the summer went completely to hell. One was the fanatics, the beheaders, the 'my god is better than your god' set. Armitage was working on a long feature, the latest in a series, about those who ran off to join these men who shimmered in the desert. How did the influence get in? It was coming down the wires, trickling through the routers, leaking out into nice family homes.

Lonely?

Angry?

Confused?

Have you considered murder?

Madness, the hacks muttered. But was it so surprising people want to believe in something bigger than themselves? This song the dark desert characters knew well. They sang it through the screen, and those who disliked the tune considered it a fresh and modern sort of evil, though in truth what the screen told was nothing new. Everything it showed was already in the mind. All thought, it's said, begins as a duet.

The other big story was Tima Blum. The Russian had recently bought the local Athletik football team ('Arthritik' and 'Asthmatik' also accepted) to the great ecstasy and disbelief of the one man and his donkey who watched its matches. In the happiest of coincidences, no sooner had Comrade Blum announced the sky was the limit on wages, several superstars in the European leagues declared it their dream to play in this ramshackle city. Nor was that the end of Blum's ambitions. His name popped up everywhere. On the glut of high-rise developments going up across town, on sun-kissed billboards around the centre, on estate-agent placards in hushed reserves of greenbelt land on which people were absolutely under no condition allowed to build. On the recently completed Grand Theatre, rumoured to have cost FIFTY MILLION DOLLARS, which everyone agreed was total madness, balls-out-in-the-fruit-aisle crazy, since there was already one theatre in town for everyone not to go to. Fifty million down the pan and it mattered not to Blum. His name became shorthand for all that was lavish, magnificent, ridiculous, criminal, sublime.

Between the Russians and the extremists, the hacks had plenty to eat. And these were only the most prominent contenders. The place was a ball of wool between many sets of claws. The Turks raised skyscrapers of their own, the Chinese loaned vast sums, the Americans had a university and a nearby military base, European NGOs offered training and jobs and the whole-grain diet of democratic values. Every visiting foreign charity seemed an occupying army, every grassroots movement a direct challenge to the suspicious government, every street ranter a potential crown prince. Even on Ellis's first day at the paper, Urvin had some fresh claimant he wished to cover. Cornelius wasn't buying.

'Please, a little filler, a nib, that's all.'

'No, Urvin.'

'You don't understand. The quotes are golden . . . There is nothing, literally nothing, they won't blame on minorities.'

'Yeah?' said Geffen, fanning himself at his desk. 'Who's to blame for this weather? It's too much.'

'Weather . . .' Urvin consulted an imaginary notepad.

'I'm sure it's funny, Urvin,' said Cornelius. 'But why promote this rubbish?'

'We're not promoting. We're showing why it's foolish.'

'It's silly, bigoted drivel. Flat-earther stuff. Medieval.'

'That's where you're wrong,' said Urvin. 'This is twenty-first century ignorance. Incredible advances in knowledge have also meant incredible advances in stupidity, and this fact is often overlooked.'

'And you're going to be our Stupidity Correspondent?'

'I don't think that's necessary. We've already got Geffen. Any actors bought a coffee recently, Geffen? Has a woman been seen in a skirt?'

Geffen raised two fingers and applied a little vibrato for emphasis.

Urvin turned to Cornelius. 'We write about rubbish all the time. But this is important rubbish. The sort of rubbish people believe. The sort of rubbish that becomes fact, if you let it.'

'Then the believers and the bigots deserve each other,' Cornelius replied. 'They can wallow in their important rubbish together. But we won't roll around in it with them.'

With that the story was spiked.

This holding of strong opinions was also a side of his father Ellis had seldom seen. He enjoyed these insights into Cornelius's character. It's rare to see people one knows well in new capacities, and always a relief when these glimpses go some way to proving these individuals are not complete stooges, cretins or frauds. These glimpses joined the small museum of things he knew and admired about his father, to be looked at often, grateful for their presence, though their lessons remained under glass.

One exception to the 'never out of sight' rule: every Tuesday afternoon, in penance for his crimes, Ellis was required to spend an hour in the company of Dr Peabody. Flattered and delighted as he was to add another voice to his chorus of trolls, he wished his parents hadn't gone to such effort on his behalf. Groans, door-slamming and threats of emigration were the most eloquent expressions of this wish. To no avail.

'He's a smart boy . . .' From the waiting room next door he could hear his mother explaining. 'He's just . . .'

'Smart in some ways' – this was his father now – 'but impressionable.'

Impressionable? Him!

'It's a difficult age,' Peabody replied. 'Plenty of ways it could go.'

Spoken as if he were a pet or a country, a washing machine out of warranty. Ellis resolved to sabotage this shrink in any way he could.

Slumped on the worried couch, staring at drifting dust particles and twisted window-blinds, he was expected to submit notes on his existence. Peabody knew the who, what, where and when – it was the why he was after.

'Now young man,' he'd say, clapping his hands and letting his watery eyes focus on the patient. 'Let's begin. And please, feel free to tell me anything.'

The blinking old face waited for the confession.

'Try to put it into words.'

Silence filled the room and fat lazy bluebottles scudded about as if maybe they could be a source of motivation. The second hand of the clock dragged miserably round.

Feel free, said Peabody. What a joke! Ellis had thought sixteen was going to be the big one. The year of girls and liberty and manhood. The year when the world revealed its secrets and cheat codes. The year of his ascendance. Yet eleven months later, here he was on Peabody's couch. Something had gone horribly wrong.

How did he feel?

Ho ho. You wouldn't get him that easily, doctor.

Was he angry?

'I'm turning out all my pockets here,' his face would say.

How did he think they felt?

Tick tock went the clock.

'Well,' Peabody would say at last, 'perhaps next week.'

Ellis did not consider torture too strong a word for the circumstances. The world was treating him very badly. Having donated a large and generous slice of scandal to the community, he was now forced to go door to door with a placard round his neck. Could people not accept the provision without questioning its source? It seemed not. Peabody was determined to milk this sacred cow. He kept talking, kept saying Ellis could tell him anything, occasionally breaking off these encouragements to clear the contents of his throat into a dented brass pot at the foot of his chair. The patient felt the naggings of remorse: a lot of blank space was crying out to be filled and he was failing to fill it. Every session the silence got louder. He would have cracked in the end – they always do – but the sessions abruptly stopped. The old goat told Cornelius and Stella their son was 'resistant to discourses on empathy', and, like St Joseph's before him, washed his hands of the boy.

TIMA BLUM was the black hole at the centre of the universe. One day he would swallow everything. Faced with such a threat, Cornelius considered no story angle too obtuse, no line of attack too slight. In the grand journalistic tradition, the editor had a vague dislike of something which he now sought fairly and professionally and without bias to prove correct. When the opening of the new play at Blum's theatre was delayed, he was straight there looking to stoke the flames.

'No explanation given,' he told Ellis on the walk over. 'Did he run out of money? Is he bored of his new toy? Or maybe someone put the frighteners on him. But who would put the frighteners on the Russians?' He was excited and wore his best silk pocket square in case they met anyone important. (In the grand journalistic tradition, he also sought the approval of the rich and famous he pilloried.)

On the sticky afternoon in question it was supposed to be Urvin pushing the theatre people for comment. But Urvin hadn't shown up for work and Jonquil made the motion of a bottle being drunk and no more was said about it. So Cornelius went instead, his prisoner moping silently in tow.

Ellis was not much interested in his father's work at this time. Journalism, as far as he was concerned, was a lot of people making a big deal out of stuff that wasn't a big deal. That or they squashed an actual big deal into a small space, or said the big deal was exactly this or that, or claimed they were experts on the big deal with the absolute definitive take when they'd first heard about it five minutes ago. Or they used the big deal to flog their own hobby horses *because when you thought about it wasn't this what the big deal was actually about*. And all the while, in every instance, they pretended the big deal was not chaotic and constantly changing but fixed and orderly, which was never true or in any way the case.

Now Cornelius ran through the possible frighteners. He couldn't see the Turks or Chinese angry if business were not involved. The jihadi influence was still young and diffuse. The police were no doubt happily paid off. It wasn't the Americans' style, and too far from the political frontline to incite the usual protest movements. So who?

Had he spent as much time online as his son, skimming the frothy content, trawling the lower depths, he would have known the list did not end there or indeed at all. Anyone with a keyboard and a grudge could join the party. It was an equal-opportunities bear pit.

'Free speech is retreating,' he announced, stooping to check his hair in the window of a parked car. With wetted fingertips he combed the grey on his temples. Cornelius was not afraid of being thought vain or grandiose. These were sins of aspiration. Decent, wholesome sins. What kept him awake at night was the sin of sloth, or any other which might lead to the *Chronicle* being scooped by its downmarket rivals at the *Gazette*. 'Not just here – it's retreating everywhere. A worldwide erosion. A geological shift. People speak more but say less.'

'I suppose.'

'You can miss it if you're not careful.' His father straightened up and they continued. 'You have to keep marking the tideline and gathering the data. Then you see how much is disappearing.'

Cornelius's mind had slid off down a favourite avenue and Ellis wasn't paying much attention, but this sounded a chime of recognition. Wasn't his father describing the plight of Mr Anton? Ellis's former teacher who had them studying Voltaire and discussing free will, who sometimes for a joke puffed out his chest and rolled his *R*s in an uncanny impression of the president. Who had told the class more than once about the theory of Perfectibility, the idea that with every turn of history mankind moved closer to its ideal forms of justice, equality, liberty, civilisation – who had told them this was in fact false, that Acceptability was more like it, that with every turn of history people accepted more. 'A lot of folk don't like that idea,' he would deadpan, 'but they accept it.' Good old Mr Anton, who kept on laughing and joking and filling their heads with ideas right up until the day he didn't turn up for lessons and was not heard from again.

They stopped just short of their destination at a junction where the traffic lights had broken. A police officer was hard at work trying to control the flow. His baton never stopped, it was constantly conducting. The officer's white shirt was dark around the armpits and small of the back. But he could not rest. Already the traffic was creeping forward. Busted Skodas and big new Chinese SUVs, tinted Mercs and sardine-can taxibuses whose drivers had one arm sunburned from leaning it out the window all day. Everyone was on the creep, looking for the momentary lapse, the crack of weakness, the authority not quite meant. The officer's little patch of crossroad was shrinking. Even with the raised baton, even with shrill whistle and palm of hand, he could barely hold them. He was the conductor, but the orchestra was relentless and refusing to play nicely. At last he turned and signalled to the pedestrians, who crossed over into the shade of the Grand Theatre.

Lightning. Thunder. The skyline wobbled slightly as the priest appeared. He straightened his dog collar and slicked back his hair and glided over to a four-poster bed where a tiny old face, almost lost in the sheets, blinked in terror.

'Is that . . . Is that you, Father?'

'Yes, dear lady, it's me.'

'Come closer, come closer . . . Oh, but you are not the priest.'

'The other priest is sick.'

'But I don't know you.'

'It's all right, dear lady, you must not be afraid.' The priest's eyes burned in their hollows. 'You know my collar, you know the cross around my neck. You know who I am because I have always been with you. Now, at the end, I am with you still.'

'The end? The doctor says the fever should pass.'

'Doctors lie, dear lady. With the best will in the world, they lie. Take it from me, as a priest: it is time. I see your spirit rising.'

'You do?'

'Let me help.'

'How?'

'Many find peace through confession.'

The old woman shrank further into the sheets.

'I have nothing to confess.'

'We all have something to confess.'

'Even the priest?'

'Dear lady, your mind is sharp for one so ... Yes, even the priest.'

'What do you have to confess, Father?'

'My dear, I am here not as confessor but as priest. Let me be a priest. Let the robes I wear mean something. The priest needs the sins of others in order to be holy. Our country is—'

'No!' A voice shouted from the darkness. 'No, no, no!'

'No?' said the priest.

'The whole country bit is cut! You know this, Peter.'

The lights came up on a small bald man in the stalls. His suffering tone gave him away as the director.

'Can I see the script again?' said the priest.

The old lady groaned and whacked her face into the pillow, sending up white powder in a way that shook years off her.

Cornelius saw his chance. 'Mr Romanov,' he called, stepping forward from the back of the auditorium. 'A word?'

The director wheeled round. An untucked white shirt bibbed his well-fed face. Tubby, scowling, he looked like a baby eating a mouthful of spinach.

'Who are you?' he demanded.

'I'm from the *Chronicle*. The news site?'

Cornelius advanced, Ellis close behind.

'You sent us a press release about postponing opening night. We've been trying to reach you for a comment.'

'The press release is the comment. Go away.'

'Only it doesn't mention why it's delayed.'

'How did you get in here?' Romanov looked about the auditorium. 'Dimitri, how did they get in?'

Dimitri's frizzled head popped up from the sound booth to announce, with as much competence as the statement allowed, that he had no clue.

'Just a few words, Mr Romanov,' said Cornelius.

From what Ellis gathered, this Romanov was a big fish if you went in for plays and that sort of thing, and the approach, which the hacks called 'doorstepping', required some delicacy his father was thought to possess. Although he didn't know then what doorstepping was, and was still suspicious about this whole journalism business, he took a second-hand pride in the fact his father was good at something. He felt raised by association, as a football fan says 'we' when talking of his team's skill though he has no such skill himself.

In the event it was a blunt sort of delicacy. A key part of this doorstepping method seemed to be ignoring the insults and dismissals and just keeping on talking, looking for a way in, for the comment that would lure a response. The whole episode was embarrassing to Ellis. From the stage, the actors regarded him with the pity and revulsion normally reserved for cripples and beggar children.

Later he would scold himself for not paying more attention in these early days. For not being the good journalist son. His mind should have been spongy in anticipation of signs and portents and telling reveals. How this person spoke a certain way. How that particular question made the interviewee hold the flat of his hand against the base of his spine or fumble fearfully.

'I'm telling you,' said Romanov, 'you should leave.'

'Is that a threat, Mr Romanov? Shall I say you threatened us?'

'Don't put words in my mouth, you piece of shit. I'm not the one you should be worrying about.'

Ellis had never heard anyone speak to his father like this. Once in the market someone called him a *son of a whoredog* (something about coverage of a trader dispute) – but the man was wild and easy to dismiss. An attack like that did nothing to dent his image of his father. But this Romanov was a famous director, a man with say and clout. In the bigger pond, swimming with bigger fish, Cornelius looked smaller, weaker, a pest. How to explain the effect this had on Ellis? He thought what Romanov had said was shocking and disgusting and secretly hoped he'd say it again.

'Even if I was allowed to comment, I wouldn't,' Romanov continued. 'Every newspaper is lies from start to finish.'

'Isn't it all lies, darling?' The priest on stage had taken an interest in the conversation. 'Are we not guilty of the same? You know, the great charade of the stage ...'

'Does anyone else smell old ham?' Romanov asked the room.

'I beg your pardon?'

'Just learn the lines, Peter. We're pissing time here.'

Ellis looked around the auditorium. He didn't know about any fifty million dollars, but the place was impressive. The supporting columns were the size of ancient oaks. The aisles wide as roads. He glanced up and followed the circles higher and higher. From the last row the actors on stage would be no bigger than microbes. There must have been two thousand seats – they would need an army to fill it.

Even more impressive was the substance of everything. Although the city had many fine buildings, their beauty was skin-deep. The best place in town looked the very height of glamour and sophistication, but it was not real. At some point one realised it was a front, a mask. Slipping from the velvet booth to use the toilet, the guest found a stinking hole in the ground. Passing through a hotel's marble lobby, ascending in the lavish elevator, the visitor stepped out on a floor of seventies-murder carpet and crudely patched walls. Spend enough time anywhere and it became apparent the marble was plaster, the gold spray-painted, the oak a joke. The whole city was a stage set and everyone was in on the act. 'People cannot bear very much reality,' Mr Anton used to say. Ellis had never stood in a building like this and he thought this Blum must be a great man, probably crazy too, for coming to their flimsy impression of a city and building something with no shortcuts or booby traps.

The set suggested an elegant, sparsely decorated room in the house of an aristocrat or oligarch. Except something wasn't right. Every detail was crooked: the windows, the doors, the lines of perspective. Not much, just enough to throw the eye. Curious, Ellis wandered closer and plucked a rose from a great carpet of flowers spread out at the front of the stage. The petals softened between his pressing fingers. Real flowers for a re-hearsal! It blew his mind. Not because of what it cost – more that this detail beside the others, the real with the false, gave the whole the full rich quality of life where truths and lies were often presented in a single confection. He was not sure there was a word for that quality. If there was, he had not been told it.

'Hey,' Romanov was shouting. 'Come away from that!'

This Romanov was an angry man, he thought. Who was he shouting at this time?

'Yes, you!'

Oh, he was shouting at him. He objected to the flower-squeezing.

'Ellis! What are you doing?' Now his father was shouting too. Cornelius didn't even know what his son had done, he was simply suspecting the worst.

It was not an unreasonable assumption – Ellis's school departure was not so long ago. All the same it annoyed him that

Cornelius took this stranger's side without so much as checking his. Whenever two adults were put together in a room, they formed a little club and looked to string up any young people nearby.

'Please leave,' Romanov was pleading. 'You and your weird kid.'

Weird? Besides a mild case of monkey hunch common among teenage boys, where the arms hung awkwardly in front like the body hadn't quite found the proper use for them and would just leave them there until it worked the problem out – besides that, he was a fairly regular specimen. Black hair, browny-green eyes, tall for his age. On two separate occasions girls had mentioned the straightness of his nose. Halfway to decent stubble too, he reckoned, though not decent enough to fool the Chicago Pub bouncers, damn their black hearts.

'Look,' said Romanov – his voice softer, Ellis imagined, out of regret for insulting him – 'if you must know, the rewrites are why we're delayed. Various little digs we decided were tawdry. And the swearing. Tolstoy and Chekhov didn't have to use swear words, did they? I have no regrets. Not one. I actually think it became better. So there you go. There's your—'

'Any trouble, Mr Romanov?'

A hatchet-faced bruiser had entered stage right, eyes on the conversation in the stalls below. He bristled. He brooded. He was clearly displeased. With his shithouse shoulders and pumped-up arms he moved towards them.

'No, no trouble,' said Romanov.

'You the lot from the other day?' asked the man, coming to the edge of the stage. 'Mr Romanov is not to be disturbed.'

'Which lot?' asked Cornelius.

'It's not them,' said Romanov.

'We're from the *Chronicle*,' said Cornelius.

'Doesn't matter where you're from,' said the big man. 'The door is where you found it.'

The goon raised a hand towards the exit and Ellis saw in

26

his waistband the matt-black handle of a gun. Yes, he was sure of it. He'd seen enough movies to know. And when he saw it he felt like he was in one of those moody gangster flicks. He was familiar with armed soldiers and police, but they were not people in the same way. Never before had he seen a man in a suit with a revolver tucked into his trousers as casually as a flower in a buttonhole. People didn't usually do that in real life, only in certain grubby types of story where consequences did not matter ... Or in those exceptional countries, those special countries like America where everyone was considered more or less sensible enough to own a gun, where there were rallies for guns the way other countries had rallies for peace, and where after every shooting (because accidents will happen) experts and enthusiasts trumpeted the scheme's success. So great was this success, they were required to talk about it every single day.

'Okay, okay.' Cornelius grabbed the boy's shoulder. The doorstepping tone had left his voice. He'd seen the weapon too.

This gun in the theatre was the first. The starter pistol. Later it would not seem strange to think of such weapons in the hands of strangers or neighbours.

THE SUMMER DAYS passed, one inferno after the next, and the family Dau found themselves spending unprecedented amounts of time in each other's company. Neither parents nor child had ever imagined this rare privilege might be theirs, and all parties dreamed desperately of escape.

'There are studies,' Ellis told his mother as they toured the local supermarket. 'That say it's not healthy.'

'Darling, there is a study for everything,' said Stella, steering the trolley through the sleepless, strip-lit aisles. Over the PA, to what sounded like the same four bars of Euro house, a selection of singers bravely refused to give up information under torture. Locating the eggs behind a promotional pyramid of *Grey Duck* grain spirit, Stella opened a carton and conducted a brief interview with each bald tenant, checking them one by one for breakages and cracks.

'But this study says it's bad for my development, not having company my own age.'

'Ellis, it's been two weeks. You're not going to turn into some wolf boy in a fortnight.' Stella took a sliced loaf of bread from a shelf labelled *Snacks for Drinking*.

'I'm missing important things at school.' As escape tools went, this was the thinnest nail file, but Ellis was enjoying this parent–son bonding enough to try anything. He also knew his mother was his best chance to break out. Not that she was a pushover, more that the burden of care was for her a shifting, living thing. An ongoing conversation. Whereas Cornelius . . . Discipline was his default, the act of being strict more important than the knowledge of when he should apply it.

'What things?' By nature a liberal warder, Stella wanted to believe the prisoner capable of rehabilitation. Only experience – hard, bitter experience – gave her pause.

'Excuse me, madame,' said a young man in waiter's garb. 'Would you be interested in trying a delicious juice?' He made a grand flourish towards a table of trembling plastic shot glasses.

'Is there alcohol in it?' asked Stella.

'Yes,' said the young man. His uniform was tight at the neck and he spoke with utmost pride.

'Then no.'

'I'll have some,' said Ellis.

'No you won't,' said Stella.

They went on.

'I don't know what things,' said Ellis. 'But Vincent would. If I could just have some study sessions with Vincent I wouldn't fall behind.' Ellis looked mournful but his heart was beating fast. He sensed a possible weakness in his mother's resolve.

'Excuse me, madame.' Another waiter type materialised beside them. 'Perhaps you'd care to try our new range of delicious teas?' Another trembling table was pointed out.

'Please, Mum. One evening a week.'

'Do they have alcohol in them?' asked Stella.

This waiter was older than the first. His shirt had left white some time ago in search of more poetic qualifiers.

'Er . . . No,' he said.

'Mum, please.'

'You better not be lying to me,' said Stella.

'Absolutely not,' said the waiter.

'On my life,' said Ellis.

(Both were lying.)

It was agreed Ellis could spend one evening a week at Vincent's house. The receiving parents were thoroughly briefed, and he was to go there on foot to avoid any temptation to tear around on bikes or loaf about in wastelands or splatter brain matter in the Space Odyssey cafe. All this was well thought out, but Ellis knew one thing his warders did not: the only powers Vincent's parents had over their son were suggestion and hope.

'Hello Mr Stanik lovely day you look healthy nicely rested I'm here to see Vincent can I come in?'

A grunt from Mr S., who with that face had a career posing for heartburn ads any time he wanted it.

In the kitchen Mrs S. slopped seconds or thirds on Vincent's plate as she described the gown of some starlet seen in the *Gazette*.

'So *gorgeous*. The most *wonderful* colours.'

Vincent, gobbling greedily, looked up at Ellis's approach. 'Danger danger!' he cried. 'Call the cops!'

Was there a word for when you campaigned so hard and pleaded so madly for something that you completely forgot how lousy it was? In this moment Ellis loathed Vincent for all the false promises he'd made without his knowledge.

'The most wonderful ... Oh, Ellis. You've got taller. Hasn't he got taller?'

Vincent arched an eyebrow. 'He looks bigger. A bigger idiot.'

Ellis gave him the finger while Mrs S. wasn't looking.

'Are you hungry, sweetheart? There's plenty here.'

'No thank you, Mrs Stanik. I've eaten.'

'You sure? It's meat dumplings. Vincey loves meat dumplings. I was just telling him about the most heavenly outfit ...'

'Look how much I'm going to eat.' Vincent began his own conversation while his mother talked. 'Watch now. Watch how strong I get.'

Ellis prodded Vincent's gut under the table. 'Strong meaning fat?'

Vincent slapped his hand away. 'Just watch. You'll get pummelled. There'll be nothing you can do.'

'Her and her husband never wear anything more than once,' Mrs S. was saying. 'Shoes, trousers, dresses. They don't own a washing machine. Can you imagine? All goes in the bin every evening.'

Ellis was not sure why adults enjoyed thinking about

famous people being boring, why they were so interested in the wardrobe malfunctions and holidays and shopping sprees of strangers. Why read about some celebrity looking tired when you could be at the dump making a rotten pumpkin explode like a zombie's head? It was a troubling mystery. Every few years some scientist claimed teenagers' brains didn't work properly, but they were always adults, these scientists. Coincidence? He thought not.

Though neither he nor Vincent paid much attention to what she was saying, he liked how Mrs S. spoke to him without caution or judgement, just chatted away regardless as if she hadn't heard what people said about him. He imagined she'd have been the same whoever the guest. *Oh, Adolf, do have a little spoonful, you are pale. Gosh, Pol, you should have seen it, the most dazzling dress.*

Midway through Mrs S.'s presentation on celebrities the lights abruptly died.

'Oh rats,' she said. 'Again?'

Again. These power cuts happened so often the government had invented a name for them. 'Load-shedding,' it was called.

A torch shone into the kitchen. Mr S. stuck his head round the door.

'Everything all right? It won't last long. Light a few candles.' He eyed Ellis with suspicion. 'Or maybe leave it.'

No more was said but the meaning was taken.

'Don't shit yourself, Dad.' Vincent finished his dinner and felt about his face for remnants as if stroking an invisible beard. 'We're out of here.'

It was a hot evening to be pushing around Vincent, who was not by any means the lightest. But freedom always had a price, and this was the hefty figure Ellis was quoted. So he was pedalling and Vincent's fat ass was sagging across the bars. They were gliding, zigzagging around the potholes, through the city centre, down the wide wide boulevards built with military parades rather than people in mind. Through Independence Square – known locally as 'The Four Walls of Independence' – where gloomy men sold peacock feathers and stray dogs laughed at private jokes and little kids splashed in the fountains while a ragged tannoy beat the ever-loving crap out of one folk classic after another.

It wasn't much of a centre. Certain high points of Western culture, such as the motionless metallic man and his brother the hovering man were notably absent. Living statues could not make a living here. Real statues had the monopoly. Statues of mythical heroes who battled dragons, statues of Everymen, statues of former leaders who were hated at the time, statues that once commanded the central squares of people's imaginations and now ruled over car parks and obscure traffic islands, statues of revolutionaries and the revolutionaries who in turn overthrew them.

Oh, the revolutions –

In the international press their little nation's woes tended to get overshadowed. A tremor in Peru, a volcano burp in Iceland, the death of some semi-famous European, a former pop star complaining about a neighbour's extension, and they were bumped and spiked. Seriously, their revolutions didn't even make the news *here*. During the last uprising the front page of the *National* was an account of soil types. Thirty-three police killed, parliament stormed, and they led with peat levels in the provinces. Only the *Chronicle* thought the riots and bloodshed worth mentioning.

Only the *Chronicle* and the Kazakhs, who never missed a chance to mock their neighbours. A punch-up was 'a Kyrzbek election', the scarecrows planted in farmers' fields were 'Kyrzbek ministers', a handkerchief was 'the Kyrzbek national flag' for surrender was all the country had ever done. Throughout history others had blown their noses on them. Or there was the one about the Kyrzbek in the steakhouse. 'What's the big idea giving me all this meat?' he asks the waiter. 'Where's my gristle?' (Their joke about the richer, luckier Kazakhs was that god's hand had slipped while he was making that country, bestowing fields of wheat and barley, rivers of gold, mountains veined with ore. And god realised the other countries would feel slighted, and terrible conflicts would arise if he didn't act fast, so he created the Kazakhs and balance was restored.)

One abundant local resource, out this evening in force, was what Cornelius called 'young bucks'. *Don't you turn into a young buck, Ellis.* This field boasted many experts and no shortage of students. It was practically a university course round here. First the buck-to-be enrolled in loitering. He learned how to stand in a group so no one approached. He mastered a bored hyena look. Then he waited for something to employ him.

Ellis and Vincent rolled on. What were the delicate white clusters that trailed in their wake? Spittle. Phlob. Vincent had recently learned to spit through his teeth and now he must spit all the time. Something he picked up at St Joseph's in the last month. Ellis was disgusted to see this. To think of everything he'd missed, the skills he'd never learn. Appalling. Just appalling. Anyone who said school had nothing to teach was an idiot. Since his exclusion the swear words would have been revised, the words for 'good' would now mean 'bad', the carousel of heroes and villains would have moved on a turn. And if he never went back to school, what then? He would be completely out of the loop, a cultural Eskimo.

Did that make him angry?

No question, Doc, it had crossed his mind. But he refused to worry now, swooping around on a bike, in this moment when he was free. Yes, freedom. On loan, with a 'best before' stamped on it, a thing he knew was real because he knew it would end.

'And there are places where you pick up food without leaving your car,' Vincent was saying.

'Uh-uh.'

'And the same restaurants on every corner so you always get what you want.'

'Uh-uh.'

'And in the supermarkets there's crazy choices for everything.'

'Like what?'

'Like if you want a drink it takes you three hours to decide because you're thinking, "Do I want Tropical Raspberry or, I dunno, Chinese Watermelon or some shit."'

'Tropical Raspberry?'

'Some of them leave your mouth red, some leave it orange or pink or green, depends what you like, really.'

'I see.'

'And if you don't know whether you feel like a burger or a pizza, they'll put burgers in the crust of the pizza. Shit like that. I'm telling you, El, that's the first meal I'm having. Tropical raspberry soda and burger pizza. No one can stop me.'

As soon as he and Vincent were old enough and had the money – they weren't sure how, being rappers perhaps – they were going to the West. London, New York, LA baby. Also Ashford, because Ellis had a cousin there. Vincent was stuck on the whole food thing, also bitches and hoes, who were apparently plentiful when you stepped up in the club. Ellis supported all that, of course – but he dreamed of other things too, things he couldn't tell Vincent. The West in his head was a place where people ran without being chased and graffiti was considerate and spelled correctly. Where doctors existed for everything, even politics and news. Where gentle robot shop assistants pointed out unexpected items in the bagging area. Where police required a reason for arrest, and if you got killed in a particularly horrible way they would name a law or community centre or little sidestreet after you, which wasn't the same as being alive but it was nice. These thoughts worked a sweet pain in Ellis, like an itch he shouldn't scratch.

*

'Hey beautiful! Hey darling!'

Now they were threading through the park and Vincent was trying his luck.

'Wanna lift, ladies?'

'Where are we supposed to sit?'

'On my lap?' This accompanied by a spit through the teeth.

'Gross.'

Vincent was a connoisseur of masturbation and an expert on ways to die but in matters of the fairer sex his knowledge was patchy. Not to say Ellis knew much about it, but he didn't go around acting like he did. He kept his mouth shut.

'Oh, you are the face of beauty.' Another spit.

'Go away.'

'Truly, I think you could be my significant one.'

'Nah-ah.'

'Ride with me on my chariot.'

'That's not a chariot. It's a BMX with two idiots on it.'

'Believe in better, baby.'

'What the hell does that mean?'

'I'll take you places.'

'You don't even have your own bike.'

'This is my bike. He's my chauffeur.'

'I need a picture of you two.'

Pouting Vincent pointed to the sign on his T-shirt: *Cultured in principle.*

'You going to kiss it before bed, yeah?'

'Probably I'm going to look at it and think I've never seen a bigger pair of losers in my life.'

'Hold on to that picture! Remember me! This seduction will occur!'

The sound of drums and horns announced it, pulling them close as darkness fell. In a boulevard off the main square a band was going at it, bashing out wild countdown music, the nerve-jangling runs of notes near the end of films where the hero has just found the ticking bomb and didn't reckon on it being so damn big. Threat music, though in real life that phrase was something of a contradiction – any threat that hired a band surely wasn't much of a threat.

In front of the band stood a large and much-used scaffold, painted in circus whites and reds and blues, ropes coming off all sides. It was this sagging object the musicians hoped to inject with menace, and it could be argued the structure's loose ropes and generally tired appearance were doing the job for them. But this didn't stop the old drummer stroking the snare with increasing frenzy, or the bossman in the purple velvet jacket pawing violently at the synthesiser, or the trio of horn players blasting out their parps and swells.

As they played the people drew in, abandoning their park benches and soft patches of grass in favour of this unexplained promise of peril. It was the sort of music everyone thought they were better than but no one could resist. Ellis even saw a group of soldiers amongst the spectators. A lot of men here wore camo fatigues, it wasn't always easy to tell which were actual soldiers, but these were *bona fide*.

At some invisible sign from the man in purple, the song changed. Two horn players came forward, a little boy between them. They raised a pair of enormous trumpets to the crowd. The child had a smaller but still oversized trumpet he struggled to lift. These players burst into a doomy, warning fanfare. This was meant to inspire excitement in the crowd, and it did, though it was the excitement of imminent injury or death, of blood about to be spilled.

Now a little parade of performers: a boy on stilts, a tiny child in a pantomime horse outfit, a group of older, surlier boys and men in blue velvet trousers and waistcoats, a smiling clown. Each waved and did a little turn and paraded off again, except the clown, who stayed. The music lowered and the clown stepped forward to speak.

Ladies and gentlemen and dear children, what a rare honour

to be in this city at last! Why, it was even more beautiful than he'd heard.

The crowd smiled and looked at one another as if to say, 'Of course, he's right. More people would know that if they came here.'

The clown promised an evening of wonders, beyond their craziest fever dreams *et cetera et cetera*. But first he needed to assemble an army.

A few nervous titters from the crowd.

The clown po-faced. Who would join him?

People looked around. This time they weren't smiling.

Didn't they think it was time for a new lot?

Silence.

Off to one side, under the shade of the trees, the soldiers watched.

No volunteers? the clown scoffed. That was all right, they were too old anyway. He didn't want cadets with bad backs and dodgy knees. He needed fresh talent. In fact, no one older than eight was allowed to join his army.

The crowd laughed. Smiling mothers pushed their children forward to join the clown's army because now it was a joke once more. Five little boys lined up, chests puffed out. The youngest must have been about two. The clown surveyed his new recruits, mugged dissatisfaction to the audience, rearranged the squad according to height, looked again, shook his head. It would have to do, he said.

Time for drill training. The young cadets couldn't march in time, they wouldn't stop when commanded or bring their feet together when called to attention, they broke rank, they picked their noses. The crowd and soldiers and musicians howled with laughter. One of the soldiers filmed it on his phone.

'Look at those little idiots!' Vincent said over and over.

Next the children had to hold the tip of a drumstick to the ground and run around it many times, with a finger in one ear,

37

then sit on a stool. Every time one of the young soldiers fell over, the old drummer hit the cymbal.

'Oh no!' cried the clown. 'This army is in terrible shape! We're not going to beat anyone!'

And the more upset he pretended to be, the more the crowd and real soldiers laughed.

When this entertainment ended a circus boy stepped up to walk the tightrope. He was a few years older than the oldest recruit but with a look on his face that said, 'Those boys may be a joke but I am not. I am made of different stuff.' Yet it was hard to know if it was his wish to do what he was about to do.

Ellis and Vincent had pushed their way to the front where they could see the performers and musicians and also, hidden away in one corner, the families of this travelling circus: the gold-toothed and gum-chewing women, the children too small to perform who observed proceedings with cat-like interest. Ellis found himself watching one of these faces more than the others: a boy about his age, sitting in a wheelchair, legs covered with a leopard-print rug.

To *oohs* and *aahs* from the crowd the steely-eyed circus boy began to walk the rope. It was a bold act – no mat or net, only a safety rope that looked like it had been tied back together at least once. Everyone was watching except the boy in the wheelchair. It wasn't that he avoided looking so much as he didn't seem to see it. His eyes passed over the band and the crowd, they took in the trees and the other circus children gathered about him, they even looked up at the big expanse of sky where at that moment one of his brothers or cousins dangled on a thread, but they didn't linger there or mark that area of vision as special. It was strange to watch: the young boy on the rope strutting back and forth and drawing ever bigger gasps from below, and the boy in the chair, watching the old drummer or brushing crumbs from the rug over his legs, occasionally glancing up as if he'd felt a drop of rain.

Maybe he'd thought himself ready, had taken the risk to show what he could do, perhaps prove himself to someone.

Maybe he never wanted to walk the rope but was forced into it, only to lose his balance and feel the safety snap, the years of wear and tear finally too much for it and it was just his lousy luck he was counting on it at the time.

Maybe he was born that way.

None of this Ellis said to Vincent. Because he was Vincent. Because what did Ellis know? Only the surface was his to see. The boy above, light as air. And the other below, older and darker, his face not telling.

'Can you believe that kid?' Vincent said as Ellis peddled them away. 'That takes some training.'

Ellis said yes as if thinking about the boy on the rope, though he was thinking about the boy in the chair.

BIZARRE footage
come to light
men smearing bacon
on mosques
masked vandals
Tuesday night
community on edge
latest in a series of
gay rights blogger
Chinese restaurant
convention centre
Authorities investigating
Governor Jacobs told reporters
These individuals
found and brought to
Fearmongering   bigotry
no place here

Spending every day in a newspaper office, even if doing little of use, a person got a sense of more than the headlines. Patterns appeared in the stories. Themes emerged. The times took on a shape, a mindset. This was the summer people began to speak of *purity* and *tradition* and *taking things back*, when every church and mosque groaned with numbers in attendance, and disapproving eyes observed the length of a girl's skirt, the open bottle of beer, the stranger by the school gates. Gangs of men hassled immigrants and darker-skinned businessmen. An imaginary truck carrying thousands of judges' wigs had tipped over in the road and people had grabbed the haul. This was the summer the anti-gay proposals and the foreign-agents bill and a hundred other bitter pills were sliding their way through the twisted guts of the legislative system. The summer when the youth pushed insults a little further, left their middle fingers up a fraction longer behind the teachers' backs, wound up their elders whenever the situation allowed it. Every person was coming from an argument or on the way to one; everybody had a lecture on the tip of the tongue or ringing in the ear; everyone was keen to make one tiny part stand for the whole. And sure enough, as old scars reappear in sunlight, the discontent drew itself along the ancient lines of nation, religion and race.

Yet few details of this shift made the *Chronicle* website. Only Mr Urvin made serious attempts to cover it. 'Crazy makes good copy,' he'd say. 'Just give them enough rope and they'll do the rest.' But Cornelius thought Urvin was making something out of nothing, whatever the article's tone. 'You set a precedent,' he told him. Rarely was he won over. The increasingly poisonous sounds and images online he had no time for. Future or not, the old newshound refused to go any further. In his opinion the Internet was a box of rage, a chamber of highly reactive and short-lived free radicals bouncing around in search of violence. If Ellis or any of the hacks tried to draw his attention to a local threat or video nasty, he would brush it away. With ever-increasing reams of content, he believed the value of content had plummeted accordingly. People wanted an opinion? They could have it! It was worthless! This was the modern age's message for the people. And people were doing their utmost to challenge that by kicking up every imaginable cloud of dust. Was their opinion still worthless if they threatened a person's family? If a commentator could not scale the heights, he could plumb the depths. If he kept digging down, if he went low enough, he would get to worth again.

Cornelius had no time for these common crackpots. Only celebrity crackpots would do. The paper continued with its articles on terrorism (*do the eyes in this grainy video belong to a newtown postman?*), its slating of various government schemes (*anti-gay-law minister quotes Oscar Wilde*), and nursed a healthy hard-on for the developer Blum, *the shocking truth about the reclusive billionaire buying up our city* and other such articles containing little in the way of truth. Spurred on, the hacks questioned Blum's motives, the structure of his buildings, the origins of his wealth, the scruples of his friends and business partners, the legitimacy of his dealings, the colour of his money. When Blum made no response, they returned to conjuring the spectre of terror. *The jihadis who walk among us. The secret murderous plots.* So secret nothing was known about them, not even if they existed. But these were details. Details, like facts, could confuse the issue, which was one of care.

In many ways life went on as normal. Shops remained open, the rubbish collected. Chocolate and grain spirit were readily available. Stella kept bashing out her transcripts at the kitchen table and fretting that the sun would do Ellis's hatless brain some permanent mischief and saying things like, 'Do you think, darling, we could have two minutes without incident or drama?' The hacks went on haranguing and badgering and stoking fires and doorstepping dignitaries. In spite of their cynicism and education, their proximity to the news and real life as it happened, they couldn't see exactly how the mood was darkening.

Did Ellis have a clearer picture? Glued to the spare computer in the tech room, endlessly scrolling content, he certainly saw more. But after hearing his father's thoughts about the Internet a few dozen times – 'A roomful of people lighting matches and shouting "Fire!"', 'A caps-locked kolkhoz!', 'They can't even spell!' – whatever he knew he kept to himself. Ignored, he pursued his own ideas of liberty, angling his computer screen in such a way he could secretly watch urgent characters doing things to one another. Anyway, who expected a teenage boy to be constantly fighting the good fight? In general people had low expectations for him and he was doing his best to meet them.

Other times, out on some errand, he would take a detour and go back to a certain unmentionable place. To a window where if the head was kept low, in the musty shrub beneath the sill, he could avoid the telltale song of Pavel or Vassar. *Sir, he's outside again!* Because it tore him up to think what he was missing. The spitting tricks and insults, of course, but also – here was his dark confession – the lessons. Now instead of history, science, geography, reading and writing, he got the five W's (who, what, where, when, why) and Doorstepping 101. He got what mattered to his father, he lived what his father intended. Cornelius was no tyrant, but being in one person's shadow the entire time was tyrannical, and after a few weeks of it Ellis would have kissed every volcano on Pavel's spotty forehead for his old seat at the back of class.

His former classmates thought he was crazy. Sneaking *into* school? Vassar and sons pummelled his arms and legs if they caught him. *Moron! Dildo! Numbnuts!* They couldn't understand why he was there. What could he say? 'I am in this stinking hedge because I want to hear life from a different teacher, because I am undernourished in certain obscure ways.' Tall twitching Vassar, class bully and class grass (an

44

early high-achiever), raining blows, looked like one of those inflatable wind dancers seen in petrol station forecourts. What he seemed to be saying in those punches was that Ellis lacked sympathy. Sympathy for their situation, for their lives. Each punch said 'You do not understand or care about others'. But this was not true, not at all. Ellis felt for them deeply – and he missed them. He missed the whole show.

Even when he did feel part of the paper, he never felt part of the news. He thought journalism was a little enclosure where a person could watch and comment on events at a safe distance. A brick changed that thinking. A large red house-brick, a nostalgic sort of brick. It visited during the night, while they were sleeping, like Father Christmas or the Tooth Fairy. It visited swiftly and violently because bricks, like the people who threw them, were inclined to do things with commitment or not at all. It met one of the *Chronicle*'s two large front windows of mirrored glass and tore a great hole in its centre, mangling the regular reflection of drowsy businesses and softly swaying trees.

Staring out through that hole the next morning, Ellis thought the sky seemed even bigger, even more painfully blue. Glass crunched beneath his feet. A thousand tiny mirrors caught his face. On the brick was a message.

WITH LOVE FRM THE 44 HORSEMEN

'The forty-four what?' said Geffen.

'Horsemen, Geffen,' said Urvin. 'Men who ride horses. Most sports journalists can read, right?'

'I know what horsemen means, thank you. I'm asking why horsemen, who horsemen.'

'Who horsemen? Jesus Christ.'

'Are the Horsemen the lot with the red shirts?' asked Geffen.

'That's the Maoists.'

'Did they egg Governor Jacobs outside city hall?'

'That was the separatists.'

'Oh, I don't know. It's all too confusing.'

'I cherish your insights, Geffen,' said Urvin. 'Truly.'

'Did I piss off some equestrians?'

'That's it, mystery solved. It was a gang of jockeys.'

'You are having fun with me.'

'Yes.'

'What's your solution then?'

Urvin, pretending not to be excited by all this, scrunched his mouth.

'Probably just kids.'

'Just kids?' Geffen looked appalled. 'It's criminal damage.'

'It's criminal spelling. Who doesn't write the "o" in "from"?'

'Dyslexics,' said Geffen. 'Oh, could be dyslexics. They're tricky customers.'

'What?'

'Because they can't spell, their other powers are heightened. They can have super-human strength.'

Urvin, incredulous and apparently near death, appealed to the other hacks for strength.

'Who cares about the spelling?' said Jonquil. 'This was a warning.'

'All right, everyone.' Urvin raised his hands. 'Calm down. We'll live.'

'You have a very short-sighted view on things, you know that, Urvin?'

'We know who's behind this,' said Cornelius.

The journalists looked at him. 'We do?'

'Isn't it obvious? Blum.'

'The Russian?'

'Who else? We start writing pieces about him, suddenly we have bricks flying through our window.'

'True,' said Geffen. 'This is exactly how these people operate. This is how you become a billionaire in Russia.'

'Geffen, please,' said Urvin. 'You don't know a thing about it.'

At this moment a police car pulled up outside. A collective groan escaped the journalists. *Who had called these bozos?*

In fact it was a single bozo. Gloomy, wincing, unreasonably tall even with that stoop all tall men gave themselves to try to fit in.

'Good morning,' said the officer, offering no suggestion he believed it.

Up close to this beanpole, as Ellis was now, he saw mainly nostril, a bit of eye.

'Fedor.' Cornelius's voice worked hard to be neither polite nor impolite.

'Oh,' said Fedor, looking down at Ellis. 'So this is the fellow.'

'I am *a* fellow,' said Ellis.

'Unpleasant business.' Fedor nodded to the busted window.

'Don't tell us,' said Urvin. 'We need a permit for that broken glass and we can make out the cheque to you.'

Fedor did not look angry or put out. Just widened his eyes and gawped.

'Ignore this man, Fedor,' said Cornelius, taking the officer by the elbow. 'We are working on ways to silence him.'

'Then world peace and a cure for cancer,' said Geffen.

'Let's talk in my office,' said Cornelius. 'More privacy.'

As they turned away Ellis heard Fedor say, 'Still in the three-piece suit, I see.' An oil and water comment, that – it separated if left a moment. It sounded like a compliment until you considered the 'still' and the wisdom of a three-piece suit when the mercury was touching 38. Cornelius held his hands out in an 'as you see me' gesture before he shut the door.

Of course, a son should accept a father's wishes. The son of a journalist, however, was in a trickier spot. Particularly if the matter was in the public interest. Was he the good and true son when he accepted the request for privacy or when he eavesdropped? Room for both possibilities. Urvin grinned when he saw Ellis pressing his ear to the door. Geffen shook his head and retired to the tech room.

'Truth is,' Fedor was saying, 'it's starting to make you look bad.'

'We're a newspaper, Fedor. It's what we do.'

'Don't give me the noble sword and shield routine. You put the fear of god into everyone over this terrorism business when you know no more than the rest of us. You make a bunch of vague accusations about this Russian—'

'Sometimes you have to shake a few trees.'

'Could you shake ones that aren't blowing themselves up in crowded areas or investing a fortune in this city?'

'You'd prefer we were like the *Gazette*, is that it? Writing articles about shoes and bum fat?'

'It's called cellulite. And why not? The *Gazette* has ten times as many readers as your rag. You could learn something.'

'They aren't readers. You can't read that crap. You skim over it and try not to fall in.'

'People want happy news and film stars, not tales of businessmen and terrorists.'

'This isn't about what readers want. This is about a brick through my window.'

Ellis wondered whether that was a strong or an arrogant thing to say about readers. In any case, Fedor ignored it.

'I know,' he replied, 'and I'm asking you to think about how you could prevent it happening again.'

'*I* should think about how *I* could prevent it? I'm not the one who threw the brick! Find that person! Ask them how to prevent it! Honestly, that's the first approach that comes to mind? It's the most ass-backward thing I've ever heard.'

'And where should I look, Cornelius? How should I do my job? Please, tell me. You make so many enemies I wouldn't know where to start.'

'Start with Blum. The man would scalp his mother if the price was right.'

'Come on. You really think a guy like that needs to bother with you?'

'Do you have a better theory?'

Fedor paused. 'I notice your boy's working here now.'

On the other side of the keyhole Ellis froze.

'What are you saying?'

'He's been here, what, a few weeks and this happens?'

'Oh, that is total magical thinking nonsense.'

'I'm just saying.'

'Well stop saying.'

'The school could have pressed charges.'

The officer proceeded to recap Ellis's great disgrace. It was fairly accurate, unpleasantly accurate ... Ellis had hoped no more needed to be said on the matter. Unfortunately this was not the case. The law had changed: prior convictions were now admissible, the public gallows were back in business. Everyone wanted the shame parade. The cops, the shrinks, the trolls – even the gentle readers in their slippers. Who didn't feel a little cheated when a suspect on the news dodged the perp walk with a coat over the head, blundering through the rabble as the bulbs flashed?

'There were problems,' said Cornelius. 'And we are sorting it out. But this ... This is not him. For one thing he can spell.'

Ellis realised he hadn't breathed for a while and took a few gulps.

'I'm telling you,' his father continued, 'it's someone we've been hounding.'

'Then stop hounding. Stop giving people a hard time. Maybe your problems will go away.'

'No, Fedor, that is not the lesson here.'

'All right, Cornelius,' said Fedor, moving to the door and causing Ellis to pull his head swiftly from it. 'It's only friendly advice. I don't want to see you come to grief.'

'I'm touched by your concern. Write it on a brick next time, why don't you?'

Smack! thought Ellis. *That told him!* His own life was full of people saying, 'Look, you don't know how the world is, let me tell you. You mustn't do that, let me show you.' He had never considered his father (one of the people who said this to him most often) might be plagued by the same types. Not only that, Cornelius had the same response – the one-fingered salute. The old man would have put it more classily, of course. Whatever the phrasing, this was an inspiring discovery. Inspiring, though sort of depressing too. Ellis had always assumed his predicament was due to being young and having to follow all the bogus rules adults set in place for the young. So it was a knee to the groin, spiritually speaking, to learn even adults and newspapers had people who wanted to curb them – that another set of laws existed, beneath the actual laws, which people looked to inflict on others.

FIRST, A CONFESSION: he liked school. To admit this at his age was a violation of every code there was, but that was the truth of it. He was not some waster or shuffling no-hoper. The twisted dropout who hid in the toilets hating everybody and plotting his revenge, that was not his style. He liked the hub-bub of the schoolyard and the riot of the hallways. He liked the faint butterflies he felt walking into that each morning. He liked how the teachers, after many years in the company and judge-ment of teenagers, were pinched or worn into extreme versions of their characters. Mr Arzak was always furious, Mrs Kuper away with the fairies, and so on. Even the St Joseph's rules and regs he secretly liked. Was there a more pleasing sentence than *Please keep feet off seats*? These were proper commands, carved in stone and brought down the mountain, weighted with long histories of obedience, not chalked up on the spot as and when it suited. Or at least this was how it seemed after his expulsion: like yodelling or the treatment of sewage, education was best appreciated at a distance.

Head boy material he was not, but he had loved some of the classes. Reading and Writing especially. In that class he paid attention, he applied himself. Mr Anton had them reading *Candide*, which even Pavel and Vassar enjoyed.

'Let me get this straight, sir.' Vassar gripped Ellis's wrist under the desk. 'If Dau punches himself in the face, that's free will?'

Dickens was another Anton favourite. *Whether I shall turn out to be the hero of my own life, or whether that station will be held by anybody else, these pages must show.* Wasn't Ellis waiting for the same reveal? He didn't know his own story. Here he was, still waiting to find out. In his future he saw only blank space, a bank of sky neither blue nor obvious cloud. It struck him that no one in this class had control over their stories. He looked around for signs of lightning striking brains. Did Vassar and Pavel feel this too? Their gormless mugs gave nothing away. Oh, the secrets that hid in an idiot's face!

He handled words more gently after that, seeing within each a germ of experience, a stealth upgrade. (Though he handled them quietly, for that sort of talk was a guaranteed smack from any number of parties). So imagine his devastation, walking into class one morning, to find Mr Anton gone and in his place Mr Arzak aka Buzz Killington furiously scribbling on the board.

'Mr Anton is MIA,' was all he would say.

Pavel wanted to know what MIA was short for.

'It's short for mind your own business,' Angry Arzak replied.

Pavel squinted, performed various internal computations, found the explanation sound.

Rumours percolated as the week wore on. *Mr Anton had been spotted making sweet love to Mrs Kuper, no, to Miss Gropnik . . . He'd stolen the caretaker's prosthetic arm . . . The principal had caught him puffing weed behind the bins and fired him with immediate effect . . .*

The real reason only became clear, to Ellis at least, when they received their new study texts. Dickens and *Candide* were out, replaced by the lowest and dullest examples of their national literature. Ellis thought once you had read one of these dry fictions you had read them all. There was always a poor noble farmer who lived in a hut with a silent faithful wife, the two of them beset by drought and metaphor. The British or Americans arrived and stirred some wickedness, the farmer died and the wife threw herself in a lake, only to discover it was a mirage, there was no water, and she was still miserably alive. Or the farmer was a cruel man who stood for something bigger and it was the wife who must kill him or the son who must flee, and every scene was a parade of breast-beating and shirt-tearing and *we may not have much but we have hope.* These stories were always claiming to be some relation to 'the people', and going by the popularity of this junk the people were always looking to adopt.

Such tales he could do without. He seethed through the classes now. 'It's just one dumb book or another,' said Vincent. 'Who cares?' But Ellis saw what they had done. It was two fingers up to everything Mr Anton taught or asked them to consider: screw your free will, screw your narrative and your 'hero of your own life', screw yourself. They'd swapped an open book for a closed one.

His grades went into free fall. You know things are on the skids when Pavel and Vassar know more than you, when they *care* more than you. Sorry, no room at the inn for facts and figures, he had a full house of anger and contempt. For a while he took great pleasure in secretly hating St Joseph's. They couldn't punish him for thinking it. How could they know?

But after a time this wasn't enough. Hate and fury are those sort of lodgers, unfortunately. They push every allowance made. They take all the space they can get.

So to the event in question: his last day of school.

The summer was not yet stupidly hot, it still had some charm to it. A pleasant breeze, what Mr Anton would have called a *zephyr*, greeted the students that morning. From the outset Ellis knew what he was going to do. A nauseous tickle – of danger, of doom – played in the pit of his stomach, but it wasn't saying, 'Let's stop.' It was curious, puppyish. He wanted to see what would happen, just for the hell of it, as a child nibbled the leaves of unknown plants, wondering if they were the poisonous varieties he'd been warned about.

The classes dragged by. He could take nothing in, too busy willing time forward to the main event. His worry was that in all this boredom the momentum would be lost or someone would rumble his plan having nothing better to do. This he felt from a position slightly outside himself – he saw himself sitting tightly at his desk, he read the look on his face. Three times he was asked the answer to questions he hadn't heard. His classmates were delighted. They were excited by his academic slump, they sensed the trouble he contained.

After several lifetimes the bell rang for the end of the day. Dawdling in the corridors, skulking about the back stairs, he waited for everyone to leave. When all was quiet he slipped up to the second floor, to the storeroom where the teaching materials were kept. The storeroom door used to have a lock but it was faulty, apparently – it kept locking teachers in so they took it off. (Bad luck, teachers.) Besides, there were only books in there. Who was going to steal those?

Quite right, St Joseph's. No one was going to steal those.

They were going to set fire to them.

He had often wondered since why he chose fire. His theory was that people favoured different ways of saying things at particular times in their lives. If you were out in the wastelands burning stuff most weekends, if you were cutting the heads off hundreds of non-safety matches and stuffing them in tennis balls to throw at Vincent, if this sort of activity was not just a form of entertainment but a sort of language for you, well, it was not hard to guess what you were going to do when up against it.

The storeroom was dingy and humid, with a strong smell of mouldy cardboard. A smell of despair. How many teachers had stood among these stacks and sighed? Might as well try to count the stars in the night sky. He was willing to bet he was the first person to stand in that room *without* sighing. He was invigorated, alive, arsonist's tool kit at the ready. Matches, lighter fluid, blanket. The last just a precaution in the unlikely instance things got out of hand. If he couldn't do anything about the books in circulation, he could at least destroy whatever garbage was lined up for the future. Finding the stuff wasn't a problem. The culprits were obvious a mile off with their pulpy, washed-out covers of suffering faces or farmer, wife and flag.

He built his pyre in the aisle at the back of the storeroom. Not a lot of space, but not a lot of boxes either. Five in total. He took a breath. This was it. As he lit the match a flash of silver in one corner caught his eye. Where the wall met the ceiling a spider sat tense in his web. Poor little guy was about to have his narrative well and truly hijacked. If the heat didn't shrivel him up the smoke would probably do him in. The young flame in Ellis's hand, aware it didn't have his full concentration, dwindled and died.

Focus, he told himself. *Sidetracked by a spider. Bigger ideas are at stake.*

Another match was lit and held to the pyre's edge. The cardboard blackened beneath the flame and . . . nothing. The boxes were oddly damp, the fire wouldn't take. The second match went out.

Okay, calm down. Stop messing around before you use up all the matches. Do what you should have done at the start. A good douse of lighter fluid all over, now try.

Would he see at any stage the madness of his plan and call it off? Would common sense intervene? To these pertinent questions, the answers were: 'What do you think?' and 'No'.

Third time was a charm. The match flared and dimmed and grew to fire. When it was happy he put it to the paper and this time, this time it took. Boy, did it take. With a great inhaling *whumph* the pyre came to life. This was more like it! This was him claiming something for himself, becoming the hero of his own life. Something had been roughly handling him and he was aligning himself with a force bigger than it, a more powerful ally . . . Looking back he would think all this so odd. He had to keep reminding himself he had really done this and didn't watch it in a film or read it in a book.

The fire burned. The flames clawed.

At this juncture it should be said that fire has more than one face. The gentle flicker of the candle, the pale Bunsen blue in

Chemistry, the spit and sizzle of the hearth. It can be a sleepy element or a raging beast. It can be friend or foe. Perhaps that's obvious to most folk – before this moment he hadn't given the matter much thought. But this specimen was livelier and hungrier than anything he'd flirted with, and growing all the time: its flames were now taller than him and its smoke was blackening the ceiling – *sorry, Mr Spider, I think you lost this one* – and the crazy flames were starting to lick the boxes of books on the nearby shelves, boxes not earmarked for destruction, so yes, now he was giving the matter thought, now he was finding it worthy of consideration.

Fortunately he had prepared for this. He unfolded the blanket and threw it on top of the blaze. End of story, right? No. Not so. The blanket only muted the carnival a moment before the flames poked through and it too was on fire. (Turned out you couldn't use a regular woollen blanket, you needed a special fire blanket. Who knew?)

Now the fire was roaring – not just blackening the ceiling but destroying it, not just licking the books on the shelves but devouring them. The storeroom was about a thousand degrees and smoke was belching thick enough to blind him or lay him out for lack of breathing. Wow, things had escalated quickly. The thought crossed his mind, it just flitted through, that perhaps he was not entirely in control of this new ally. He was no expert on fire – 'Clearly!' the audience cries – but it did seem like if he stayed here this fire would eat him too. And when you got down to it that didn't seem like the behaviour of an ally at all.

So he fled. What else could he do? The place was unsafe. Choking and spluttering, he ran through the empty corridors, down the stairs to the double doors. Locked. He hadn't considered that. Quite a lot he hadn't considered.

How quiet the school was then. Like no one had ever walked the hallways or sat in the – *the classrooms!* He dashed into the first he found (Year 5, a project on witch trials lined the walls) and worked a window until it gave enough for him to squeeze out into the evening and run and run . . .

When he was a safe distance he slowed and tried to catch his breath. It was most strange, the city was its usual self. He felt sure there should be sirens and red lights streaking past to tackle the inferno by now. He was equally sure every cop in town was heading towards him. In truth he was sort of hopeful about these things. Those people might know what to do.

Instead, nothing. Couples sat in the soft twilight of the parks staring at their phones or each other. The usual array of entrepreneurs and hustlers thronged the street corners. Beside a hotdog stall a group of sparrows fell to in-fighting. Mysteriously, miraculously, life went on.

He tried to relax. *Hello, Officer, just out for an evening stroll.* Only was it his imagination or was he walking differently, as a guilty person would walk? He didn't know what that looked like but he was sure other people did, that they would notice him and whisper and inform the relevant authorities. He felt the parts of his body as individual components: his loose arms, the hair sitting on his scalp, the sticky armpits, the useless end points of his fingers and toes. His face was fixed, tense. He was aware he was holding it against its will but could not stop. It had been so long in this position it felt like a mask.

No blue police haze outside his block either. What was wrong with people? They didn't appreciate the seriousness of what he had done. 'You've got dirt on your face,' said his mother, as if it were the most normal thing in the world. *It's not dirt!* he wanted to cry. *It's the ashes of my school!* He was appalled by how flippant his parents were about these things they didn't know. Really, he couldn't be in the same room. He lay on his bed wondering if anyone had found the fire yet. Should he call the emergency services and tell them himself? No, too risky. Still a slim chance he might get away with this. He saw his name plastered over the top of the newspapers. *Firebug teen guts school.* Did he want that? Perhaps he did. It was hard to know what he wanted or was thinking at that time. Above all he felt pained that he had let it happen, and that they – the school, its teachers, everyone – had let it happen too. He should have been supervised better! Pained also that in all this talk about the self as hero it hadn't occurred to him a person could just as easily, perhaps far more easily, be the villain of his own life too.

Next morning he sloped in to police tape and worried faces and a house-sized black crater where the top right-hand corner of St Joseph's had been. The fire brigade had arrived the previous evening after a call from inside the school: Mrs Kuper had been working late in her office. Smelling smoke, the poor woman opened her door and nearly died of fright. She nearly died again, of suffocation, before the firemen got to her.

She could have died!

And he felt terrible about that. Bad enough to hand himself in and confess his crimes – except there was no need. They were waiting for him. The caretaker, one-armed Woyzeck, had seen him loitering on the stairs after everyone else left. The detective and the principal had a few questions. Things fell apart pretty quickly after that.

There it is, ladies and gents and trolls: the cautionary tale of the grubby arsonist. Regard this shifty convict, this cold-blooded crim. Look at those eyes, but don't come too close, stay away from the bars. He didn't want or expect sympathy (though it should be said Mrs Kuper was all right). He deeply regret-ted the whole business and wished it had never happened. Sometimes he thought – 'Better late than never!' the audience cries – that it pointed to a fundamental flaw in him. *A lack of empathy*, as Peabody would have it, or something else less clearly worded. Setting fire to things you didn't like was not an eloquent solution. Historically speaking, it did not put you in good company.

At other times he thought it was, as he felt then, a problem with the outside world, which he had tried to answer foolishly. He had good intentions – 'Oh, those are the worst!' the audience cries – but really, how many arsonists started their fires because a favourite teacher was sacked or because they were made to study certain books?

Lastly, perhaps in honour of the departed Mr Anton (whose whereabouts remained unknown), Ellis wondered if he had any choice in what he did. Was this the course decided for him in the best of all possible worlds? Would there always be, no matter what version of the story, that storeroom and that spider and that fire, waiting for him?

GORGEOUS Mia Zarkovia looked
            every bit the dream
      white chiffon halter
                        denim hot-pants
      in town to watch her hubby
                  stuck to mineral water
      fuelling rumours
                        pregnant with
      superstar footballer
                  A close friend told The Gazette
                        home in Milan
Roberto's first start for Athletik
            mega-bucks   private jet
      All eyes on Mia
                  watching for that
                        bump

THEY GATHERED at the eternal flame in Victory Square. A host of young men chanting, clapping, shouting, feeding mobbishness to one another. Roll cameras! This was the good stuff. Even grumpy Mr Kozlov couldn't help grinning behind the lens. 'Hooligans' wasn't quite right, but they were something more than what they were. See the closeness of those buzz cuts, hear the fullness of those voices. Notice how easily they fell in step as they marched, how quickly they picked up the tribal cries, the relish with which they chanted the names and slurs.

Oh, some might say, it's just good fun. Nothing to complain about, nothing to cause concern. It happens in every country in the world. And this is true and yet . . .

They marched on the stadium, red and blue flags flying, their voices as one.

Ellis was on mic duty, running alongside Kozlov, the pair of them puffing and sweating. Why were they here? To cover the football match, of course. A momentous day in the country's sporting calendar. Blum's golden new team of millionaires unveiled. But let's be honest, Kozlov and Ellis were looking for other things too. Dirt, chaos, bad practice. Anything which might nail this Blum to the wall. That was the real sport now. Stella was not best pleased Ellis was involved. 'I thought we agreed,' he had heard her telling Cornelius. 'You wanted him to see the paper,' his father replied. 'Well this is it.' 'I wanted him to see the good stuff. Not you hounding folk and confirming your own bias.' 'Stell darling, you're asking for a peach without a stone. Why does everyone imagine journalists are saints?' 'Believe me,' she said, 'I do not think that.'

*

61

Down the street the young men stomped, the traffic snarling and honking behind. The fans didn't care. They were one, they were many.

At the stadium gates the crowd clotted and came to a standstill. Police blocked the entrances.

'What's going on?' the fans cried.

'The stadium is full,' came the reply.

'That's not possible. We have tickets and we're not yet inside.'

'We're telling you, it's full.'

'How?' the fans cried.

'How should we know?' the officers replied.

The mob at the gates couldn't believe it. They had come so far, they had paid so much, they had loved their team so madly. They had to be let in.

The officers shook their heads. That was no good to them, was it?

What they meant was due process must be observed. Before the last revolution the police would turn a blind eye for a nice blue hundred note, but these new police were not built that way. They were inscrutable, upright to a fault. The rate was now five hundred.

A description of this process. The person who is close enough to the officers, who hasn't already given all his money to the ticket office or the tout, produces the appropriate notes and makes eye contact with his nearest law enforcement agent. This requires a carefully timed flash of the cash – long enough the other officers nearby see and don't stop him when he goes to jump the gate, short enough they don't think he's being unsubtle or even perhaps insulting by so obviously giving money to only one of them. It's a tricky line to tread, many ways it could go wrong, but the process has started, and the worst thing the punter can do now is have second thoughts. He must press on. The notes are slipped into the nearest uniform's shirt pocket. It is traditional for the face above the pocket to make no show of receipt. A hard moment for the customer. Everything hangs in the balance. He twitches, uncertain the donation has been registered. If he guesses wrong and goes ahead he's breaking the law. How can he tell? To ask the officer is considered most disrespectful. It might also lead to arrest. But if he doesn't move then his bribe has been for nothing. Difficult. He doesn't have much time to decide. The officer might forget he's paid, or someone else will see his indecision and go in his place. He's got to move now. He rushes to the gate and scrambles over. If everything's gone smoothly, if he's made no stumbles in the earlier negotiations, the cops will stand by, their heads angelically poised at such an angle that the crime, it could be argued, goes unnoticed. But if some aspect of the ritual has been skipped, if the invisible contract has been incorrectly filled out, then the officers will leap upon the scrambling man and tear him from the gate, and they will punish him to the full extent of the law, to infinity and beyond, as the fellow says.

A cynical amusement trickled through the crowd. This was why the stadium was full: the cops had their own ticketing system in place. That was how it was. Lining the pockets. Crossing the palms. *Sure, sure.* There was even some sympathy for this outlook, and cries of 'Nice work if you can get it'. But the amusement soon dwindled as the bribers climbed the gates and left the rest behind. Seeing their sour beliefs proved true offered the remainder no comfort. They were only human, and as such, despised in others the cynicism they praised in themselves.

The crowd pushed forward. Some had no money left for the police. Others refused on principle. They'd paid good money, why should they pay again? They were here to see the new international stars, the geniuses of the game. The first unveiling of the great Roberto. What did a man who earned a quarter of a million dollars a week look like up close? Perhaps seeing such a specimen would provide some secret to success. Perhaps seeing such success was success in its own right. They squeezed tighter against the gate. The cops shoved back. The mass rocked to and fro, threatening to tip.

'Hey,' people cried. 'Quit this! There are kids in here!'

'Let us in, you crooks!'

'Don't make us break your heads!'

The officers drew their batons and shouted for people to stay back. There was fear in their eyes. They knew they had no chance if the crowd turned violent. Possibly they remembered the last revolution, or the one before that. Other countries had elections every five years, they had uprisings. Well, five years was up and those officers knew it.

'And turn off that camera!' they cried.

The film crew did not comply. That is, Kozlov did not – though Ellis, fired up too, disobeyed in spirit. They were journalists, this was their job. Sticking their nose in things and shaking stuff up and giving the two-fingered salute to the high and mighty, that was their privilege. *Bite it, suckers!* They had the special invisible reporters' badges that said this was okay. Besides, the cops were too far away to do anything about it.

The crowd kept pushing. The fans jeered and booed. All the taunting they'd been practising and saving for the other team was poured on the police, and the cops said nothing, made no attempt to communicate, knew nothing of softly softly, only looked angry and confused and scared and radioed for backup which arrived in a fury of stomping boots as column after column of soldiers pushed through the crowd and took up positions in front of the gates.

Far from calming matters this made the situation worse. People, furious they weren't trusted to behave, started misbehaving. Now there was violent shoving on both sides. Ellis saw a hand slipping into someone else's backpack and rough wicked faces he hadn't noticed before, as if their masks had fallen to the floor. It seemed at any moment something would be done which could not be undone. He hadn't seen proper unrest offline before and it was different from what he had imagined. It was possible to be in it and part of it without ever deciding, without having any particular feeling on the matter. He felt like he was in one of those sci-fi movies about brain-eating parasites from outer space.

'We should go,' he told Kozlov.

'Just a minute,' Kozlov muttered. 'This is gold.'

Though Ellis appreciated the gold in this report, and for once the privileges of reporting, now he wanted out. This would end in stampede, riot, maybe death – and he didn't want to die. He had never popped Kristal or made love in the club. He had never eaten food off a slate or drunk tea from a jam-jar or had cause to say 'Let's pow-wow Monday'. Damn it, he had never promoted his brand, or found out what the phrase meant.

A shove knocked the crowd and Kozlov lost his footing, pitching sideways. The sheer numbers meant he couldn't fall, but he hit the sea of bodies hard, sending up a howl. In the melee someone tried to grab his camera and from his half-standing half-fallen position he wrestled a hand which may have belonged to a man with missing teeth or to a shouting woman. Other hands made to grab the camera and it was unclear whether they were trying to get it back for Kozlov or also lay claim. The genre of this movie was now less sci-fi and more straight up zombie apocalypse horror. Kozlov fought them off, biting a hand in the process. *Bedlam at the ballgame,* the headline would read on the site next morning, but at that moment this was not the main concern.

'Stay back!' Kozlov shouted. 'We're press.'

Who knew what the crowd thought of that. They were embroiled in their own little scuffles even after Kozlov prised himself and his camera away.

'We should go,' he said, and the look on his face was such Ellis didn't bother pointing out this was what he had just said.

The match was underway and the air was thick with roars of excitement and frustration and dissent. Cops and soldiers linked arm in arm for long stretches of the stadium wall, though its circumference was far too great for them to cover. Circling the exterior, Kozlov filmed hordes of punters scaling the unguarded sections or climbing trees and radio towers and streetlights to get a view. So many people got on the roof of one building it collapsed. They pulled themselves from the rubble, this crazed zombie swarm, miraculously unscathed, and climbed another building. From a shady stretch of trees opposite, a dozen exquisitely bored female officers watched them brawl and push and climb.

Ellis saw all this and was sorry for his country. He felt certain that in better places you wouldn't see fights at football matches. There'd be no good reason, no need. He wanted to rewind the footage in the video camera and put these actions in reverse: the army would leave, the people would pluck their money out of the officers' pockets, the angry crowd would settle and thin, the stadium would empty, everything would be calm again.

Perhaps he wouldn't have been so disgusted or thought any of this if he'd got in instead of being stuck outside. But that's as it may be.

EXCLUSIVE VIDEO
Gazette drone
(city's only working newspaper drone)
gets YOU inside stadium
Sneak peek
yesterday's sell-out football
Top of Roberto's head
More shiny than the rest
Hair gel
THE go-to product for European footballers
Improves heading
Science
Unfortunately momentous day
tarnished by bad elements
Some in   crowd
thought they were still at dead goat polo
famous Kyrzbek 'goat-boy dance'
no sight for gorgeous pregnant Mia Zarkovia
or her handsome hubby
Disgusting scenes
Click here to watch

ACCORDING TO PEABODY, Ellis didn't know the meaning of empathy, but he did, he absolutely did. He was always watching his parents in particular, trying to work them out. Perhaps everyone tried to know their mother and father in this way, but just then he was welded to his, had almost every aspect of his life decided by them, suffered their authority more than most his age. So of course he tried to understand them, to consider them with an open heart and mind, even if the heart especially was not so full of affection at that time. Talk about rewinding the footage, being parented was like that kidnapping syndrome in reverse: first you swooned over the big dumb beasts, and they let you coo and seemed to cherish you, then *boom*, they went and locked you up. The final step for the child, he decided, was where the hostage started – with freedom.

Perhaps it was fairer to say that empathy for his parents came and went. It had its seasons. But there were moments, undeniably.

The night they got the phone call from Urvin. Cornelius took it, centre stage as usual. But that night Ellis's eyes were on Stella. She leaned in the kitchen doorway, wrapped in herself, watching her husband talk. The paint on her fingernails was chipping (she picked at it between bursts of typing). Ellis could see the little islands of blue remaining which he sometimes felt, running his fingertips across the bumps where paint and nail met. The line between what was real and what was not, and he could feel it.

What was she thinking? This woman who was seven days a week on that laptop ferrying other people's words from headphones to page. Not much of a job and the pay was poor but she had done it long enough to strum the keyboard without stopping to correct mistakes or rewind the audio. What did this woman – wife of an internationally ignored newspaper editor, mother of a son who let's just say had veered a little off course – make of the plot she was hearing?

Now she left the doorway and perched on the arm of the sofa where Ellis sat, one eye on the news.

'Don't you want to watch something else?' she asked.

She'd be completely into her typing, too absorbed to look up or return a 'hello' – then click, the laptop would close, the breath would exhale, and she'd want to know every last thing about what he'd learned at school or what he thought of this or that. He couldn't fob her off either. If he said he didn't like something she always made him explain why, which could be a major hassle. If he said something without thinking it through she'd frown and say, 'Is that what you really mean?' Not in a nasty way, more quizzical, but that was enough when it came from her.

'This channel is fine,' he said.

On evenings when Cornelius was home they watched the news and its sisters: the hard-hitting exposé, the political panel shows of 'Who can shout the loudest'. But if he was working late she watched other programmes, about travel, heartbreak, ghosts, adventure. Ordinarily Ellis did his own things, only just then he didn't have a choice. This was the one screen he was allowed.

'Isn't there anything funny on?' she asked.

He didn't need to change the channel to know the answer. Low farce, bad wigs, all manner of mugging to the camera.

'Shush,' she said, seeing his look. 'Let's have something fun.'

She often watched these shows, with a fond exasperation, but this time, call him paranoid, he thought the suggestion was for his benefit more than hers. Like the news was not a suitable item for his young brain. Like it might damage him in some way. Not to say she wanted to keep him a child forever, maybe just to fast-forward him through the stretch where the footage went fuzzy or violent or kinky, and press play again when he was safely on the other side, all responsible and mature.

'Security though,' his father was saying. 'That's bound to be heavy.'

With his free hand Cornelius checked his trousers for fluff. A special brush for this purpose rested on top of his bedroom dresser, a special brush he was separated from at this moment. Stella watched him picking at fluff, discussing his tabloid intrigues, and her look was not unlike the one she wore for the tired comedy routines on TV. The *Chronicle* was not the best newspaper – not even Cornelius would claim that. On the other hand it was his baby and she was respectful of that, or at any rate polite, which admittedly was not always the same thing. Sometimes she'd say to him, 'If they don't want the interview you shouldn't push them' or 'You gave that one an easy ride', but that was the most critical Ellis ever heard her.

It didn't occur to Ellis that she might dislike the newspaper in any serious way. The *Chronicle* was part of their family after all. As a former cynic now glimpsing the paper's potential for action and kicking out, he no longer saw how it could be tiresome or dangerous or unwelcome to anyone.

No, he thought if the fault lay anywhere it was with her, not the paper. She introduced uncertainty. She was not like those other mothers who prowled the house for stray hairs and rug blemishes, who shuddered at bad grades and dirty shirts and dinner getting cold. Normal mothers didn't leave sweet wrappers lying around or ghosts of old loo rolls on the spinner (yet also didn't go down six flights at 2 a.m. to pick up a can rolling around in the wind). Their idea of a good time was not hiking out to the mountains and finding a nice tree to sleep beneath. They didn't make their sons hot chocolate during a blackout (three tablespoons of salt?) or carry everywhere those little mumbling songs or ask 'Is now a bad time?' when they called someone or have it in their nature to question anything and everything, as his mother did.

None of which was to say he would swap her for a minute, of course.

She reached over to stroke his hair, but this to him was more child's play and he shook himself free. At the time his theory about parents was you had to occasionally give them the talk-to-the-hand treatment: if they knew you were soft on them they could cause you all kinds of problems.

She gave a little *hmm* like she'd expected as much and took her affections over to the bird. Shadows in that corner fell across her face stealing certain lines, details, aspects of substance. She looked much younger than his father just then. Through the birdcage bars she offered a handful of sunflower seeds. The cage rocked at the touch, it was only a cheap thing, not solid, yet still in a way more solid than the hand rocking it. The bird's maniac eyes regarded the offering.

She had found Basan at the state fair, tethered by the ankle, flapping limply to mockery from the crowd. 'Animals!' she cried at everyone except the bird. Cornelius ushered her away and thought the incident forgotten, but she snuck back and returned with the parrot on her arm. What she paid she wouldn't say, the matter was settled. At first there was no cage in the flat, only a stoop, and the bird flapped about the apartment as it pleased. Cornelius put a stop to it. 'It's either free or it's not,' he said. 'You can't have it both ways.' Very philosophically put, though the main reason was it was crapping on everything and abusing the soft furnishings. In the end, reluctantly, Stella agreed to the caging. Those were the two moments of history for that parrot: the day it was freed and the day it was caged. They did not sound like they were in the right order, but they were.

Now Basan took the seeds one by one, working each thoughtfully between beak and tongue. Black beak, bronze bars, grey seeds striped like undertaker's trousers. Husks fell to the cage floor thickening the carpet of chaff already gathered there. Stella used to make mosaics in the evening, cutting plates, smashing ugly vases (see her poised with the hammer, about to right the wrongs of taste) but she abandoned the habit. Too much mess, she said. The parrot was not exactly squeaky clean but she didn't seem to mind that.

'Right.' Cornelius spoke loudly and seemed pleased. 'Too good to miss.'

She withdrew her hand from the cage and the bird craned after, hopeful for the remaining. No, she was done feeding and threw the last seeds back in the bag and brushed her hands clean. She looked out of the window, out towards those mountains of hers, but it was dark and no mountains could be seen. That remained her position, turned away, looking out, when Cornelius got off the phone and announced Blum was throwing a party tomorrow and the *Chronicle* was going to crash it.

HOLY MOTHER, the cars. Was Ellis dead? Was he dreaming? Rolls Royces, Humvees, Aston Martins, Lamborghinis with the doors that opened up, Ferraris with the super-sweet light displays under the chassis ... Vincent would have busted a nut. Right there in the street outside the Hotel Excelsior he'd have whacked off like a loon. And this was not to mention the ranks of Mercedes and BMWs with chauffeurs who polished the paintwork or sat in the dark interiors holding their bellies as expectant mothers receive the ultrasound, ready to wait any length of time while their masters drank and danced, ready to spend their lives in that car, to grow old in that car, to feel the teeth loosening and the limbs stiffening, to see the hair turning grey in the rear-view mirror, ready to turn to dust in that car.

Where were they heading, Ellis and his father? Past this motorcade, away from the hotel's front entrance, seeking a suitable alley for subterfuge. In his month as a hack Ellis had learned there was always a weak spot, in people and in buildings. Every hotel or grand hall had its tradesmen's entrance, its unguarded window, its fire exit where the staff nipped out for a quick smoke. The two of them were looking for this fault together, a father-and-son hunting trip. They walked in step, the son watching the father for pointers and copying his stride, which was a little awkward: the feet splayed, the body tilted forward like a jug being poured. As if he was in friction with the elements and could not move smoothly through them. But at this moment Ellis was not doubting. He was kicking his legs out importantly just the same. If Cornelius noticed he pretended not to; if Cornelius was nervous he didn't show it. He had campaigned for Ellis to be here, despite Stella's protestations. Actually asked for the boy's help. Apparently after his success at the embassy Ellis was the go-to party-crasher.

Tonight the weak spot was an unmarked handle-less door left ever so slightly ajar with a stub of folded cardboard. A waiter who popped out to the shops perhaps. Who cared? They were inside, heading through a labyrinth of service corridors, sniffing out the celebrations. The trick was to act like you owned the place, Cornelius said. Brisk but never rushed, gracious but brooking no nonsense. You did not register the rushing bus-boys and shouting chefs. They were not of your celestial sphere. This was what he said and it seemed to be working: they were through the back of house without incident and pushing into the hotel proper, walking along marathon corridors with barely a door to be seen, only endless walls that existed merely to make a hollow sound when knocked on which Ellis was told to stop doing sharpish.

Ahead of them a grand reception area loomed and if Ellis slowed a little it was because he saw at the edges of the room big serious types with earpieces and dark suits and he remem-bered their friend in the theatre, the dull glint of gun at his waist. What did the gun say, besides *Bang* and *You're dead*? It said directors could be directed. It said bricks could fly through windows and you will shut up and like it. He feared any mo-ment one of these security types might spot them and this time be less friendly, not that they were friendly before. He could not tell if his father was thinking this too: Cornelius's jaw was set, his eyes fixed on the swirling party beyond.

The heavies at the doorway noted them, their gaze passed slowly over, then – was this the moment? – nodded them through. Now they were really in. The sacred centre. Cornelius's jaw relaxed, his eyes took on a hawkish quality. Father and son observed the scene.

And what a scene. A great many fine-looking women, pinned and preened, coiffured and collagened, botoxed and bursting forth. No strangers to upgrading and accessorising. The latest in luxury trim and twin-airbag technology. Surrounding them a great many old men, suddenly attentive to youth. A room

full of grandfathers reunited with their darling granddaugh-
ters after many years apart. The old boys really stoked at how
their little girls had grown. (Here these men were known as
Forbses, and the women, there was no direct translation, it was
a local term with a long poetic history, but the closest dictionary
equivalent was cattle.) Also a frenzy of waiters and waitresses
carrying everything the heart desired while just there on the
other side of the window, Ellis knew this for a fact, were can
collectors and used paper merchants and dark faces that lived
in flies. You could see them while you sipped your champagne,
if you looked. It's the funniest thing, the big pimping rich men
told one another, stabbing the air with their cigars and stroking
the chest hair which sprouted madly from their shirts, laughing at jokes they'd told before and would soon tell again. The
amplified and fat-brained Forbses, the glittering females, the
bustling waiters . . . And around and in between, like rocks in a
sea, the blank unsmiling faces of the security detail.

One or two things Ellis didn't understand. Some guests
did these stage whispers where they covered their mouths
then talked loud enough for the whole room to hear. Others
laughed like they were going for the world record while their
eyes scanned the room to see if others were having a better
time. For some reason people kept saying they were speechless.
They snapped their fingers at waiters, which in his neighbourhood meant 'Please break these bones' but here seemed to
mean something else. And while the food streaming past (rare,
obscure things like prawns) looked and smelled incredible,
hardly anyone ate a thing. Occasionally one of the girls put
a morsel in her mouth and looked miserable about it. Also
(no lie) one platter had a sign saying French carrots. French
wine maybe, from what he understood that was a big deal, but
carrots? Whoever did the catering was maybe not the sharpest,
because you could get carrots here no problem without hump-
ing them over from France.

Even if he didn't understand it all, he figured this was how it was done and made mental notes for his own birthday party the next week. His father's look, however, was moody blues, *Taxi Driver*. He was working himself up to despising everyone present. Was it that the man hadn't watched MTV, he was ignorant of all things bling? Or that, surrounded by these costly creatures, he no longer made the same impression? Okay, there was the three-piece suit of midnight-blue merino wool, bespoke cut in the English style by his little man on Constitution, but look closer and see the loose thread where the suit had caught, the fraying shirt cuff, the motionless second hand of his fancy watch. Observe the dried flakes of skin about the shoulders, the slight shabbiness of the whole enterprise. Add to this the fact it was his only suit. Ellis was not seeking to undermine him – there would be plenty of time for that – it was just, brought into contact with the outside world, the man was occasionally exposed.

'Mr Dau!' cried a voice. 'You made it!'

A squat little man was sailing towards them, chin held high, an entourage of beauties and bodyguards in his wake. So this was Mr Blum. Three fingertips clutched a champagne flute at the base of the stem. Though Blum weaved a little drunkenly, such was his poise he never spilled a drop. Ellis had never seen someone hold a glass like this before and wondered if it was something taught at billionaire school.

'He chose the scenic route,' Blum told his hangers-on. 'Ivan showed me on the dooberry. No need, Mr Dau! Delighted to have you and your . . .'

'Ellis,' said Ellis.

'. . . and your Ellis.'

The billionaire up close: midget ears, delicate eyes and nose, hair thin and neatly combed, a pursed mouth and the faintest sketch of a moustache, all encased in a great slab of face, a slab that correctly employed could have made at least three such faces. Whatever creator one believed in, it was indulgent work. The effect was not so much good or bad as expensive.

'Will you have a glass of champagne, Mr Dau? Perhaps a prawn?'

'No thanks.'

'People make a great fuss about prawns. What you dredge up with them, the child slaves who peel them. Are you one of those people who makes a great fuss?' Blum did not wait for an answer. 'It's nonsense, of course. Might have been an element of truth to it once – not now. But people don't want to know that. Put all the facts and figures in front of them and they'd push them away. They'd rather get angry, and it's so much easier to get angry about something you don't know anything about. Isn't it, Mr Dau?'

'I know about threats,' Cornelius replied.

'Now really, if you mean the little hello goodbye in the theatre you can't be too upset. You were trespassing, dear man! We had to step up security. Outside elements. Haven't even seen the play yet and already they're unhappy about the content. People do *love* getting their backs up ... It gets harder and harder to keep the flag flying for free speech, don't you find, Mr Dau?'

Cornelius said nothing.

'Mr Dau doesn't like me,' Blum explained to his entourage. 'He writes nasty little stories about me in his newspaper. Apparently I'm the big bad wolf.'

'That's ridiculous,' said a sour-faced blonde at his side. 'Tima's dragging this dump into the twenty-first century. You should be writing about the Turks. Building their shoddy condos. First earthquake those things will be rubble.'

'Our guests don't want to hear about the Turks, darling. Mr Dau holds me responsible for every evil in this town. Isn't that right, Mr Dau?' Blum widened his eyes. 'That kind of thinking is dangerous, you know. Never trust the theory which appears to explain everything. Some things are too true ...'

He grabbed an olive from the tray of a passing waiter.

'That sounds like a crook's defence,' said Cornelius.

Blum chewed the olive thoughtfully and spat the pit into an aide's waiting palm. 'Have it your way. I'm saying there are worse things than crooks.'

'Mr Blum gets emotional when talking about his projects,' said a thin, owlish man. 'For the record, he is in no way saying he's a crook.'

'Uri's my PR man,' said Blum with a dismissive wave. 'Uri knows best. I could bugger a choirboy and he'd ensure no sniff of it made the papers.'

'Mr Blum is in no way saying he has intercourse with boys.'

'That's right. Only choirboys.'

'These are jokes, you understand. Mr Blum has a wonderful sense of—'

'Give it a rest, Uri,' said a voice. 'You'll have a fucking hernia.'

The bodies parted to reveal a girl. Excuse Ellis if he paused here and had a little moment, he was not so crazed with hormones that he fell at the feet of every female he saw, but this was the genuine article. Real beauty. Tear-your-heart-out stuff. No need to wax lyrical about the shape of her nose or the size of her eyes, no need to seek obscure words to describe the colour of her hair, her beauty was present in these places but that wasn't the source. All the women at that party had exquisite noses, eyes, hair and so forth. If they hadn't always, someone had bought these things for them. Yet this girl stood out in a crowded field. How to explain this? Modern scholarship will be delighted to learn Ellis had a theory about female beauty. Some girls hid it; others – particularly at his age – had just got it and wanted all to know it (Vincent called these *the nouveau bitche*). Some had been told it so often no further word could impress them. Some were trapped by it. All these sorts of beauty could trip a girl up. But a final category existed of girls whose beauty was a simple fact: they didn't plot their preciousness, nor did they suffer it, they just were. She belonged to that bracket. Maybe a girl could only be beautiful in this last way if she had money, the money to be left alone all her life, to not have her beauty made a commodity. Or was that unfair? God knows life was tough for these poor billionaires. Everyone blamed it on the money.

'You'll have to excuse my daughter Joan,' said Blum. 'This is what they teach them at English public schools. Fifty thousand a term and it's fuck this and bugger that.'

Joan. An old-fashioned name. Ellis bet she loathed it sometimes and wished for another, like that would change everything.

'Ellis Dau,' she said, looking straight at him. 'I know who you are.'

A number of feelings went to war in Ellis. He wanted her to know him very much, though he feared what she knew of him would not be good.

'My friends told me about you.' She fiddled with the back of her dress like it still had the tags in. 'You're the boy from St Joseph's. The one they kicked out.'

Great. Just perfect. It was as he had thought.

'Oh yeah?' said Blum with bleary half-interest. 'What d'you do, son? Look down a lady teacher's blouse?'

The sour-faced blonde scowled at Ellis. He, in return, tried to look like he was the very chairman of the female-decency preservation society. Mainly for the sake of Joan, he didn't care what the rest of them thought.

'No,' said Joan, looking at him like she knew who he was in a way he did not. 'This one really screwed the pooch.'

'Language, sweetheart.'

She kept on looking at Ellis, not exactly friendly or un-friendly. She had this way of pushing her mouth to one side, bolshy and shy at the same time. He noticed her fingernails were short and dirty. Dirtier than his and he was a boy.

'Go on,' she said. 'Tell them.'

He didn't know if she approved of his actions or what she knew. There had been a lot of stories.

'Well,' he said, 'I didn't mean for it to—'

A security crew-cut approached and whispered in Blum's ear. 'So get rid of them,' Blum told him.

The crew-cut whispered more. Guests were gathering at the windows, drawn to some commotion outside.

'All right,' said Blum. 'I'll deal with it.'

The entourage headed for the entrance, Daus following. Past white-faced concierges and through the revolving doors and out into the festering evening. In the middle of the road, oddly framed against the supercars, a motley band of protestors shouted and shook their fists. It looked downright illegal to Ellis, these people so close to those cars. A few of the chaffeurs stood listening, arms crossed.

'We won't be ignored!' shouted a figure at the centre. A dozen flat-faced young men in tracksuits and tall white hats echoed the statement.

'We won't take it any more!' the first man cried.

He was a nose taller than the rest, this speaker, in a soldier's uniform covered with irregular badges and medals with dirty ribbons like he had made or awarded them himself. This and the paleness of his skin made him catch the eye.

'Oh!' he said, seeing Blum approaching. 'I can tell immediately that you are the proprietor!' His manner was approving but also sly, like a merchant who knows the apples he sells are rotten inside. 'Check out that suit! Very nice, very nice . . . How many dollars would a body need to buy a suit like that, I wonder?'

Ellis saw the man's smooth face was in fact a block of muscle and jaw. Looking more, he realised the extraordinary whiteness of his eyes was mostly because of the extraordinary blackness of his pupils. He noticed the opening and closing nostrils of a bull about to charge. A smile lurked beneath, with a large gap between the upper two front teeth, but by now he had seen the hard jaw and the black-and-white eyes and the bull's nostrils and he was not much in the mood for smiling back. By this point he was thinking this was a person of particular suspicion.

'Tonight is a private party,' said Blum. 'You can't be here.'

'We're not at your party,' said a white-haired thug without a hat. 'We're in the road. That's public property.'

'And you never know,' said the soldier with the bull nostrils, 'we might be on the guest list. The name is Anders Grotz. If not, try 'the Forty-four Horsemen'. Do check. We would so like to be on the list.'

'You're not,' said Blum.

'It's a new name,' the white-haired thug explained. 'Nothing to do with membership numbers, just sounds good.'

'I'm asking you nicely,' said Blum.

'You've got the Four Horsemen of the Apocalypse,' said Grotz, 'so imagine if there were forty more of them.'

'Why not the Forty-five Horsemen?' asked Joan. 'Or the Eight hundred and ninety seven horsemen?'

'Because it's the Forty-four Horsemen,' said Grotz.

'Why?' she asked.

'It just is,' said Grotz.

'This one is a real *Murder She Wrote*,' said White Hair, staring at Joan.

'Why are you bothering us?' Blum seemed quite sober now.

In the background the bouncers massed.

'Do you like our hats?' Grotz asked, unfazed. They were the traditional goatherd numbers occasionally seen on old men. Hats to keep the sun off weak minds. 'No man can be killed or harmed when he wears this hat. You see this brush design at the front? This symbolises juniper, which is associated with eternity. I don't know what the other curls stand for, but every one has meaning and history. The hat is a symbol of our superiority over other nations and our hatred of perversion.'

'Just get rid of them, Tima,' said the blonde.

'The wool is delightful against my skin,' said another goon.

'We're bringing it back,' said a third.

'I never thought I'd say this,' said Joan, ' but can we go inside?'

She'd taken off her shoes and with a look of deep reverential boredom swung them back and forth.

'All my life,' said Grotz, running his hand along the paintwork of a scarlet Porsche, 'I am thinking, "What is my purpose?" I am a good soldier. When my country asks me to kill, I kill. But always I am thinking, "Is there more to me than this? Will I ever be the household name?"'

Gently, worshipfully, his hand traced the bonnet's curve.

'Then I see the gene pool being corrupted, the Western gay agenda spreading, the men with long hair in our streets, and I understand the cause of our problems and I know something must be done, I know I must do it . . .'

Oh boy, thought Ellis. *We've got a jumper.* Leave an easy conclusion near a certain type and they leapt straight into it. Crazy how many people must be violently against everything in sight or pathetically for it. Like everything must fit these narrow boxes. *Will it make?* the hacks at the paper were always asking each other. *Will the story make?*

'Now you come here with your disrespectful plays, with your homosexuals and foreign agents – it distresses me, it causes me concern. I'll be honest with you, I lie awake at night worrying about the purity of our people.'

'What a crock of shit,' said the sour-faced blonde. She rummaged in her handbag for a cigarette which she found and lit.

'Women should not smoke,' White Hair told her. 'It puts their babies at risk of gayness.'

'And you're a medical expert, I suppose,' said the blonde.

'What do they know?' said White Hair. 'They're only experts.'

'Tima,' said the blonde. 'Our guests are waiting. Leave these numbskulls.'

'Anna is right, Dad,' said Joan.

'Anya,' said the blonde.

'Whatever,' said Joan.

Blum did not rush to answer. For all the talk of him being

ruthless and dangerous, this didn't look like his scene. At the hotel windows, the party guests watched. These thugs had everyone's attention.

'Burn the flag, Rolo,' said Grotz.

An acned henchman stepped forward, tricolour flag in his hands.

'Take this, Russians,' he said.

'That's the Dutch flag,' said Joan.

'I don't think so,' said Grotz.

'It is,' said Joan.

Grotz, seeing Rolo falter, told him, 'Don't listen to her. Ignore this negative thinking. Be the bigger person.'

Rolo lit one corner and the flag went up.

'See how foreigners are?' Grotz asked his men. 'It's always someone else's fault. "That's not our flag." They could have just gone along with it. Didn't have to be so difficult about it.'

'A real *Murder She Wrote*,' said White Hair, staring at Joan.

'I've heard enough,' said Blum, signalling the nearest security guard. 'Call the police.'

'You're removing us from this public space?' said Grotz. 'Because we displease you?'

Blum was no longer listening. He was ushering his radiant daughter and others back inside.

'You see that?' Grotz asked his supporters and the listening chauffeurs. 'You see this rudeness? You see this arrogance?' He turned to Cornelius. 'I know you're with me on this, Mr Journalist. I've seen your picture by the articles. I know you're sick of the Muslims and Russians and out-of-touch elites too.'

Cornelius was alarmed by the association. The idea that he or any of the media could share, far less induce, these grievances . . . It was preposterous. Simply preposterous.

'Why does everyone keep insisting I'm like them?' he demanded. 'I'm not like you. You're thugs! You trashed my newspaper!'

'You're upset,' said Grotz.

'He's totally upset,' said White Hair.

'You think we hate you,' said Grotz. 'Not so. We are not your enemies, we are friends who do not like you.'

'I fail to see—'

'A difference? Oh there is. Oh certainly. We do this out of love, you see. The brick is a gift of this love. It says, "Hey friend! Why do you ignore us? Don't ignore us! We love you!"'

'We will love you in the face,' said White Hair.

'Like I said,' Grotz continued, 'I have a great regard for your paper. Lot of powerful stuff therein. Only thing is, you don't know what you want. We know what we want.'

'No sex before marriage for women, do *something* about the Muslims, deport immigrants and gays, death penalty for paedos or we sort it ourselves,' said White Hair.

'And ban Chinese food,' said Rolo.

Grotz's eyes, alive at the mention of these hopes and dreams, abruptly deadened.

'It repeats on me,' Rolo explained.

'We'll discuss the Chinese food,' Grotz replied.

How wrong it was to say demagogues knew nothing of tolerance. True, they didn't spread it about, but for their cretinous supporters, for their foot-in-mouth fans, the tolerance was off the charts. To have every slippery denial of bigotry immediately undermined. To overlook all the other types of personal awfulness even 'the cause' couldn't explain or excuse. To share every car journey and pub evening with those peers. A lifetime in the company of men who thought science was witchcraft and art was for fags, who considered it the acme of wit to tell cleaners they had missed a spot. Who else had such space in their hearts? No one knew tolerance like the promoters of intolerance.

'It repeats on me,' said Rolo. 'That's all.'

'There's other stuff,' Grotz told Cornelius, 'but that's the gist. That's why we should be working together, you and us. We need a bigger media presence. Need to get inside people's dreams, you follow? When you get into the public unconscious, that's when you become a real thing.'

'And why on earth should the *Chronicle* want that?'

'Because it's all changing. Can't you tell? Because soon we won't be asking. Because the falcon is turning wider and wider in the thingy. You see? I'm an educated man like yourself.' Grotz clicked his fingers. 'Hey, you should interview me!'

'Great idea,' said White Hair.

'Come on, ask me a question.'

Cornelius did not reply.

'Go on,' said White Hair. He pushed Cornelius, hard enough to make him stumble back. Now this Ellis had never seen. His father treated like that? A professional and respectable man pushed around by thugs. Ellis had never put much stock in words like *professional* and *respectable* before but he realised he had been counting on them to mean something, to have a certain currency in the wider world. Apparently these Horsemen did not recognise or deal with such ideas.

And his father, his father did nothing. Just stood there mutely, head lowered as if waiting to receive further blows. Prior to this moment Ellis knew two versions of his father – the quiet home man and the chivvying reporter. Alone, that first Cornelius had been too small, too limited. That second Cornelius, the editor and smasher of idols, seemed to complete and explain the man. But clearly that second version also had its limits. Faced with actual violence, a third appeared: Cornelius the pragmatist, Cornelius the looker-away, Cornelius the 'please let's not have any trouble'. Ellis understood why – of course, he was scared too. Still, it took some sucking in of breath and lowering of hopes to align this grey and sketchy version, this pencil study, to the man he had imagined his father to be.

'You look stressed, Mr Dau,' said Grotz. 'Don't be stressed. Stress is the great killer . . . If you're thinking, "Why are they giving me a hard time?" that's the wrong question. You should be asking, "How can I make my new friends like me? How can I get on their team?"'

The sound of approaching sirens tore Grotz from his reverie. 'Time to go,' he said. He didn't seem disappointed or angry at being moved on – he looked happy. Happy that he and his goons had stood beside the grand cars and troubled the host. Happy to have caused a scene and ruined something.

'Think on those questions,' he called back as his ragtag unit took off into the night. 'This is the start of something beautiful!'

HE DIDN'T think about the girl again. No time for senti-mental hooey. Serious matters afoot. The fate of a nation. What was needed were hawks and tigers, not big-eyed puppies off Valentine's cards. So no, sorry, he didn't think about her again.

All right, that's a lie. He thought about her constantly.

Okay, full confession: he thought about her constantly and he followed her.

He didn't want to be some throbbing adolescent basket case. He didn't want to obsess about her. Only he had no choice. Problems on problems: these thoughts wouldn't let him be, yet his memory of her was blurred and shady, a low-resolution job not up to task. All that unquestioning beauty had burned out his retina, he saw the outline only. Craving someone so much and unable to summon even a decent picture of her face . . . Pure misery.

In days of yore people went to extreme lengths to know the whereabouts and private lives of strangers. Journos of a certain persuasion rooted through people's bins. Armed with a target's mobile number and the right know-how, one could tap in to their texts and answerphone messages. 'Everyone was doing it,' Urvin more than once said wistfully. This sounded to Ellis like a lot of effort. Nowadays it was all at the touch of a button. Nowadays people made it so easy to stalk them. Nowadays they volunteered the information, stacking it up in little boxes for the happy shopper. Yes, the Web was providing incredible new opportunities for weirdos, blackmailers and gutter hacks. It was a brave new world for the men who hid in bushes. His sympathies went out to those old time stalkers for whom progress came too late, those footsore stooges with the permanent sniffle and the snooper's bad back. They didn't have the resources he had today.

Slouched at the tech room desk, he put her name into the usual sites. Six profile pages across the lot. Her face in a thousand different photos. *Ah, that's what she looked like – hold on, power cut, lost her, no, there she is, we're back . . .* He was still in pain (let's face it, no resolution was high enough) but at least the pain was focused. Here she was: a living breathing girl built from likes and reblogs and hyperlinks. She had a thing for eighties synth bands and snarky gifs, wanted to save the rainforest and tax the rich, harboured the usual fears of spiders, politicians, clowns. Big on Americana, she posted picture after picture of strip malls and manicured lawns and motel swimming pools, of sullen boys and girls dressed in something called 'charity shop chic', their hair lop-sided, their faces bleached with flash. Was ugliness her thing? Hope for him yet, Vincent might have said. Perhaps this wasn't her character so much as the Web's for that age and calling – don't ask Ellis where the person ended and the era began. All the same he got worked up. He had a feeling, yes, a growing feeling that she was his—

'What's this?'

The horror. He hadn't noticed his father approaching. He couldn't close those windows fast enough. Genuinely could not have been more embarrassed if he'd been discovered looking at the usual tangle of flesh. Without it being said, he knew this girl was off limits. A Juliet to his Romeo. He hadn't read the play, but he'd seen the film with the gold guns where she said, 'Prodigious birth of love it is to me, that I must love a loathed enemy.' *Tough break*, he thought when he watched that. *Good luck to her*, he thought. *Also respect* – all that anguish and catastrophe and she never stopped speaking in verse.

He braced himself for the telling off. But the reality was far worse.

'Ellis, it's natural at your age to have certain feelings . . .'

Oh god, here we go.

'Women are magnificent . . . inspirational . . . the very essence of . . .'

And so on and so forth.

'But you mustn't let your emotions run away with you.'

Shoot me now.

'This girl, she's not . . .'

'Not what?'

'What I'm saying is there's a type. A type you should stay away from. You've seen her family, the company she keeps . . .'

Bit rich coming from someone who spent practically every day with Mr Urvin, a man who talked nostalgically about tapping people's phones and going through their bins. But he didn't argue. It would only have inspired more. Cornelius, reading this silence as contemplation inspired by his wisdom, squeezed his son's shoulder in commiseration at the unfairness of this world, and returned to work.

Did Ellis listen to his father? Anyone thinking 'I hope so' should perhaps stop reading this account. It will only cause further heartache.

He brought her web pages back up and followed the trail. It didn't take long to find what he was looking for. She'd never visited the National Museum and was planning to go this afternoon.

'If anyone asks,' he told Mr Kozlov, 'I've got an errand to run.'

In a park of bright pink flowers with a sickly rotten perfume and trees whose long flossy paraphernalia blanketed the ground and itched the skin, he began his stakeout. His mind was set, his middle finger raised to all the haters. A person needed to push against the world to find out where the limits were – that was how you grew up. If you never climbed out of the cot or touched the naked flame or in some way tore the wallpaper then you never learned, you remained a child forever. You could not wait for people to hand this stuff over. They could be pretty stingy about it, you couldn't give them that sort of power. Control the authority figures in your life, that was the thrust of his thinking. He was nearly seventeen years old after all, the big one seven in less than a week.

Sound as that was, he was still performing mental cartwheels trying to make this decision something his father would have supported. Didn't he say a reporter must look for motive in all things, must build his story, must establish the characters of note? Wasn't Joan such a character? Wasn't following her the best way to do these things? Ellis didn't know for certain whether this was true or what he wanted to be true – it was not always an easy distinction to make – yet even as he told himself to be careful he knew nothing would stop him. The headline was already written. *Lovestruck newshound begins his investigations.*

His observations then, for the benefit of a full and proper report. An hour or two at most and there she was, crossing the sun-drenched plaza, smooth and nimble as a spirit that moves on air and makes no footprint. She wore no fancy outfit today, just an old T-shirt and black jeans. A scruffy rucksack over one shoulder. Super-understated. If he hadn't seen first-hand the privilege surrounding her he might have thought her poor. Round here no self-respecting female carried a rucksack – even cashiers and high-school girls wielded designer bags. Wouldn't show their faces in real life without the fake Louis V. Yet this girl, who could've bought the actual megabucks version, who could have strutted head to toe in solid gold, chose to dress like a can-collector who lived in a bush.

Did that put him off? Ha! She could have worn pure rubbish, she could have worn a swarm of bees – he still took a powerful hit at the sight of her. If anything the hit was greater than previous. He felt because he had been forbidden to see her he had the right to harbour wild, dramatic emotions for her. And in another sense this ban put he and her on the same side, made them bedfellows, so to speak. Without her knowing it, without sharing much more than a glance, they had become co-conspirators.

He half expected the museum to be shut. Weeds and trees sprouted out of the back of it, for god's sake. But Joan strolled straight in. It just went to show. *Never assume* was his father's first rule of journalism and a good rule in the here and now. Following the suspect (this was what he was calling her, this was how he hoped to save face) into the cool lobby, he found it was business as usual. Usual being sleepy, exhausted, on its last legs. Pinned across one wall, a huge and faded tourism poster struggled to capture the enchantment of their country. *The only way to leave is to never visit*, the slogan claimed. A pair of attendants at reception competed in the category of Most Inanimate Object. Yet history was still readily available. History on tap, history galore.

She headed into the first room. Worried he was too close and would be seen he paused beside a map of the country. The map was large, the country small, the lines of its borders drawn and redrawn many times. To deter thieves and vandals, layer upon layer of Sellotape armadilloed the map's surface. Without the tape, did the country fall apart? What else held it together?

But enough of the map – the girl!

She was not among the first room's crude masks and hammered blades. Nor in the second room where Islam and Christendom revealed their mysteries and cast doubts upon his ancestors' small unpolished gods. He hurried on into the Twentieth Century, where his way was blocked by a great crowd of suits and their wives.

'And you can guess who came calling,' a nervous and pasty guide was saying.

'The Russians!' they cried.

Indeed. Who else? (The British perhaps, Cornelius said they had gone to war for less – for an ear in one case, on another occasion for a stool.)

Ellis pushed through, elbowing fat folds, mindful of his

quest, until he saw Joan near the front. She was stuck too. They were going to endure more of this lecture before they were through.

'That's right,' said the guide. 'They had seen the oil and gas of our neighbours—'

'Screw those guys!' a man shouted.

'But such treasures have dodged our country.' With this admission the guide's eyes lowered and his long lashes fluttered as if he were personally to blame. 'In terms of resources, we have—'

'Nothing!' cried the crowd. They were getting the hang of this, and their happiness at knowing the answer outweighed the grimness of the word.

Joan, however, was not interested in audience participation. She was squeezing and jostling, trying to escape. Ellis strained in the same direction, only to find himself wedged against a woman plumply whispering observations to no one in particular.

'Isn't that peculiar. Really so peculiar. Really odd . . .'

'Each step forward for the wider world put us one step back,' the fluttering guide went on.

'Just funny, when you think about it. Just mad . . .'

Joan had broken free and was moving away. Ellis fell to his knees and crawled through the forest of legs. Dignitaries quibbled and squawked.

'Oh my!'

'Look at that boy!'

'Isn't that the most bizarre thing? Isn't that odd?'

Back on his feet and finally on the threshold of Culture he watched her strolling on, admiring the wood carvings of which their country was so proud, contemplating the better examples of their propaganda posters which might by some definitions be called art. Why did people like museums anyway? He couldn't figure it out. Everything was old and falling apart, the jugs didn't hold water and the swords didn't cut, and even the stuff that might still do the job was stuck on the wall or pinned under glass. Framed blankets. Silent guitars. Books with the pages sealed shut. It was all so crushingly useless. A shadow of sadness hung over the whole show. If he hadn't been on a mission he'd have crawled into a corner and wept.

Perhaps Joan had a finer appreciation of these things. She seemed to know how long to stand in front of each exhibit though that information wasn't written anywhere as far as Ellis could see.

In any case it was a relief when she left the museum, stepping out into the bull's-eye of another cruel hot day. Whew, this spirit girl moved fast. He could scarcely keep up. The clatter of his flip-flops he thought would wake the very dead – yet perhaps this was paranoia for not once did she look round to question the commotion.

He followed her past the Courts of Justice and its attendant bars: The Alibi, The Verdict, The Greased Palm. Past the brownfield sites where cadets rehearsed manoeuvres by moonlight like girls who did not wish their routines seen before the village dance. Past the enormous plot of land once claimed would be home to the tallest building on the continent: 'Kim Tower', named after a foreign leader the previous President admired. The city was littered with this negative memorabilia, these corsages of marriages that didn't last.

Question: Were these absent spaces the real monuments here?

Question: Was the city under construction or in decay?

On they went, past the Blum plazas and Chinese condos, past grand houses where gardeners pulled tiny weeds from immaculate drives. Here were the Royale and the Crown, the two main cinemas, opposite one another. Their owners were at war over dimensions – at last count they were on twelve apiece. Past the central police station outside which Nestor's legs still stood, long after the rest of him was toppled, and into Independence

Square, home to the Palace of the Parliament. It was said the first whorehouses in the city stood on this spot, before they were knocked down and replaced with this steroid-jacked city hall. Though Ellis was very small when Nestor appeared triumphant on the balcony to make his promise to the people below, he had seen pictures of the happy crowds straining excitedly against the soldiers who kept them in place, and the whole nation was familiar with that first historic speech so peppered with good serious words like *cleanse* and *open* and *candidates*, plural. Cornelius said these words were not exactly untrue. Yet somewhere in the cleansing all desire to challenge the leadership had been lost, along with many of the candidates.

Now the spy got a nasty surprise. Joan abruptly swivelled to face him and made a shooing gesture with the back of her hand. *A shooing gesture.* That almost did for him. Right then and there he nearly threw in the towel. He was folding himself into a doorway, about to start the great post-mortem, when a Range Rover with tinted windows rolled past. Further down the street he saw her shooing again. She was shooing the car, not him.

'Go away,' she shouted.

The Range Rover stopped a short distance from her, looking big and dumb and hesitant. Ellis watched with growing disgust. Disgust that someone should be following this girl. Couldn't they leave her alone? Couldn't a young woman do as she pleased without sleazebags shadowing her every move? What a time this was, what an awful thing to see.

'Get lost,' she shouted.

Off she went. He followed – and if there was a hint of sleazebag in his actions it was of a well-meaning sleazebag, a sleazebag of good character, a sleazebag on whom you could depend. Drawing level with the Range Rover, he saw two security bruisers conferring inside. Her father's people. No sooner had he passed, the car resumed its trundle, speed set to kerb-crawl. Joan strode on, the SUV creeping behind, and the sight made him wonder if being a billionaire's baby might not be all baths in bank notes and which-diamonds-shall-I-wear-today?

With a sudden shimmy she darted off the road. Into the main market where she was swallowed in the chaos of SIM cards and knock-off Levi's and sprigs of fir and weird rubber boots and car keys sold for the bragging rights with no car included, also every type of grain and flour and dried herb, every manner of tailor and fixer, and ladies washing vegetables and salesgirls playing patty cake and horse butchers and beef barons and grandmothers who'd bussed in from the provinces to sell one scrawny chicken and a DVD salesman with his TV set up in a ditch and a stall of rotten corn for a penny a cob and a great convention of starlings in the eaves that never let up chirping and a market drunk asleep on a porter's trolley who when shaken by disapproving passers-by cried, 'Do I come to your house and wake you?'

She weaved through the teeming alleys, dropping her shoulders, slipping her hips, while he blundered on behind, upsetting baskets, vaulting dusty goods, raising squawks from indignant poultry. The narrow streets seemed on her side: their rubbish slowed only his feet, their jutting details caught only his clothes, their strays tripped only his legs, their snaking paths confused only his brain, exhausted only his lungs. She was not apart from it but in it, shoulder to shoulder, face to face. Cool, level-eyed, the billionaire's daughter reared on king prawns and French carrots, wearing her extreme beauty with no more care or ceremony than an old coat slung on to pop to the postbox in the rain.

He had almost lost her when she stopped at the famous orange seller. Famous because his stall sold the best, or so he was always claiming in a foghorn bawl. While Joan bought fruit Ellis caught his breath and listened to the traders' talk. The Horsemen had been here this morning, hassling possible immigrants, turning over stalls they felt did not reflect their values, smashing livelihoods they thought spread the wrong message. It was a mystery to him how these yobs did exactly as they pleased without reprisal while others like yours truly got walloped for every misdemeanour. Where was the justice? He told himself it was just a few people inconvenienced. Thanks to these Horsemen the *Chronicle* had one more brick and one less window, but he didn't take that as a sign of life as a whole. It wasn't the true reality, surely.

The true reality was the suspect had now purchased her orange and was eating it in a most compelling and un-billionaire-like manner, all teeth and lips and tongue. Perhaps that was not a journalistic observation of the highest quality, but what was a boy to do? She was really a lovely suspect.

Finishing the fruit she used the back of her hand as a napkin and was off again with he, the determined sleuth, in pursuit. It was exciting to watch her and discover her secrets, if only the surface of them. To be so close to her without her knowing. Exciting also to think he might be discovered, that she might at any moment see him and know him, that his cover might be blown.

Behind the market she found a working water pump where she gave herself a birdbath, turning the water into her thin strong wrists one at a time and rubbing it with insistence about her fine and twisting neck and stroking it over every uncovered inch of her skin, letting the drops run off and into the earth. From behind the dusty wares of a nearby carpet seller he observed the rivers running along the contours of her body, on occasion disappearing into her clothes and what lay beneath. Those droplets that trailed and lagged after the others would sometimes catch the sun in a million tiny mirrors that made her shimmer and dance in the heat.

Safe to say St Joseph's and the *Chronicle* were a million miles from his thoughts at this time. Instantly he could appreciate this new field of study. Her movements were so lingering and unrushed he began to feel like the chewed-up orange himself. Schooled by his parents as to what was decent and upright, he knew it was inappropriate to be watching her, just as he knew men were the reason women crossed their legs. But he thought there was some encouragement in this instance. As if she knew he was there and was playing to the gallery. Like she was alive to the desire around her. Thinking this did not help with his feeling of being chewed up.

Around this time the carpet seller, ignorant of Ellis's need for stealth and secrecy, began to inquire of his interest in the rug he seemed to be admiring so intently. The whispered replies were not heeded. Violently the trader beat his wares to expose the quality beneath. Ellis was provoked to sneezing and forced to retreat.

When he returned to his observation spot – tragedy. She was gone and could not be traced. He had lost her.

'Holy mother of Jesus and god, all right,' Vincent said when he heard about Ellis's investigations. 'Let's not lose our shit entirely. It's crystal clear what's needed here.'

'It is?'

'Sure . . . You need to get laid. Badly.'

NATURALLY Ellis was the only one who thought a girl sprinkling herself with water was front page news. Him and perhaps the *Gazette*, and he shuddered to imagine what their strapline would have been. *Daddy's princess sets pulses racing in wet T-shirt comp for one* or some similar car crash of perv, sneer and cliché.

Otherwise the Horsemen were the big news. Like the great St Joseph's nit epidemic, one minute no one had known or cared about their existence and the next they were the only thing anyone was talking about. This Grotz and his associates seemed to be everywhere at once. Videos of their recent raids, which these hard-working head stompers filmed and posted online, got thousands of views in a few short hours. Who knew whether the viewers liked or loathed it, people were enthralled. In their knee-jerk hatred of all things different the Horsemen had a certain moral clarity. They knew their position, nasty as it was, in a way many did not. Everything they did said, 'Who will challenge us?' No one raised their hand.

'We are monitoring it,' Ellis heard Fedor telling Cornelius (his ear was once more glued to the door).

'And you want us to keep quiet? I'm all for not giving idiots a platform, cutting off the oxygen of publicity and so on, but silencing conversations about terrorism isn't the same as fighting it.'

'Turning over a few market stalls is not terrorism, Cornelius. This is exactly the problem, when you use language like this. It's sensational. Dangerous. You do not help a delicate situation. Everything has to be a scandal with you newspaper types.'

'And nothing would be a scandal if you had your way.'

'We are trying to be sympathetic to the nuances of the situation. You are trying to take those nuances away.'

A dull man, this Fedor, Ellis would have described him as 'unigmatic' if that was a word.

'You lecture me while these thugs openly harass people.'

'They've been warned.'

'What good is warning them? Why don't you arrest them?'

Though Cornelius was loud in his criticism, he didn't do much either. Only one piece about the nationalists made the website that week: a surprisingly neutral report on the Horsemen's violent online videos.

'We've become a fucking news aggregator,' Urvin grumbled. 'Just churning out rehashed versions of whatever pops up on the Internet. No checks, no follow-up calls, no opinion. No idea how to amp something up in the true and time-honoured manner.'

Bland as it was, the article still caused a spike in traffic to the site. Someone even wrote a comment, its tone ambiguous, in the box below:

who will they come 4 next?

This question was answered on the evening of Ellis's seventeenth birthday.

'A wild success' is how he would have liked his party to be known. Unfortunately that wasn't true. Probably a lot of parents kept their kids away after the snafu at school. Whatever the reason, the numbers were . . . small. 'How small is small?' the journalists are asking. Well, counting the parrot, who hated him, and his parents, who didn't trust him, there were five of them. In terms of people who didn't live in the apartment already, if that sort of data were needed, there was Vincent.

The first hour or so was watching Vincent trying to teach the bird profanities while his parents ignored them in the kitchen.

'Wanker . . . Say it. Wan-ker.'

'Ellis has a boner. Try that. Ellis has a boner.'

The second hour was blasting the undead in the head or

heart for maximum points. In a special one-night-only deal the games console had been freed from his parents' wardrobe. *Oh yeah, zombies, you can't hide from the Grim Reaper. 'Specially when he's got a bazooka.* This was also the hour when Ellis tried out etiquette tips from Blum's party.

'Mother, more cake!'

'Don't you click your fingers at me, young man.'

The third hour was mostly spent in Vincent's armpit. A bad hour.

'Watch this now. Watch how I do this. There's nothing you can do. Death grip. Boom. Letting you know right there.'

The fourth hour, technically his bedtime, was when things got interesting. Halfway through the haunted care-home mission, as they gave those cannibal grannies a make-over they wouldn't forget, a loud hammering at the door made him and Vincent look up. No one was expected. A zombie jumped out of a grandfather clock and ate Ellis's brain. *Too bad, sucker.*

'Hey,' cried a voice. 'It's Urvin. You've got to see this.'

Not just Urvin. It was the whole *Chronicle* team bar Kozlov.

'What, you don't pick up your phone?' Urvin asked Cornelius, pushing in with Armitage, Jonquil and Geffen behind. He clutched a bottle of grain spirit in which he'd already made considerable inroads.

'It's my son's birthday, Urvin. We're trying to have a quiet evening.'

'Not any more you're not. It's all kicked off.'

Urvin fumbled with his phone, a wild gleam in his eyes. Ellis had spent long enough at the paper to know the look of a hack with the scent. It meant a heap of trouble for someone, which meant news for Urvin. To those who shook their heads at such distasteful excitement, Urvin would have said that every trade put callouses on its tradesmen – in journalism the hard patches developed not on the hands or feet but on the inside, the spirit. Hacks and human misery had a business relationship. Not to say they were heartless, but they didn't let themselves get dragged under and they didn't look away, and those who complained didn't get it, and those who couldn't handle it should take up something else like flower arranging or playing the flute. 'Happiness writes white,' he liked to say, by which he meant the joy and wellbeing of others merited no ink.

'Balls to this.' Urvin gave up on his phone. 'Jonquil, you show him.'

After a brief search Jonquil brought up the image in question.

'That's a photo of Jacobs,' he told Cornelius. 'Taken tonight.'

'Governor Jacobs?'

During the last election Governor Jacobs made a name as the country's most progressive politician by pasting campaign posters on every stray dog in the district.

'Hard to tell, isn't it? They say he's got a broken jaw, fractured cheekbone, smashed ribs. They took him to Central an hour ago.'

'This can't be real.'

Who knew when this became the first response, when everyone started working backwards from the assumption any picture or video or story was false and whole troll farms were churning this stuff out day and night.

'No reason to doubt it,' said Jonquil. 'Kozlov is outside the hospital with a camera now. The staff confirmed it. He'll ring us if anything changes.'

'Who did this?'

Urvin looked like he'd been waiting for Cornelius to ask.

'Who do you think?' he said.

Here was the scene in the Daus' apartment that evening: the adults gathered around the kitchen table, smoking, drinking, debating, while in the living room Ellis and Vincent kept the zombie hordes at bay.

We will see peace on Earth if we have to murder these fiends with our bare hands.

Actually it was mainly Vincent holding off the zombie

hordes. It was hard to explain, Ellis had been praying for that console for a solid month, but ever since the journos arrived with that bad-news gleam in their eyes he'd felt distracted. Tonight was supposed to be his ascendance to adulthood, the big upgrade, Ellis 2.0, yet it still felt like he was on the wrong side of the door. Somehow he'd managed to get excluded at his own birthday party.

'Hey dickbreath, are you playing or not?'

'Just a minute.'

He went over to the kitchen door and listened.

'I'm telling you,' Urvin was saying, 'I'm begging you . . . We have to go after them. Both barrels.'

'Don't give them too much credit,' said Cornelius.

'What can the cops do now? They let it go too far. Either they look weak or make martyrs.'

Ellis leaned closer and accidentally creaked the door.

'Darling?' said his mother. 'Is that you?'

Nothing for it but to own it. He stepped into the cave of smoke. Six worried faces. Five nervous hands taking turns ashing cigarettes on one tiny saucer. In the window behind, the setting sun framed their heads with fire. Typical of nature in its throwaway glory to explode with no one watching. Just typical. And there were other matters to consider, like the pattern of pigeons which freckled the blazing sky and the faintly swirling brushwork of the clouds and those giant sleeping mountains in the distance. A tip-top display, though it didn't help his mood. It felt like pretty tactless timing so hot on the hooves of these Horsemen. He didn't know where he was in a world that punched you in the face and seconds later stroked your hair. He had his work cut out as it was.

'Do you want something, darling?' asked Stella.

He wanted to delay matters so he could take it all in. Mr Geffen slumped in the nearest chair, scowling at the picture of horses made of felt as if they were in some way responsible. Miss Armitage wearing the expression of someone permanently being flicked on the forehead by an invisible assailant. Mr Urvin pouring shots. Blurry, with the ability to get much blurrier. Mr Jonquil, speaking now about the need to get something online as soon as, pushing the words through that letterbox mouth like a ventriloquist who'd mislaid his puppet. Cornelius, the only one who didn't smoke, sat with the fruit bowl in front of him, turning a grape between his fingers as he listened. All hell breaking loose and the man was polishing grapes. At the far end, Stella, watching with wise dark eyes, pulled the birthday cake towards her and blew off the ash that had drifted onto its icing. She raised her eyebrows at Ellis as if to say 'What can you do?' and cut two slices for two saucers.

'You want more cake, I bet,' she said.

For some reason that annoyed him. He didn't like her second-guessing his wants and desires, talking to him like he was still a child with childish tastes. That version of him was not relevant to his life now. His needs and dreams were more complex, more grown-up, they could not be so easily read.

Of course he did want more cake, but that was not the main thing. Above all he wanted to know what was going on.

'Twenty more minutes then bed,' she told him, pushing the saucers across the table. They came to rest beside a box of matches. He noticed her grab the matches and hide that hand under the table. He knew it wasn't easy for his parents, that he'd done nothing to deserve or reclaim their trust. He knew questions still hung over him – about what he'd done, about what it was in his nature to become – but all the same that little action hurt.

He took the cake. As he left, the room kindled to life again.

'Mr Geffen,' he heard his mother say. 'Would you shut the door?'

Yes, an odd night. More than odd. He had this awful feeling. Apocalyptic levels of badness. Without knowing it, people were no longer quite themselves, like they were in the gravity of a thing bigger than them. Everything was becoming unhinged.

Geffen, yawning heavily, made his goodbyes around ten. 'Get bent' were his last words of the night, in response to something Urvin yelled about euthanasia. Vincent cackled – all night he'd been enjoying the profanities, mainly from Urvin, coming through the walls – but he couldn't laugh long because he was next for the chop. Mr S. was on the phone and this lateness was beyond a joke.

Lingering over his teeth in the bathroom (the kitchen was next door and the walls were not much), Ellis heard more news coming in. Via social media the Horsemen had claimed responsibility for the attack. Far and wide this claim was being clicked and shared, and now the first *Gazette* and *Gazette*-ish articles were sprouting online ... *This Just Happened And It Is So WTF We Cannot Even Handle It* and *You Will Not Believe Who Just Got Their Head Kicked In*, soon to be followed by *Five Things We Learned From Jacobs Getting His Head Kicked In* and *The Twelve Best Celebrity Responses To Jacobs Getting His Head Kicked In*. Some would lay into the Horsemen and others would try to defend them or claim it was a conspiracy to frame them and a few might discover the attackers' identities or what they imagined were the correct identities and seek to wage an attack of their own, and all those who wished to cause offence would cause it, and all those who wished to take offence would take it, and with each comment and think piece and declaration that this alone was the true reality while all else was propaganda – *I think, We need, My take, How dare* – the volume rose in the craterscape of open mouths.

'Wannabes, that's what they are.' Cornelius sounded drunk. 'Plastic gangsters.'

'They seem real enough to me,' said Jonquil.

'Real or not,' said Stella, 'let's not feed them.' She sounded more sober than the others.

'I agree,' said Miss Armitage. 'There's what interests us and what's truly in our interests ...'

'We've got to report it,' said Jonquil.

This is how the *Chronicle* hacks should be remembered: arguing, spirited.

'Exactly!' said Urvin. 'They want to screw this country? We'll screw them!'

Ellis could sense Stella's frown through the wall. 'It would strengthen your case, Urvin, if you didn't make reporting sound like a sex act.'

'Who said anything about sex?' asked Urvin. 'I wasn't talking about sex. Did you hear me say anything about sex?'

'You just said it three times,' said Armitage.

'You did,' said Jonquil.

'Come on, Stella,' grumbled Urvin. 'Now you're jumping on the puritannical bandwagon too?'

'Do you see me blushing?' she replied. 'That's not what I'm getting at. I'm saying macho, shouty coverage is the wrong approach. They want a fight. Why give it to them?'

'But they broke the guy's jaw!' cried Urvin. 'And they admit it, they're proud of it! It's happened. It's news. We report the news . . . Someone has to say, "It is happening." You know, like that Goya picture. Someone has to say, "I saw it."'

'*I saw it!*' the parrot's old-child voice echoed from next door.

'Right, boss?'

'Sure, publish and be . . . you know,' said Cornelius. No doubt about it, thought Ellis, his father was loaded. He wasn't a big drinker. Coming home from Uncle Mart's second wedding he had to stop their cab to puke at the side of the road. 'But I think you all overestimate our influence . . . I mean, who apart from us cares what we put up?'

'Boss . . .'

'No, let's be honest. Who do we oust? What do we stop? You talk like we're going to fix the problem, but we don't fix problems.'

Ellis was still prepared to defer to his father on matters of the wider world, but the way Cornelius was talking now was nothing he wished to copy.

'Tomorrow morning,' Cornelius continued, 'the *Gazette* will have a story about someone's handbag, or a fucking *hamster*, with more hits and comments, more discussion, than anything we write about this now.'

The hacks, amused by his tone, familiar with the neediness and contempt all editors felt for their readers, laughed and clinked their glasses. Only the eavesdropper next door failed to see the funny side. He knew adults were full of smart things to say about the world and in some ways questioned everything, like what words were insensitive in what situations and how long to wait before making jokes about a crisis, but in other ways they didn't see how they got stuck in patterns of thought. Faced with the new or dangerous, they relied on the framework they had bolted together in order to make sense of the world. Listening to them talk, he thought knowledge was not always an aid to understanding. For some things a young brain was needed, a brain not yet set in stone. The young brain understood things were always moving. Change for it was a part of life. Also it was not drunk. Out of the loop maybe, 'registered useless' perhaps, but useless was not always a useless position.

When history arrives on the scene, late as usual, appealing for witnesses, the same shifty informants always come forward. The experts, the boffins, the mandarins. They turn up with it all written down: the names of the relevant politicians correctly spelled, the cabinet debriefs reported word for word, the big picture drawn out. Shuffling, overworked history is happy to take what's offered. It does not bother to ask around. It does not question the youth on the corner. Why bother with the hopeless crushes and hormone-raddled moods of a teenager who must be in bed by 10 p.m.? History has better things to do. Except – up in the star chambers of the political sphere the wise men digest a baffling glut of considerations, of points and counterpoints. Down at ground level it is a matter of what each individual feels in their heart, what a seventeen-year-old boy can smell in his nostrils. When an excluded teen, halfway through a zombie killing spree, feels the hairs rising and senses something is up. He and others like him, they're the ones who have to live this history. And who knows, they may play a part in it too, before things are through.

'Ellis Dau.' His mother leaned in the doorway. 'This is not a conversation for you to be listening to.'

'How am I listening? I was using the toilet.'

'Come on. Bed.'

He came out into the hallway and hugged her. It was not something he normally did – there was an age a boy should stop embracing his mother, he felt – but tonight was not a normal night. He had this awful feeling of things slipping away and wanted to hold on to what he could. His mother smelled as she always did, of smoke and rose sweets and something like earth, though the smoke was higher up the register tonight. He drew it in. He held the thought of her, the smoky shadow of what she was to him.

At that moment the bulb failed and the room fell dark. Oh, and it was bigger, much bigger, than that. Through the window he saw darkness stealing across the windows opposite, devouring every pinpoint of brightness, eating up the tenements and distant highways. Block by block, neighbourhood by neighbourhood, the city disappeared. It was there one moment and not the next. His mother was gone, they were all gone, only darkness remained.

'Stella?' said his father's voice.

'I'm out here.'

'Oh. Good.'

'Bloody power cuts,' said Urvin. 'Where are the matches?'

Glass smashed to the floor.

'Balls to this,' said Urvin. 'I'm pissed as hell.'

'*I saw it! I saw it! Balls to this!*' the parrot screeched in the next room.

'My phone was on this table,' said Armitage.

'Soon as the power's back, we put something up,' said Urvin.

'Where's Ellis?' said Cornelius. 'Where are the matches?'

'Don't worry,' said Ellis. 'I'm here.'

'I've got the matches,' said Stella.

'All right,' said Cornelius. 'Everyone relax. The lights will come back. Just wait. They'll come back.'

Just wait . . .

Lying in the humid night, waiting for sleep, he heard his father repeating these words. The open window, instead of cooling, merely brought the traffic and sirens closer. He kicked the sheet from under him. Flipped the pillow. Appealed feebly to the mute electric fan.

They'll come back . . .

He couldn't settle. His body announced strange prickles and itches which disappeared as quickly as they'd arrived. Close to his ear a mosquito whined. Things danced on him in the night.

Just wait. They'll come back.

Over and over, like a mantra or prayer. Like a plea. Because his father didn't have control over any of this. Not the electricity, not the Horsemen, not the people or the police. That plea didn't come from the first, thoughtful Cornelius, or from the second, newshound Cornelius. It was Cornelius the third speaking now, Cornelius the small, the neutral. Though it pained Ellis to see this incarnation, what hurt most was the realisation there was no other: his father had only ever been this third type, this minor version.

CUTS

THIS NEWSPAPER does not have to tell you things are bad.

If nothing has changed by the time you read this, our city has been without power for three days. The routers and phone lines remain down. Our country has fallen off the map.

We know this single page of paper isn't much. But we feel it is important you know we are still here, even if for now it is a bare-bones operation.

Please understand, we are as upset about this blackout as you are, and we are doing everything in our power to find out how it happened and how much longer we must suffer it.

Other news organisations like the *Gazette* have gone silent. They are waiting for the lights to come back. While we have the utmost respect for our competitors, we do not believe a newspaper should only be a fairweather friend.

Of course the power cut is not the only trouble we face. Let us not forget the hideous attack on Governor Jacobs, and the assaults on others too.

We must not be intimidated by bully tactics, we must not be swayed by fear-mongering or won over by the rhetoric of hate. We must be strong where others are weak.

Good readers, keep your eyes open in these dark times! Remember the old proverb about one's shadow: if it is not watched, it will start playing tricks.

THREE DAYS and strangeness had crept over the threshold, into the family Dau. No more transcribing for Stella. She smoked to keep busy. Instead of scattering rose sweets across the table and working her way through, she would take them from the tub, one by one, replacing the lid and twisting it each time. No more smiles from her when Ellis ate or calls of *pelican, gannet, hungry horse*. Now she was ... absorbed. The bird got more conversation than the men did.

Cornelius, who used to remain at the table after dinner reading or buffing his English brogues to a mirror shine, had taken to standing at the window and eyeing the street below. One evening, tormented by the creases in his three good shirts, he tried to heat the iron on the gas stove – now he had two good shirts. He talked more but said less, and had adopted little flourishes such as 'don't you think' and 'that's what I'd like to know' which were absent from his speech before. When he ran out of words he was uncomfortable with silence, preferring instead the wind-up radio and those state-sponsored bulletins he once mocked.

This, he said, was a *wayzgoose* time. An old word from before electricity existed. When summer came to an end and the presses began working by candlelight, the master printers threw a party for their workers and there was a goose for eating.

Ellis did not think this time so much of a party. For one thing he was fed a lot of these facts and tidbits. Horror of horrors, his father had decided to take an interest in his education.

'But school's finished,' he told Cornelius. 'It's the holidays.'

'One should never stop trying to improve oneself,' said his father.

Fine, but could they stop trying to improve others? No, it

seemed Cornelius had various nuggets of wisdom he was keen to impart: the boy must practise writing.

'I can speak the language,' Ellis told him.

'Writing is not the same as speaking,' Cornelius replied.

At his father's insistence – 'Trouble comes from people trying to make fine points with a blunt instrument!' – Ellis had spent the previous day wrestling the odd sentences and thorny conjugations of *Grimbold's Grammar*. Now that was hard work. To read those dog-eared pages was to fall asleep with his eyes open. To pick up that book was to be hit on the head by it. *Be prepared for kisses when you give your girl this merry scent* and other such statements. Ellis was full of questions. What did merry smell like? How did you prepare for a kiss? Cornelius, rubbing his eyes and breathing deeply, reached for another example. *Lamont never would have bit a forest ranger*. But who or what was this Lamont? A bear? A priest? Surely it was important to know. Could you ever say 'never' with certainty? Was the sentence complete? Didn't it need a *if the ranger had not bit him first* or a *if he weren't so tasty*? Ellis tried to pin things down, much to his father's annoyance.

'The things he asks,' he heard Cornelius saying to Stella that night. 'I don't know whether any of it goes in.'

'Give the boy a break. Perhaps he doesn't wish to be moulded in your image.'

Don't think Ellis enjoyed all this eavesdropping. Only he suspected his parents were protecting him from certain details.

'He shouldn't even be in that office,' she added.

'That was your idea!'

'I know, but things were different then.'

'It won't be like this for long.'

'But it is like this now.'

He smelled cigarette smoke. Edging closer, he saw them sitting at right angles across the kitchen table, his father in profile, his mother turned away. In a pleading voice, like a salesman desperate for the commission, Cornelius ran off a well-worn list of reasons not to worry. That wasn't how things were done here. They weren't breaking any laws. This was a free country last time he'd checked. Besides, things were undoubtedly as bad as they were going to get and must improve soon. Actually, salesman was too kind a word for him in this instance. His guilty tone, his soft posturing, was that of a husband sent out for medicine who'd returned with a new hat.

'You always push these things,' she said, then something Ellis didn't catch, and his father said, 'It wouldn't happen like that.' She laughed, not happily, and he added, 'All right, if it comes to it, but it won't.'

'Leo, you are a shaolin monk of bullshitting yourself,' she said.

Ellis saw enough of his father's scowl to know a point had been won. He thought she didn't used to be so curt with him, that the sport of contradicting him was once more kindly played. He thought his father also sensed this and the knowledge had caused some wear and tear, perhaps not on the surface but at some deeper level, to the calm and certainty he hoped to project.

'You're reading too much into things,' he told her.

Ellis stepped forward.

'What are you talking about?' he asked.

His father looked up and blinked. 'Everything is fine,' he said.

'I can hear it.' It was no picnic for Ellis, forever cast in the role of gormless youth when he was seventeen years old already with many worldly things known to him and hair in all the correct places. Really, he'd been a child for the longest time. He was ready to retire from childhood.

'Your mother is anxious, that's all,' said Cornelius.

He looked over, expecting Stella to deny it. She just carried on smoking, though that act alone seemed a response of sorts. Ellis moved to the counter and mixed an apple water. When he looked around his parents were watching him.

'What is that?' Cornelius asked like he'd never seen anyone drink before.

'It's concentrate,' said Stella. 'I buy it in the market.'

'Natural identical apple flavour,' added Ellis.

'You don't like water?' said Cornelius. 'What's wrong with water?'

'Leo,' she said.

Ellis looked from her to him.

'Your mother wants us to be careful.' Cornelius gave him a smile and wink as if to say, 'We will have to humour her on this one.'

'I'm talking about real consequences,' she said.

'Do you think I want trouble?' he said.

Stella's expression in no way suggested she was won over. With thumb and forefinger of one hand she rubbed at the knuckles of the other.

'We must all keep an eye out,' Cornelius added, trying to make this statement sound cheery and not like an order or a concern. He smiled, though the clenching and unclenching vein in his temple was usually a sign he wasn't in the best of moods. 'All right, son? You'll do that, won't you?'

'Sure.'

'You see? The boy's not worried.'

A flick of her wrist brushed his words away. A typical national gesture, that flick. It meant: forget it, who knows, it is gone, it is neither here nor there, thankfully I do not care, sadly I care very much.

Cornelius's look was no more comforting though perhaps easier to read. He was counting on things not to turn against him. Otherwise his own judgement could not be trusted, it would be a black mark against himself.

Each night the citizens went to sleep hopeful; each morning they woke to disappointment. More heat, more blackout, nothing but stones in their stockings. Some internal confidence began to falter. Dependence on the premise looked increasingly foolish. To live without TV ... Without Internet! The human spirit could only take so much spinning disk. If the sun had failed to rise, it could scarcely have stung more.

Yet Cornelius would not give up the *Chronicle*. Despite the difficulties, he insisted on keeping the paper open. Refusing to fight or quit, he had decided to just hang on, a limpet on the blasted rock. Limpet wisdom said existence alone was a victory. He would not surrender like those flubbers at the *Gazette*.

Here he was on day four, in stiff three-piecer and cruel shoes, taking the streets with long strides. His son trailed a little behind him, holding back. Around them the city twisted between different stories. Bloom of blossom on the Boulevard. Grandly useless government buildings. The wide cold plazas. The not exactly straight avenues. These things had stayed the same. What else? Starlings and potholes remained in abundance. Roadside women continued to sell eggs and dusky strawberries, or for a few pennies weighed the curious on their scales. A soldier still stood on duty in the glass box outside the Palace of the Parliament (during the summer this shift was known among locals as 'the microwave meal for one'). The whole look of the place – the wires hanging from the tenements like vines, the trees with lower reaches painted white for obscure reasons of disease or presentation, the breezeblock left bare as a legitimate kind of decoration, the beggars on the underpass stairs posed in sunlight like witnesses to a revelation – none of that had changed.

But look elsewhere. Look at the wealthy properties, where buzzing generators now kept the fences electric and gates secure. Generators everywhere, powering everything, this season's must-have item. And, often to be found in close proximity, burly blockheads standing guard, fresh off the peg from wherever the Blums bought theirs, the picture of watchfulness and vigilance. The luxury developments unfinished, all work ceased. On the plywood hoarding of one promised development, a mock-up of a rooftop scene: a businessman staring at his phone, a dancing and possibly drunk blonde, a second woman looking over the edge as if considering ending it for good. The cinemas battling over dimensions were both shut. A shame, as the Crown had just got X-D – *The most dimensions you can possibly get!* Few shops or restaurants remained open, but more young bucks than ever whispered and plotted on the streets. And soldiers and police everywhere, often guarding nothing in particular. Sometimes they stopped people for no apparent reason. Not to question, just to see if they would do as asked. *Wait a moment, friend. Wait now.*

Other phrases heard in the streets today: *parasite, agenda, violate, modesty. Our country. Overrun. Reclaim. Go back.* Each slur charmed more snakes out of the long grass. All the pre-historic nasties raised their heads and said, 'Hey, did you hear that? We're not dead!'

Now the more commercial neighbourhoods. *Johnny Pub, Cafe Concord, Rich Man Fashion Boutique.* See how the streets are darkening. See the figures in the doorways, the scrawls on the walls. *Light will shine. Better will come.* Rubbish swept back in a gallant please-after-you. At Victory Square, the eternal flame switched off.

And beyond, the slumped and faded premises of the *Chronicle,* board over that one front window like a pirate's eyepatch. Inside, Jonquil was collapsed in his chair, fanning himself in the manner of those American tourists occasionally seen during happier times, so flabbergasted by the heat they thought nothing of paying three dollars for a bottle of water or a cold beer to be drunk between murmurs about the resilience of the locals. (Everyone was very fond of these tourists and hoped they would return soon.) Opposite, Miss Armitage rearranged her desk again for want of something to do. Around them, the blank computer terminals rested with their ancient secrets.

How quiet the place was! Without the dry spidery scuttling of fingers on keyboards. Without the phone calls: the fluid negotiations and angry denials of bias, the respectful imploring for confidences not yet shared. Without the outrage and teasing and farmed quotations of social media. Without the constant flood of information coursing easily and pointlessly through the phones and servers, the raging torrent of promotion from government departments, supermarkets, charities, businesses of all sizes, aspiring restauranteurs, pushy mums, gushing PAs, sad-mouthed managers in search of lost traction, self-made men who worried the message was not getting out, controversy peddlers, professional meddlers, public relations gurus who wanted to *push the envelope* and *get a conversation started* and *think outside the box.*

'Just the man!' cried Jonquil, straightening at the sight of Cornelius.

'No, Jonquil,' he replied, rooting through the post by the door.

'Who said anything?' said Jonquil. 'I didn't say anything.'

'We're not running it.' Cornelius looked around. 'Where is everyone?'

'Oh, come on.' Jonquil was on his feet and coming over.

'Geffen and Kozlov are in the back,' said Armitage, blowing a strand of hair from her forehead. 'Haven't seen Urvin.'

Cornelius headed for the tech room, Jonquil on his heels.

'You think you're being objective sitting on the fence?'

'I know this argument, Jonquil. Journalism is artifice and sleight of hand, truth is what we make to look true, things aren't going to stop moving and we can't possibly wait for all the facts.'

'We could just float the suggestion. Denial of conjecture is a story in itself. Can they refute these troubling allegations about the cuts? Can they prove they didn't do it? Make them sweat a bit at least . . .'

In the back, Mr Geffen, making the impossible look easy, slept blissfully in an office swivel chair. His shoeless feet explained the murderous face of Mr Kozlov nearby.

'Damn it, Geffen.' Cornelius kicked the old hack's chair. 'Could you at least look like you're making an effort?'

'It's just so hot,' Geffen mumbled.

'I don't want to hear it . . . Kozlov, how much juice have we got?'

'One full can. Plus a little in the genny.'

'Can we get more?'

'We could just float the suggestion,' said Jonquil.

'Maybe,' said Kozlov. 'You'll pay twenty times what you did yesterday.'

'Jesus.'

'That's a conservative estimate,' said Kozlov, angling his chin into his neck to stifle a squib of indigestion. 'It's going up every minute.'

'Above thirty degrees my body starts to shut down,' Geffen explained. 'It's actually a medical condition.'

'The merest suggestion,' said Jonquil.

'Well, go out and get another barrel if you can.' Ignoring the others, Cornelius peeled off a stack of notes and handed them to Kozlov. 'And let's hold off on printing tonight.'

'Hold off on printing?' said Jonquil. 'I know resources are tight, but that right there is the thin end—'

'I tell you,' said Geffen, 'I feel bereft of life.'

'All of you shut up!' Cornelius cried. Softer, he continued, 'And Kozlov, if this goes on much longer we'll need to dust off that thing.' He nodded towards the old proofing press and boxes of type in the corner.

'I don't know how to use that,' said Kozlov. 'I work with computers and stuff. You know, technology.' Pained, beseeching, he gestured to his sickly drone.

'That was technology once,' Cornelius told him. 'I'll show you how. We'll print it together.'

Ellis, standing quietly in the corner, doubted it would ever come to that. It seemed a lot of labour. And his father was less the type to do the dishes than the type to speak eloquently and at length about how the dishes should be done.

'That could be your job, Geffen,' said Cornelius. 'Since you're at such a loose end. Find some ink for this press, just in case.'

'But it's so hot out there. My body starts to shut down.'

'Yeah, well, we've all got problems. And will someone please find Urvin? Where the hell is he?'

By way of explanation Jonquil and Geffen both made the traditional sign of the bottle being drunk. Only it didn't really explain Urvin's absence, not in the current state of things.

'HEY BABY, need someone to keep you warm?'

'It's thirty-five in the shade, idiot.'

'All right, need someone to cool you down?'

'Oh you're doing that nicely.'

Call the police, summon the fire brigade, alert social services: the Fabulous Bonzo Brothers were back. The silver tongue of Vincent was once more cutting a swathe through the ladies. As if a little blackout could stop this. As if soldiers in the streets and queues round the block for diesel could silence this raw sexual power. As if a little thing like a country could cockblock them. Wrong. Dead wrong. It was the holidays and Ellis's curfew had been lifted. This elite seduction unit was highly trained and ready for anything. Nothing could surprise it – it had heard every rejection. It was mobile too, a mobile seduction unit, as they were on Vincent's bike again with yours truly working the ones and twos. Was it Ellis's imagination or did people make the sign of the cross as they passed? *Holy mother of.* They had never seen the like. They had never seen two individuals so unflinching, unbeatable, unstoppab—

'Stop!'

The seduction unit stopped. Vincent rolled off the bars and stooped for a scrap of paper in the grass. By the last of the daylight he examined it.

'Look.'

Formally, preciously, he held out the torn fragment. They stooped together in concentration, two curators of a mystical and priceless text. Ellis studied the artefact. He mustered a second opinion. Flesh tones, a curve of something, a wiry tangle of hair. There wasn't much of it, but what there was looked *bona fide.* Solemnly he gave the nod. It was confirmed: they had found pornography at last. Vincent's puffy face was on the verge of tears. Ellis put a hand on his shoulder. Three days without Internet had been hard on them all.

A little longer in this spot searching without luck for other shards they might piece together to form some exquisite and explicit corpse, then the seduction unit was on the road again, pedalling onwards in its search for romance, adventure, love.

'Hey sugar plum, hey darling . . . Who's your daddy, baby?'

'Ask him yourself. He's right behind you.'

'Drive, Ellis! Drive!'

After some more of this, with little (no) success, the decision was taken to visit Chicago Pub. That is, to try their luck getting in. One of the great mysteries of Ellis's life, one of the great injustices too, was how despite its reputation for indecency and uncleanliness, and a general mantra of anything goes, Chicago Pub remained resolutely prejudiced against underage teenage boys. The bouncers were on it. But there was a first time for everything, as Vincent reminded him. Tonight might be their night.

They stashed the bike behind a bush and approached the temple of their hopes and dreams on foot. Edging towards the live, tumbling bass (Madonna, the timeless classic), their hopeful young eyes beheld the flashing red neon of *GIRLS – MUSIC – LIQUOR*.

All hail the holy trinity, now let us pray.

A clear mark of the quality of the establishment, that sign. Burning through the diesel to keep those words in neon reflected the bar's dedication to those ideas, they felt.

What was the door looking like? Only one bouncer this evening, a good sign. They had clashed with this particular gorilla before but tonight he didn't seem to recognise them. Probably because they had on the big man swagger, the Full English of airs and graces. Absolute entitlement, that was the look, like the ancient aristos in the London members' clubs (there had been a recent Russian documentary on the subject) with their little silver bells tableside to ring for the wet nurse whose breasts they might suckle until they were content.

The gatecrashers approached. Chests puffed, a pinch of adult boredom around the eyes, voices on a low growl setting if asked anything. The gorilla watched them walk right up, scrutinised them closely, read with scepticism the message on Vincent's T-shirt which said *SMALL PARTY HURTS NOBODY*.

'No kids,' he said.

'We're not kids,' Vincent gruffly answered.

Mr Gorilla breathed deeply. Conversation was evidently something he had hoped to avoid. Implied in his manner was a faint recollection that others still practised this outlandish fad and that there was no accounting for taste.

'No,' he said.

'We were just in here. We went out. For cigarettes.'

'No.'

'It's true.'

'No.'

'No what?'

'No is the what.'

'Okay,' said Vincent, 'I didn't want it to come to this but fine . . .' He looked left, looked right. 'I have in my possession a pornographic picture – *of a lady* – which I will let you look at if you let us in.'

The gorilla was strangely unmoved.

'No kids allowed.'

'Come on, Vincent,' said Ellis. 'Let's go.'

But Vincent was in a fighting mood. He felt certain things were owed to him. The younger bodies were always on the wrong side of the door, they were forever outside looking in. Well, maybe he was tired of that. Maybe he wanted more and would take it if it were not given.

'Who are you calling kids?' he said. 'We're not kids.'

'What are you then?'

'We're men.' Vincent bashed a fist against his chest. 'We're businessmen.' Again with the fist. 'We're big pimps.' A third time with the fist. Personally Ellis thought he'd overdone it with the fist.

The gorilla's eyebrows lifted.

'Big pimps?'

'That's right . . . Dammit.'

'Oh.' A change in the primate's expression. 'Why didn't you say so? Moses!'

'What's happening?' said a grainy voice from inside.

'I've got a pair of big pimps out here. They want to come in.'

'Big pimps, eh?' A leathery-skinned man came to the doorway, idly fingering the lapels of his burgundy suit as he appraised them. So this was the legendary Moses who owned the place. Who mothers warned their sons and daughters about, who church groups prayed to be saved or struck down. Whose life was one never-ending party. This was the great man himself. He looked a little malnourished, a little unwell.

'Oh yes,' he said. 'I see what you mean. The pimpishness is strong . . . What are your names?'

'I'm Teflon Don,' said Vincent.

Moses didn't blink.

'That's your actual name?'

'Er . . . Yeah.'

'Not a nickname?'

'No . . .'

Ellis shot Vincent a look of *you better not be screwing this up*.

'So Teflon is your first name.'

'Yeah.'

The gorilla got some dust or something stuck in his throat.

'I see – and you are?'

'Ellis.'

Now it was Vincent's turn to shoot the look.

'Okay. Teflon Don and Ellis. Well, you gentlemen must come in at once.'

Ellis and Vincent exchanged a glance. Very quick, they were

trying to play this cool. Thank the sweet merciful Lord it was finally happening, the doors were at last being opened. They were becoming men. It seemed almost too good to be true. They stared into the face of this Moses, seeking confirmation, answers, promises, but found nothing definite there. It wasn't that sort of face.

Over the sacred threshold they went, into the excited gloom . . .

Squinting and cautious, they made out only fragments. A long dark room with thick drapes across the windows. On one wall a painting of the original gangster Mr Al Capone. Also bull horns and wagon wheels and a large array of penis-shaped fertility symbols one can only assume were common décor in prohibition-era Chicago. But mostly they were aware of music and shouting and funking colliding smells of bodies, smoke, drink. Girls with bruising eye shadow and punchy red lips swayed to the rhythm or smooched soldiers, of which there were a concerning number, though here they didn't look stern or miserable like they did in the outside world.

'It's . . . so . . . beautiful,' said Vincent, his voice raw with emotion. First the scrap of porn, now this. It had been quite a day.

A brief conference followed. It was agreed that as men they should drink. Something classy, exotic, mature. Something debonair. A drinker's drink. In a word: Malibu. It just ticked all the boxes. Unfortunately their wallets had not caught up with the rest of them, there were budgetary constraints to consider. They were talking pocket lint, not much more. The only thing for it was to start a tab. But as they stepped up to the bar they felt the mitts of Moses on their shoulders.

'Leave that stuff,' he said. 'That's for the riffraff. I'm taking you two to the VIP room.'

There is no need, presumably, to explain what a big deal this was. The VIP room was everyone's dream, the ultimate goal, the one shared vision of humanity. A primal urge. A driving force.

Humans hadn't got to where they were as a species without it – it's the reason they came down from the trees and started walking on two legs. Since the dawn of man he had been trying to get into the VIP room. One day, on the wall of some yet-to-be-discovered cave, archaeologists will find a painting of a little stick person outside a fancy rope cordon, looking hopefully in.

They tracked through the bar behind Moses. The sea of drunkards parted before him. Smiling faces turned in their direction, a surprisingly friendly crowd. At the back a door led into a darkened room full of bottles and ripe fermenting alcohol smells. *So there was a secret VIP room behind the storeroom. Supercool.*

'This is it,' said Moses, gesturing to a final door, a big steel job with another gorilla guarding it.

'You're serious about keeping out the riffraff,' Ellis said in his deepest adult voice.

'It's a top priority.'

'I respect that,' said Vincent.

'Thank you, Teflon. I respect that you respect it. Tony?'

The gorilla handed Moses a Polaroid camera.

'Let me take a quick picture of you two before you go inside,' he said. 'For my collection.'

Before they could say cheese or anything else he'd snapped the shot. *Was that flash bright or what* – it blinded Ellis completely. He was blinking and trying to regain his sight as the bouncer cracked open the door and Moses guided them into the darkness beyond.

'Here it is, guys!' their host cried. 'Have a ball!'

This was it, this was really it. Stumbling gratefully forward they charged into the VIP, into the future, into adulthood, into . . .

'An alley?' said Vincent, his sight restored.

The door slammed shut behind them.

Ellis took in their surroundings. He noted the overflowing dumpster, the dogs grubbing in sour tracts of waste, the questionable ambience. He had to admit this VIP room did look a lot like an alley.

'It is an alley, numbnuts,' said Vincent. 'He kicked us out.'

Thus concluded another evening in the lives of the Fabulous Bonzo Brothers. Oh, send the clowns home. Please don't make them do this any more. They're tired and they want to go to bed.

'Soldiers get all the pussy,' Vincent said.

For a while they smashed an old TV with sticks. As a night-cap of sorts. This saddened Ellis as much as it cheered him. He was sure people his age in better countries didn't do this sort of thing: their lives were full of better options. He had seen pictures of bathrooms where the toilet had another smaller toilet next to it, sweetly confusing people just for the hell of it, so they had to think, 'Which one shall I use today?' These were the sort of options he meant.

It was time to fast-track a solution. Tomorrow night, they decided. A foolproof plan was forged.

But Ellis's evening was not over. No, his evening was not done with him. As he sloped home past the White Rabbit, his evening had a nasty surprise lined up.

If Chicago Pub was at one end of the scale, White Rabbit was at the other. In terms of prestige, that is. While Chicago Pub was a sticky place run by liars and frequented by scoun-drels, White Rabbit was all table service and leather banquettes and the crème de la crème. Everyone was a VIP in White Rabbit, the whole place was one big VIP area. Alas, the door policy was simple but brutal: foreigners only, unless you were a woman who looked like a movie star or a man who spent like one. Vincent and Ellis wouldn't stand a chance. Forget the bouncers – the ground would swallow them as they ap-proached, lightning bolts would blast them, birds would swarm screeching out of nowhere and tear them to shreds, anything to ensure this perversion of nature did not occur.

To give some further impression of White Rabbit: Joan was

a visitor. She mentioned it online, back in the good old days.

So of course as Ellis passed he craned a hopeful neck, angling for a glimpse of that vision. No luck. But what should he see instead? An ugly little cluster of white hats bickering with the door staff. Either a group of goatherds had won the lottery or the Horsemen were on the prowl.

'You encourage it,' one of them was saying. 'You allow it to happen.'

'Please step away, sir. This is a private venue.'

'But a public offence,' said the Horseman. 'You are harbouring gays. I can feel their tingly presence, I sense their pink handprint all over.'

This man Ellis recognised as their leader, Grotz. On the other side of the street he kept his head down and picked up his pace, these Horsemen being the sort of individuals a person could live without. All he wanted was to go home, commit a little thought crime about that Blum girl, and pass out.

He had got a few hundred yards when someone cried, 'That's her!' Then echoes of many pairs of feet giving chase, coming his way. A blur brushed his shoulder, leaving in the air a heady perfumed trace. Seconds later a dozen or so Horsemen careered past in the same direction, trampling that feminine scent beneath their own cologne of dumplings and polyester.

Maybe he was tired, maybe somewhat demoralised after the evening he'd had – whatever the case, he didn't respond. It was also possible that, without knowing exactly how or when, he had come to accept such sights in this city, that shouting men pursuing a girl no longer pressed the panic button in people's brains. What could cause that? There were no nice answers. Either these events had grown so frequent people had become callous, or they were telling themselves it was nothing serious, no big deal, as though remaining peaceful and good-natured in the face of hate and suffering was a solution.

That young woman must be out for a jog with those men and those shouts simply friendly encouragements . . .

*

He was shaken out of it when the running girl crossed the street in front. Back to reality. Back with a bump. He knew that profile – it was Joan.

He was sprinting before he could think. No time to ponder the finer points, he was already on the move, on the heels of the Horsemen who were on the heels of Joan. In this menacing and broken conga they darted through the streets. The city was a graveyard tonight: everyone was asleep or pretending to be. He'd been like them, hoping to dream this all away, but now these grunts were threatening people he cared about and something must be done. Was that empathy or because he wanted to get in her pants? One for Dr Peabody, perhaps.

Other thoughts contended in him as he ran, like how to stop these thugs without getting straight up killed. Of course the chivalrous death was the height of romance, to have one's head caved in for a special someone was truly a charming gesture, but where the elements and fates allowed it he preferred a softer sort of romance, a living breathing sort of romance. It was sort of a personal rule he had, to not be brutally murdered if at all possible.

So he held back, he let the Horsemen lead the charge, following close behind. Close enough it sometimes seemed they were running together, these magnificent goons and him. Now as any banker who has swum with dolphins will testify, being so near such wild creatures casts a powerful spell. In the case of these homophobes and bovver boys the enchantment was violent and unpleasant in nature. The closest thing he could compare it to was that football match where the crowd was rocked and buffeted on a sea of dangerous sentiment it neither entirely invited nor understood. It would be nice to say that both times he was stronger than this outside pressure. It would be nice to say he did not feel it. Instead, let's say he never forgot where his loyalties lay. They were up ahead in a little black dress, shoeless and moving fast.

Alas, now Joan made a big mistake. She took a wrong turn into a dead-end street and the Horsemen piled in after. He pulled up short. What to do? Cautiously he crept forward. To the casual observer or informant he might have been a lookout for their gang.

'Move from me, vermin!'

Joan was kicking up dust, slapping the dirt with bare soles while these others encircled her with whoops and hollers. One grabbed her hips while she repelled another and when that grip was lost a third party launched an advance and managed to hold her a short time until she wriggled and twisted and bit herself free. No, free was the wrong word. The chain of Horsemen was tight around her. She had nowhere to go.

He watched from afar. Disgusted as he was his feet were no longer so keen to lead him forward. In this moment he felt every bit his father's son, heir to the same special principles that lost their value when taken out of the packaging.

'Wow!' said Grotz. 'I'm sweating! I'm really sweating after that . . . Blum's girl, right? She's a good runner, isn't she, boys?'

Whoops and cheers and kissing of teeth decided it was so.

Joan spat.

'That's not very ladylike.' Grotz crooked a finger at her. 'That's a foreign mentality at work, spitting. It's not in our mentality, in the mentality of our womenfolk, to spit.'

'Get fucked,' said Joan.

'Again with this bad mentality,' said Grotz. 'You see what we're up against, boys? This coarseness and vulgarity, tearing our country apart. If it's not the gays, it's the language. What can be done?'

'She needs to learn,' said the white-haired thug, 'that saying things like that, to good people, to young men with their whole lives ahead of them, could be very hurtful.'

'Oh no,' said Joan, heavy on the sarcasm. 'Did I hurt your feelings?'

'I didn't mean hurtful to me,' said White Hair.

There was about this individual a certain desperate quality: when he spoke the others seemed to sense it and recall their own grubby purposes. The fan of faces constricted around Joan. Violence was never far from the mind of this White Hair and his desires were contagious to the impressionable souls who studied him. Ellis liked him less every time he spoke, and he hadn't liked him to start.

In the alleyway under the stars a terrible stillness fell. Watching a dust speck hang in the air, time can seem to stop – this was how it was in that silence. All parties watched one another, waiting for a sign.

In a flash Joan came to life and made a dash for a gap between the bodies. But White Hair was faster. He threw himself forward and knocked her to the ground. She cried out beneath him, writhing in vain. Ellis's fingers were squeezed numb inside his fists.

'Did you lose your bodyguards, baby girl?' White Hair crooned.

Writhing, biting, scratching, Joan fought with everything she had.

'Did you lose them to come and see me?'

'Get off,' she hissed.

It was no good. She was overwhelmed.

'Not so many wise cracks today, uh? Not so mouthy now?'

Her face, wresting this way and that, fell at last towards Ellis, its features blank, the fight drained out, something like an old and fearful acceptance in its place. He didn't know whether she saw him or not. Her legs stopped kicking. She moved no more. White Hair ran a hand over her body, groping, claiming, taking. She lay faintly breathing, her empty eyes still turned towards Ellis. In that stillness she admitted real terror. God help him he wanted to kill this White Hair for what he had made her, for what he had made him, for what he was about to do.

'Stop!' cried a voice.

To his surprise and horror Ellis realised the voice belonged to him.

Great, crowed the internal chorus of trolls and Peabodys who plagued him in times of stress. *You have one simple rule about not getting killed and you screw it up. What were you thinking?*

Simply that he couldn't believe what was about to happen, he couldn't believe even these idiots would let this happen, and some remote, restricted part of his brain decided it was all part of this awful spell. That these Horsemen, far from being the conjurors, were under it too. He thought if he could just break the spell they might wake up.

The faces turned towards him. It was unclear whether the violent spell was broken or whether they wished to include him in it.

'Who's that?' said Grotz. 'Come forward.'

Slowly, unhappily, he moved towards them. He wanted to leave himself a way out of this alley if possible. Two Horsemen, reading his thoughts, grabbed him by the arms and brought him closer.

'He's just a kid,' said one probably a year older than him.

'I think the police are coming,' Ellis told them. He was trying to break this horrible enchantment however he could, though as soon as the words passed his lips he hated himself – it was what a lookout would have said. So far he'd done very little to prove he wasn't one of them.

'Let them come, we welcome their input,' Grotz said, though Ellis noticed he moved towards the struggling couple and prised White Hair gently off. 'Enough of this hurly burly,' Grotz told them fondly, like they could get a room later.

White Hair picked himself up, wiping a trickle of blood from the corner of his mouth where Joan had caught him in her struggle.

'I like you,' he said, talking down to where she lay. 'You've got *je ne sais quoi* . . . You could corrupt me.'

'I know this boy from somewhere.' Grotz was looking at Ellis. 'Are you a national, boy?'

'Yes.' Here Ellis felt he'd failed again. Who were they to ask him this? Why should he answer and give them this power?

'Should you be out this late? There are bad people about, you know.'

Grotz nodded towards Joan, who with some labour and un-certainty was getting to her feet. Ellis caught her eye and saw anger. Did she think he was involved? All he knew for certain was after the empty surrender of those eyes he was glad to see anger. Anger was a friend next to that.

'You bruised my wrists,' she muttered.

'How do we know those bruises weren't there before?' Grotz replied.

Approving murmurs from the other Horsemen. They were watching a master at work. History was being made in this humble alley and they knew it. Those touchstone moments observed in art when chaos coalesced into form, those glimpses of the sublime – these existed for racists too. They had their own equivalents to the first performance of the Rites of Spring, the Lumière brothers' train, *that* jazz fusion festival in Minsk. In years to come they would ask each other, 'Were you there in that alley, when we were harassing that girl and it all just made sense?'

'You shouldn't be out,' one of Grotz's rat-faced associates told Ellis.

'My parents don't mind,' Ellis lied.

Grotz snapped his fingers. 'I know where I saw you. Outside the party. You're Dau's boy.'

'Ellis Dau?' asked Ratface.

No point denying it. Yet he had a bad feeling about where this was going.

'You're the guy from St Joseph's,' said Ratface. 'I heard about you . . .'

He proceeded to recount Ellis's vandalism in graphic detail.

The only omission, for which Ellis was eternally grateful: Rat-face didn't seem to know he'd torched the national stuff.

'No!' said Grotz when the story ended. 'You're that guy?'

Again Ellis had to own it. But at what cost? Threat and savagery was still very much the ambience in this alley. Although this Grotz did a lot of smiling, it was not the sort of smiling that brought any comfort. Yet Ellis didn't want him to stop smiling either. An unhappy position to be in. Apart from foreigners, minorities and hats, he had no idea what these Horsemen liked or disliked. They banged on about protecting their culture, but the culture of bullying was the only culture they were ever seen to pursue – and that seemed to be doing just fine, that needed no protection. He might have read it wrong, this nationalism lark might have finer points he was missing, but it seemed these thugs were stuck in a strange loop where they cracked skulls because it was sickening how the noble tradition of cracking skulls had been lost and no one – *smash* – could remember – *crunch* – quite how it was done.

Grotz spread his arms to crush Ellis, embrace him, who knew.

'You're a legend!' he cried.

This was news to Ellis. As he understood it, legends weren't grounded by their parents or bamboozled out of nightclubs. Their birthday guest lists did not consist of one pervert and a parrot. But who was he to quibble? The mood in the alley relaxed. The spectre of his caved and dying head receded.

'You're one of the reasons I started the Horsemen,' Grotz went on. 'I heard about the school and I thought, "People are fighting back."'

The faces which had been cannibalising him for parts now softened. A couple of morons even came forward and shook his hand. He wasn't sure how he felt about all this. Joan, he could see, was also undecided. *Grey grey*, they called this sort of good-bad tangle round here. Her look was pure grey grey.

'Hey,' said Grotz, 'you should join us . . . Have you ever fired a gun?'

Ellis had not.

'I bet you'd like to. Every man likes to fire a gun. It's in their DNA. We're getting guns soon. Got to keep this country safe, you see. Stop them overrunning us, polluting the gene pool. The team could use someone like you.'

Ellis mumbled that he'd think about it. Of course he didn't want any part of this hell – although, purely as an observation, it felt pretty good to be called a man and offered a gun. He looked at a person like his father, who wouldn't let him hold a notepad, then he looked at Grotz. He could see why one was struggling and the other was on the up and up. Grotz offered opportunities to those who never got opportunities. Weaker individuals than Ellis might take him up on it. Again it was an old story.

Come in, South Patrol. Come in.

A two-way radio on Grotz's belt crackled into life.

South Patrol, are you there?

'North Patrol, we hear you loud and clear,' Grotz told the radio. 'What's your status?'

South Patrol, be advised, we have eyes on two possible homosexuals, the radio squawked. *I repeat, possible homosexuals spotted.*

'Roger that, North Patrol. Try to keep calm. What's your position?'

Er . . . We're by the fountain?

'Is that Rolo?' asked White Hair.

Grotz nodded grimly.

'North Patrol,' he said, 'we're going to need more info on that location. There's potentially homosexuals near a lot of fountains. Over.'

Oh, right . . . Um . . . The fountain near McDonald's?

'That's better, North Patrol. Now how do you know they're homosexual?'

What?

135

'How do you know they are gays?'

They smiled at me and I got a weird feeling. Like all fuzzy.

'It'll do,' said Grotz. 'Roger that, North Patrol. We're on our way.' He turned to his knuckleheads. 'All right, men, sounds like a gang of homosexuals are trying to infect the water supply. Let's roll out!' He looked at Ellis and Joan. 'Mr Dau, think about our offer. Miss Blum, please leave our beautiful country before some accident befalls you.'

Off they went. Others needed terrorising and mustn't be kept waiting. They reminded Ellis of this boy Oster at the lake where he used to go swimming every summer. All the kids would be playing in the water when they'd hear, 'Here comes Oster!' and this great lummox would come charging off the jetty and jump feet first into the middle of everyone. Wouldn't even look. He'd just shout, 'Here comes Oster!' like they should be delighted to have the pleasure of his company. Then he'd strong-arm every kid in the lake and generally be a total pain. If anyone tried to reason with him or tell him to stop he'd dunk them or pull down their trunks which would make everyone else glad it wasn't them being treated like that. It got so people were anxious in the water even when Oster wasn't around. Everyone lived in fear the big goon would show up. Eventually Oster jumped in and almost killed some little kid and everyone said it was awful and they banned Oster from the lake. And for a while it was nice and quiet and everyone remembered the kid that nearly died, but the next year some new kid was shouting and bombing and doing all the Oster nonsense. The thing with these Oster types, *they always had a great time.* Never a cloud in their sky. One of life's major riddles, Ellis thought, was how the dumb-asses enjoyed all the certainty while those with any thought or consideration were up to their necks in worry and doubt. Really, he almost envied the Osters.

He and Joan stood a moment in silence. Sod's Law, a boy has all these things he wants to say to a girl and when he finally gets the chance a Nazi death squad ruins the moment.

'Looks like you made some new friends,' she said finally.

Phrased as a snarl, this statement. Yes, definitely some anger there. *They weren't my friends!* he wanted to cry. *Did I look like I was enjoying that? I nearly got killed! For you!* But the words wouldn't come out. He was a little confused by her talking to him: he was meant to be the observer and she the subject. He knew her mainly with his eyes, that was their arrangement.

He was still mulling his response when she turned away. She was leaving? He wanted to go with her, to never let her out of his sight. It tore him up thinking he might never see her again. And no, he didn't know how to say these things without sounding mad or desperate.

'You're going?' he asked.

'Oh yes.' She wheeled round in this dazed clumsy way. 'I'm going to make those bastards pay. I'm going to have their houses bombed. I'm going to have their fucking throats cut . . . One word, one word from me and they'll have their faces smashed in!' To demonstrate this smashing she began pounding an old aluminium bin minding its own business.

He thought about holding her – he considered this proposal and rejected it. Didn't seem a wise move with all the bin-smashing going on. Also maybe something he hadn't earned.

'No,' she said, stopping suddenly. She shivered like she'd walked through a spider's web. 'No, I won't . . . I won't do that.'

She slumped into a crouch, arms clasped behind her neck.

'I didn't scream,' she said, partly to him and partly to herself. 'Why didn't I scream?'

He felt awful. Like he'd failed her. He knelt beside her and put a hand on her shoulder.

'It's not your fault,' he told her. He didn't know what else to say.

Now something devastating: she took his hand. Full contact for he couldn't say how long. If the Ellis of a few moments earlier had told him this he would not have believed it. (And

ON *the fourth night of the blackout, Kozlov and Armitage drove out to Urvin's bungalow in the twelfth microdistrict to look for their missing colleague. Kozlov took a video camera.*

The footage lasts barely a couple of minutes and is shot entirely in night vision, which does the sketchy atmosphere no favours. After knocking on the front door and getting no response, they decide to go around the back of the property and force the screen door into the kitchen. They eventually gain entry and there follows some rooting and crashing about in the dark and shouting for Urvin which can be fast-forwarded or cut should other news agencies wish to use the material. At one point Armitage says, 'Signs of a struggle' and Kozlov says, 'You haven't been to Urvin's house before, have you?'

The money shot is at two minutes three seconds, when Armitage calls Kozlov and the camera over.

'Look,' she says, pointing to a dark silver square on the kitchen table.

'What is it?' asks Kozlov.

'His hip-flask,' she says. 'Five years working with the man, I've never seen him without it.'

BLEAK was the mood at the *Chronicle* entering day five. On the wind-up radio, the authorities blamed a stray cat for the power cut. 'Are you kidding me with this shit?' Jonquil yelled at no one in particular. The gleeful unrelenting heat was frying everyone. Geffen's snores were a fairly constant soundtrack – 'My dreams are air-conditioned,' he whispered when confronted – and even the usually alert Armitage had a drugged look about the eyes. No one had a clue as to Urvin's whereabouts or wellbeing. Kozlov had failed to find more diesel; the newspaper was down to its last can. Up against it all, Cornelius's mind turned to the dusty press in the corner.

'There comes a time in every boy's life,' he told Ellis, 'when he must stop goofing about and dreaming of girls.'

His tie was off and the top button of his shirt undone. He slouched in his chair, which ordinarily he considered a crime. 'Posture makes a gentleman,' he liked to say. But today he looked crumpled, second-hand. Even if the electric iron were still working, Ellis thought it had never worked that well.

'A time . . .' Cornelius drifted off.

'A time?'

'When he must step up.'

'To the plate?'

'Yes, Ellis. To the plate. Exactly so. Your help may be needed printing.'

'Printing? I thought Mr Kozlov was going to do it.'

'Between you and me, I worry about Mr Kozlov's dedication. I want you to learn too. Wouldn't you like that? To be a printer?'

Dangling it in front of Ellis like it was his dream all along did not make it so.

'Do I get paid?' he asked.

'We must remember the bigger picture,' said Cornelius, which Ellis took to be a no.

So began his brief training as apprentice or devil. Devil being the industry word. Not, as it has been suggested, because they gave the printer grief, but because casting the lead type smudged them head to toe in soot. This was how his father told it as he readied the old machine. Cornelius said many things that morning, such as how *j* was the youngest letter and the origins of *getting the wrong end of the stick* and the purpose of the hell box and the story of Gutenberg, whom he had a book about in his office. Before this fellow, he claimed, words were carved whole from wooden blocks or copied by hand, copies of copies of copies, riddled with error, full of mutant meaning. Knowledge was hard to come by. Gutenberg made it cheap and easy. His moveable type changed the world as much as gunpowder or the wheel. And was the road to greatness easy? No, it was paved with hardships. In saying this Ellis thought his father suggested some similarity with Gutenberg, like he was also in the rank of those who would improve the world if only it would let them. A little high-mindedness was okay with him. Better Cornelius talked himself up than down.

But mostly the apprentice had to concern himself with the type. And it was a concern. An amateur designed this alphabet, he thought. The *n* and the *u* looked identical when one of them was upside down. The letters *p* and *d* and *q* and *b* were all the same character just mirrored or rotated. Some letters were worked almost to death, others utterly idle. It was the effort of a student who did half his homework and hit the bottle.

'One must work within the parameters set,' his father said when he complained. 'A *b* is a *b* and a *d* is a *d*. The convention must not be harmed. Otherwise you are making art and not communication.'

Ellis did his best to order and control these characters and bring them together in the meaning his father intended. He set the type, upside down and left right. He filled out the *chase*, building spaces with *furniture*, before he locked up the *forme* and *laid it to bed*. He kept the heavy-as-anything proofing press maintained with catches of grease and cleaned the rollers so they ran smooth and true. The sticky crackling ink he was careful to mix to the appropriate *viscosity* and *hue* – too thick and the words would *mackle*, too thin and they would be as ghosts or spirits with no meaning in the living world. Sometimes he was entrusted to do the pulling too and this was his favourite part, the bump and run of the letters beneath the paper like a train on the tracks or a hand dropping down the steps of a spine saying, *I am here, I am here.*

'Keep practising,' said his father. 'I have some things to do.'

But without Cornelius it wasn't the same. Working together, it felt like newspaper business, when it was just Ellis, it became a diversion to keep him occupied while the adults got on with the real work. He had heard of a theme park like this in America where children played at being adults by doing boring office jobs like filing and writing reports while the adults were off drinking beer.

In the office next door, the heat-crazed hacks pitched blackout stories to Cornelius.

We do a piece on how with the Internet down everyone is knitting again. It's a knitting renaissance.

We write a piece on how everyone is drinking rancid milk.

We write about how crime has gone up. Or down.

We write about how something everybody loves is not going to exist any more. Don't know what. Whatever people love.

We write about candles. 'Boom time for candlemakers.' 'Candle Fever.' 'Candle trade burning at both ends.' We follow a candlemaker for the day. Favourite candles of celebrities. Candle trends. What are they doing with the candles? What are they actually doing?

Meanwhile in the print room, Ellis's attention wandered. Daydreams took over. He stared so long at the letters that landscapes rose off the block and he was trekking through lowercase shrubs and streams or else surrounded by the sky-scrapers and high-rises of the capitals, big business in his heart. His eyes dawdled around the inner spaces of *f*s and *c*s, they took naps in the tails of *g*s and the cubbyholes of *a*s. It was lonely lost in words. At times he could have sworn the dot of an *i* was a head looking at him. Those stupid lamppost letter *l*s made him wish he were a dog . . .

Raised voices broke his thoughts. He had been at the paper long enough to know how journalists talked to one another – the briskness and rudeness he didn't even notice any more. But he was also familiar enough with the office bustle to realise when something unusual was going on. He heard strain in the voices, the strain of people trying to resist various damaging outcomes, which wasn't usually much of a concern round here.

He tip-toed down the corridor and listened in.

'. . . being invisible, turning a blind eye, that won't help us,' Jonquil was saying. 'The reality of the situation is no longer escapable.'

'Reality?' said Geffen. 'Are we going to talk about reality? You say the word like it's just been invented. But the rest of us have been living in it for some time, Jonquil, and the rules are simple: If you don't want your hand burned, don't put it in the fire. *Leave. It. Alone.*'

'But fire spreads. It finds you.'

'Please, both of you, keep it down,' said Cornelius.

Ellis peeked in. Light from the room's remaining window illuminated the bickering journalists. His distinguished and uncomfortable father leaned against Armitage's desk. Jonquil paced the length of the room. Geffen slumped despairingly, well on his way to breaking another chair. It was the last day this could be called a newspaper office, though none of them knew it at the time.

Allegation and distrust was the theme. The news editor was of the opinion the blackout was an inside job.

Geffen shook his head and muttered about theories like they were corns on his feet. Bloody Jonquil, casting aspersions.

Jonquil was highly respectful of his elderly colleague's opinion, but the issue here was what the blackout killed, besides sporting events. Information. It killed information in almost every form it was received. Today's revolutions started with a link and a click. And not just revolutions but slower creeping things (he doffed his cap to the usual suspects: the Horsemen; the zealots; Mother Russia, drunk on her own skulduggery; Uncle Sam, blind surgeon to many in the region). Cutting the power stopped those connections being made.

Governments were not above deliberate blackouts, Cornelius agreed.

Jonquil nodded vigorously. Egypt and Tunisia during the Arab Spring, the Burmese in 2007 . . .

The office had watched these foreign conflicts keenly. The feeling was that in due course the lens of history turned on every country, even those small places no one had heard of, and the light caught it and shone through and the fire was lit.

Today TV and Internet were basic human rights, Jonquil went on. Remember Romania? They suffered Ceausescu while he was starving them but when he cancelled the TV channels, the soap operas, they rose up. Turning off the power was not an act of power a government could display.

That was all well and good, but Geffen wanted to know if Jonquil had any evidence relating to *their* situation.

Yes, he'd heard things. From sources, if Geffen knew what those were.

Cornelius would not run conjecture, as he'd told Jonquil many times.

Jonquil laughed. Ah, the ethical journalist. Must be a rainbow nearby. You swore by two sources for every fact – until you couldn't find a second. You put allegations to the accused – usually. You printed only established evidence – except when reasonable doubt was enough. You never accepted an unchecked story – unless you couldn't resist it. Everyone bent the rules. How good the story was, that was the thing.

No, Geffen shouted, getting to his feet. That was not the thing.

Jonquil wanted to know was Geffen all right, he looked a little stressed.

Too right he was stressed. This was going to end badly.

Jonquil agreed these weren't pleasant thoughts. But once you stopped voicing unwelcome thoughts, you forgot how to think them, or how to think freely at all. Any challenging ideas you killed as soon as you had them. Then you were no better, he went on, his voice rising, *than a cretin*.

But Geffen was leaving. Let them suffer if they wanted, he muttered, pushing past Miss Armitage who was returning from a cigarette.

'What's up with him?' she asked.

'Mr Geffen has stepped down to spend more time with his anxiety,' Jonquil replied.

Even now, in spite of everything, Ellis imagined they would soon go back to their previous lives. At any moment the lights would come on and the computers would start whirring and the reporters would return. Their problems would shrink to more manageable dimensions. He assumed (yes, tsk tsk, the journalist's son assuming) that as a small concern in the margins of the country's affairs they would be spared any lasting damage. What he failed to see was that the world was always making plans behind a person's back, outside badness was forever being thrown his way, lines were shifting without his knowledge, consequences were spawning that he could not or did not wish to acknowledge, and at some juncture, 'the shit', to use a Vincent phrase, 'cannot be unshitted'.

Maybe Geffen had a premonition, because a few hours later the men with guns arrived. To give them the title they gave themselves, one should call them the police.

Of course it was not unknown for cops here to walk into businesses tooled up and looking for trouble. A lot of books were not properly kept, a lot of taxes not paid, and that bothered these officers, it pained them a great deal. So they came around sniffing for a cut, the boss or manager paid them off, and they went away soothed and life continued. It wasn't hard to tell when someone wanted a sweetener, the whole tone of the conversation was geared towards *resolving the situation* and *finding a solution* and *making it work for everyone.*

So when Fedor appeared at the door that morning, deputies in tow, the assumption was he had his hand out and those words on his lips. Yes, their old friend Fedor – the hacks let out an audible sigh. They had been fearing other visitors and Fedor was a blessing by comparison.

'Leo,' he said. 'So glad you're all right.'

His voice was mild, edged with consideration. Yet his manner had shifted in a way Ellis couldn't place. Something stony lay beneath it, as if kindness at its heart were a probe by which the limits of a person might be tested.

'What's this about, Fedor?' Cornelius sensed the shift too.

'A mission of concern, you might call it.' Fedor, wandering in, paused at Urvin's desk to inspect a plastic figurine of Snoopy. Hands clasped behind his back, he studied this market knick-knack as though it were a priceless antique perhaps reported missing. 'You know my biggest worry? My biggest worry is something will happen to you. Daily I worry.'

He unfurled to his full height and looked down at Cornelius.

'Which is why I'm so upset when I see this,' he said.

Yesterday's *Chronicle* was raised aloft. Fedor wanted to know why such things had been written with times so dangerous and unpleasant. Journalists were meant to set an example, he had been given to understand, yet this was non-friendly.

'Non-friendly' was a fairly accurate way of describing Fedor's attitude at this moment. On previous run-ins Ellis had thought him dull, awkward, a bit of a pushover. A tall man without much backbone. But now the officer was leading the conversation, taking charge. No longer did he stoop or mumble. With his troops around him he had the zeal of a man with a job to do. Ellis decided he was more creepy than dull.

'We've done nothing,' Cornelius protested.

'Sometimes it's the way a person does nothing that's the problem,' said Fedor.

If Ellis still felt any relief it was police on their doorstep, this was the moment it ebbed away.

'That article wasn't intended to offend,' said Cornelius.

'Perhaps,' said Fedor. 'But as an officer you have to read between the lines. And this edition is riddled with micro-aggressions.'

'Micro-aggressions?' said Cornelius.

'Simply riddled with them.'

Cornelius seemed to be crumpling in front of Ellis's eyes. He looked so small and pale and old. Worn down, worn out. His thin elegant hands performed unnecessary calculations at his sides. His expression was that of a packhorse which, already weighed down, sees its master approaching with the saddle. Ellis saw how tired he was, how much pressure he was under, how intensely he'd been fearing confrontation. Why give him a hard time? Wasn't it obvious he hadn't meant it? He was the very Pulitzer of timid journalism and sitting on fences.

Ellis looked from him to Fedor, newly smug about the throat and mouth, the eyes narrowing in disapproval, the wet black stones which were their pupils shining darkly in this face now haughty, powerful, cold. No doubt about it, the balance had shifted.

'The thing about micro-aggressions,' Fedor continued, 'is you're not necessarily aware you're making them.' If he had a smile he hadn't bothered to use it for a while. 'All the same, we can't have it. People are restless with this blackout. Jihadis waiting for a sniff. Certain adjustments are necessary. Print the wrong words all hell could break loose.'

There seemed to be a disconnect. A huge disconnect, Ellis thought, between the mindset of the *Chronicle* and what Fedor and his cronies considered the reality of the situation. Fedor was operating on an extreme view of what the newspaper was. Only a few hours ago this cabal of insurrectionists had been plotting an article about knitting. Side by side, the two versions didn't make sense.

'Are you telling us what we can write?' asked Jonquil. It was true that this particular hack wanted to push things further, that he aspired to be a thorn in someone's side, but even so . . .

'Let's not do the freedom of speech routine,' said a scowling deputy.

'What? That boring old stuff? Those annoying civil liberties?'

'Oh, please.'

'Instead of sorting real problems you're breathing down our necks.'

Fedor frowned. 'Have you ever considered,' he said, 'that you are the problem?'

Still Cornelius said nothing. The calculating hands had reduced their movements – now his fists simply opened and closed, trying to hold on to something that wasn't there.

'That you are creating, or at least compounding, this hostile and unstable environment?'

You are the problem. This hostile environment.

We write about candles. We follow a candlemaker for the day.

In tandem! At the same time!

Their local enforcer proceeded to lay out the modern approach to policing as he saw it. Behind those stony eyes was the belief that crime was accelerating along with everything else, it was cancerously creeping into all good and worthwhile systems. These days one had to anticipate, to read the danger before it became the danger. Luckily for them, he and his gun-toting chums were forward thinking. On the lookout. A country collapsed when it failed to imagine the possibilities. Order fell apart when it failed to foresee every type of chaos.

He didn't wait for someone to detonate the bomb, he arrested the man who typed *bomb* into a computer. And they would be amazed, just amazed, at the number of times everything fell into place from there. These turbulent times called for a more theory-based approach to evidence, he was afraid to say. Yes, in such unfortunate and regrettable times, the absence of evidence was no longer the evidence of absence, if they followed his meaning.

As he spoke he brushed dust from Geffen's desk, so practised in the business of accusation his attention could wander, as a barber stares out of the window while his razor traces the customer's throat. Ellis had never thought the police had much power over them, or not any they'd dare to use, so it was maddening to see this man casually enforcing it now. Maddening also to see his father accepting it and letting these slanders go unchecked. He knew these were unhealthy thoughts; it would do no good to argue, yet he felt this was a critical moment: either his father challenged this or he swallowed it and whatever was planned for him. Yes, Ellis felt this desperately. With the total conviction of soul or spirit or the like. It was not an epiphany exactly – what great realisation had he reached? Only that blind acceptance was bad for the constitution. His father should let them know he was no chump. 'Speak now or forever hold your peace,' people said, which always made him think of peace as something slippery and alive and trying to escape, like a madly gasping fish.

'For some time the *Chronicle* has suggested a weakness of the state,' Fedor continued. 'This promotes bad thinking, which leads to violence. My officers must be able to do their job without such threats. However passive and unintended your aggressions, you are opposing law and order. Do you see how that's an extremist position? How you've become a danger to yourself and others?'

Candle Fever. A knitting renaissance.

'That is total malicious rubbish,' said Jonquil.

'I can't say I'm surprised by your attitude,' said Fedor. 'It's precisely why this paper is now closed.'

We write about how something won't exist any more.

Two officers stepped forward. They were taking Cornelius in for questioning, one announced, placing a pair of handcuffs on him. The hands, still grasping and ungrasping, made more sense in the cuffs than out of them.

The stunned journalists watched as real, uncut news swallowed them.

'Don't fret,' said Fedor. 'This closure is not necessarily permanent, this questioning quite routine. And all for your protection. You're lucky we got to you before others did.'

He was making all the sounds of assistance without providing any. And still Cornelius said nothing. Ellis was so pained by this, so choked with frustration, anger, sympathy, worry. Armitage muttered about 'censorship'.

'We don't like that word,' said one of Fedor's deputies.

'Are you censoring "censorship"?' asked Jonquil, gobsmacked.

'Now is not the time to get academic or play footsie with the big ideas,' said Fedor. 'It's just until things return to normal.'

Who decided normal, and who would cover the news in the meanwhile, Fedor already knew. State radio gave people what they needed immediately. No disrespect, but the *Chronicle*'s little piece of paper was not necessary or useful. It was irrelevant by the time it hit the newsstand. People could get all their information at the click of a button.

'What you want to tell them,' said Jonquil.

Fedor looked at him curiously. 'What did you expect?' he said.

The officers filed out. All except one who ducked into the back room and returned with the last can of diesel, for which his peers commended him. Ellis watched his father being led across the street, head bowed. It was true he had sometimes spoken harshly of the man, but it was awful to see him like this, on this adjusted scale. He realised his father had been educating him according to an era that was past. The man did not know the times as they were, he had just been hoping they'd get through this unscathed, that things would work out. As forgivable, even charming, as that assumption was, it remained only that: an assumption.

Ellis wanted to run out and help, but it was not his place to do so. His problem at this time was that he didn't quite know what was going on, yet was close enough to reach out his hand and touch it, and to be touched by it.

Looking at Jonquil and Armitage, he saw in the graveness of their faces that this was really happening and there was no newspaper to announce it. Despite all the noise and rumour, deep down he had still believed there was one true course of events and while people might contest the fringe details and argue minor points this core of truth was sacred and untouched and never called into question. It sounded naïve but that was what he believed. Now he saw this story as it would be told without a newspaper to challenge the official version. Already he could hear the lies they would be fed: how the newspaper was closed 'for their own protection', how thankful they were for police help. Reading between the lines, they were saying *thank you* over and over. He and the other journalists, his father in prison, his mother at home. Through their shouting and in-sults and tears, *thank you* was what they meant.

HOW did she meet the suspect?

She did not remember exactly. A mutual friend introduced them, perhaps. At a party, she believed. She thought him interesting but didn't like him right away.

The suspect had a different version of events.

The first time he saw her was in the university bar, playing pool. Before each shot she smoothed the torn baize. This was twenty years ago. She was with the mutual friend, though the way he told it, it wasn't a mutual friend at all. Boyfriend, more like.

'She looked up and I knew already I was in trouble. One look and I was wiped out!'

'Your father is exaggerating wildly.'

'Really, your mother was intimidating.'

'What rubbish.'

Many times Ellis had heard this. Part of the reason he asked for the story was that he knew what they would say. What he wanted, without necessarily putting his want into words, was the quiet thrill of watching loved ones present details of their lives and thoughts already known, seeing which bits they offered up and how they chose to tell them, observing the loved mind at work.

He'd push for more. How did they get together?

'This boyfriend went off to fight in the war.'

'He was not my boyfriend . . .'

'Anyway, he went off.'

'We started spending more time together . . .'

One night, as they walked back from dinner, a flash of fire tore through the old mulberry tree in the middle of campus. The blast knocked them to the ground. For a second Cornelius, looking up at the earth and flame raining down, didn't know where he was.

'My mouth was sour, and I realised it was fear. I could taste the sourness of my fear.'

She was already on her feet, reaching for him, and they found each other and locked their arms and ran together for the dorms. They were up the stairs and in his room by the time the second mortar hit.

'Then I noticed she was hurt.'

A glint of shrapnel above her elbow drew a line of blood down the arm to her trembling fingers and onwards, onto the linoleum it dripped. She let him hold her arm and pull the metal out. He tore one his vests – 'An original Marks and Spencer singlet!' – and fashioned a bandage to stem the flow.

The shelling continued. They huddled together on the bed, as far from the window as possible in case the glass shattered, each protecting the other, his arm around her shoulders, her face against his chest.

'And slowly the mortars grew more distant,' his father would say, 'and the sound of two heartbeats grew louder—'

'Oh, you corny old soul.'

'And shortly before midnight she turned her face towards mine . . .'

'All right,' his mother would say, 'that's enough of that.'

They were frequently observed at this time
At the Crown cinema. That was their date spot. In its lazy ceiling fans and vivid carbonated beverages, in the eternal night of its auditorium, they sought respite from the heat. Their friend Joseph Beale worked there as an usher. Nervous Joseph, who carried with him at all times a medical form exempting him from physical exertion on account of a hole in his heart, let them sit behind the screen without paying. Westerns and British farces and Technicolor romances were the big draws. People threw popcorn at the screen if the censor's cuts were

obvious. Sometimes Joseph came and sat with them, listening for the manager's tread on the back stairs. In moments of particular anxiety he held his card of medical exemption and ran his fingers along the folded edge. 'This is the last time,' he always said.

Once a European film made the billing. Havoc in the kingdom behind the screen: the subtitles were backwards. But Cornelius, long before he laid eyes on a letter-bed press, found he could read the inverted text. He translated for her, whispering the character's words as if they were his own. Started putting on voices and taking liberties with the language, adding his own amorous embellishments. She laughed so loud that people on the correct side of the screen began shushing each other. 'This is a serious film!' someone shouted. Afterwards the two of them staggered from the cinema, weak with glee, repeating, 'This is a serious film!'

Years later they returned to the Crown to mark their ballots, taking Ellis with them. Joseph Beale stood behind three seated matrons who handled the votes. He was the manager now and wore thick horn-rims to compensate for all those hours in the gloom. Seeing for the first time the auditorium's grooved ceiling, its walls of crimped pink, the boy was reminded of a great open mouth, a cavity revealed by inspection to be of matter and secret colour. That day a new movie star was on the billing, a matinee idol swathed in the national flag, his image plastered wherever one looked. His name was at the top of the forms too, though after 'N' they reverted to alphabetical order.

She was preparing dinner when he returned. He could hear the kitchen bustle, the air dimpled by those little unconscious sounds she made when organising or putting things away. She looked up and saw him in the doorway, alone. He tried to repeat Fedor's words. *Routine questioning. For your protection. Certain adjustments necessary.* Only the words didn't work any more. He could barely get them out of his mouth. Language, he felt, was no longer explaining things so much as getting away with things.

She listened, saying nothing. He didn't begrudge her silence. What could she say? What could any decent person, who didn't want to completely lose her mind, say? What reasonable response could anyone give to something so unreasonable? That it was unfair and wrong? That it was a disgrace? Of course, it was all these things. But how did saying them help?

His mother used to tell another story he never asked to hear. About when she was a child in her father's shop. The shop – if two shelves of dried goods in their front room could be called a shop – where people came to buy matches and salt and oil for cooking, to scoop cups of flour or corn from the sloping sacks. Where young girls brought their mothers to sniff with suspicion the scented pastes and blocks of soap that conjured white bubbles on the skin. And where one day a jeep pulled up with two men inside. Her father stood to greet them. One of the men took the collection at the church in the next village. They were gathering food for the war effort, he explained.

'Of course,' said her father, 'the best price for you.'

'You misunderstand us,' said the first man. 'We are not giving you money. This is for a national purpose. This is special privilege.' As if the privilege belonged to the person having their goods taken. Her father begged. He hadn't got much, this was his livelihood, the home a poor one as they could see. He'd thought the state was on the people's side. 'Watch what you say,' the first man warned as the other heaved the sacks out to the jeep. 'Everyone must do their bit.' This man bore no sign of the affiliation he claimed, no sign of the churchgoer either. 'You don't need to take everything,' her father pleaded. The first man drew a nightstick and brought it down quick and savage. Cut the pleading short. In the doorway the second man surveyed the scene. They got in the jeep and drove away.

*

That story always seemed to Ellis the sort that grown-ups told to show how lucky young folk were today. *Back then people used the street as a toilet and we drank dog milk and the chairs had only three legs so they fell over the whole time.* Of course he felt bad for his mother and grandfather even if the story were only slightly true. And he understood why parents thought of the world in terms of what harm it might do, not what it might owe. What irritated him was when people exaggerated this stuff to make a point. When you pulled a face and someone said, 'If the wind changes your face will stay like that forever.' He didn't like being scared into doing stuff. But when he stood there trying to explain to his mother what had happened to his father, that was the story foremost in his mind.

IT WAS absolutely not his parents' fault he occasionally did bad things: he was brought up well and had to seek his own negative influences. A self-made moron, one could say, with a little help from his friends. And if from time to time he put his hand in wickedness, no malice was intended. The night of his father's arrest he wanted to do the right thing; at the same time the prospect of having his own life had been dangled in front of him so long, he thought he was finally at the point of getting it. The world had shown him riches and ecstasies yet failed to deliver them. So he had made his own plans. He just wanted a little of what other people had. Was that so much to ask? Certain words he wished to know the meaning of, and not through reading about them in a book or watching them online. He couldn't miss this, too many opportunities had already been squandered. He wasn't going to wait around for someone to give this stuff to him on a plate or for some unspeakably fine daughter of a billionaire to take an interest. Time was running out. He worried that if he bailed tonight Vincent would do it anyway and that would be unbearable. He'd be unbearable. His smug face.

The brain can perform some interesting gymnastics when it wants to do something it shouldn't. Moves it was not thought capable of. There's the grey matter, spongy, wheezing, wincing – it would be sitting on the couch and smoking cigarettes if it could, a sixty-a-day character. Give it long division or some basic exercise and it's a horrible spectacle, a massacre. The poor devil crocks its back merely bending over to look at the sum. With an awful medley of groans and splutters it starts the heavy lifting. Was that blood it just spat? It looks about to conk out. The mathematics is abandoned, the brain returns to the couch, hopes are lowered accordingly. But if that brain sees something it wants (usually something off the curriculum, something it's not meant to have) then suddenly this lousy flabby blob is doing the splits and lifting lorries off babies and climbing sheer rock faces and somersaulting backwards through laser fields. The same brain, the same old sack of random trivia, responsible for this? It can pull off superhuman feats to get what it desires, and the same again to justify why it should.

Full marks to Ellis's brain on this one, it fooled itself nicely. *To make this trip with Vincent was proof of his freedom*, it said. He couldn't allow the authorities or the world at large to ruin this as well. By doing it he was fighting back, he was creating his own rules instead of living by someone else's. If he felt shabby about the decision, this argument raised him a little in his own esteem.

Enough justifying and politicking. The scene unfolds as follows.

It was night and the wind tickled the trees and the cicadas threw their creaks against the houses. It was night and the gentle hands of thieves were waking up and stretching in anticipation of the busy shift ahead. It was night and out in the darkened city the vendors and hagglers and card sharks and sentries and prisoners went about their business and Ellis was going about his, climbing the winding lanes into the Newtown Heights, life savings in his pocket, while wheezing Vincent at his side told tales of what to expect.

'We won't get much time so don't waste it.'

'I won't.'

'Get yourself ready before.'

'I don't know if I . . .'

'And no chit-chat.'

'We don't say anything?'

'Really. This is a big man enterprise.'

'What about the scratch?'

'Serious projects! We are not playing games like these other idiots.' Vincent made a sweeping gesture, though there were no other idiots in sight.

'The scratch though?'

'Is there a full moon?'

Ellis could see no moon.

'You only catch the scratch when there's a full moon. Trust me. My uncle is a doctor.'

'Your uncle is a dentist.'

'Same thing.'

'But don't we need to say why we're there?'

'They know why we're there!' Vincent paused for breath, huffing in shallow bursts. 'It's the only reason anyone goes!'

Ellis, as he waited, tried without success to unstick his jacket collar from the back of his neck. He had dressed for the occasion. Best flip-flops, cleanest T-shirt, real imitation Adidas shorts. The large and largely ruined black evening jacket was a hand-me-down from his father, too stuffy to appreciate, too precious to remove.

Resuming the climb, they pushed deeper into the slum. Wires criss-crossed the sky between the shabby tenements. Antennas, outstretched like pointing fingers, accused in all directions. From time to time some stabled animal snorted close at hand, offended by the indelicacies of their conversation. Eyes glistened in the gloom. Side streets bristled with barter and exchange. A jar of fireflies was shaken to inspect the wares within. Daubed over doorways, hanging in windows, were symbols and charms the boys did not recognise, the calling cards of other gods. The warm night air was thick with the smells of beasts and shit pits and charring gristle and the singsong scent of that shrub, common to these hills, which so perfectly mimicked the mustiness of an unwashed sports kit.

'I just hand over the money?'

'Exactly. You hand over the money and dive into the pool.' When nervous, Vincent would nod his head as if assuring himself this was the right and true path.

'There's a pool?'

'No, dummy. I am talking meteorically.'

Metaphorically. In his mind Ellis was forever correcting Vincent – but there was no point mentioning these things to him, no point at all. Just as there was no point flagging up this trouble with his father. Before long Vincent would only be misusing it, for a discount at their destination perhaps. Sometimes Ellis wondered why they were friends, what bonded the two of them besides this time and place and a certain grasping desperation. Maybe that was another choice – the choice of who one ends up close to – only available in better countries.

'You're sure about this?' Past claims had made this question necessary.

'I swear it.'

Ellis remembered his father's phrase.

'It's not conjecture?'

'Trust me, they'll do it with anyone. Even people who use words like *conjecture*. Even your hopeless ass.'

Ellis was pretty sure his ass was not as hopeless as Vincent's. He didn't smell of damp, nor did he stick out his tongue when reading or thinking heavily. He was taller, thinner and more factually accurate.

'Is this illegal?'

'No,' scoffed Vincent. 'It's extra-legal.'

'That sounds illegal.'

'It's the opposite of illegal.'

'The opposite of illegal is legal.'

Vincent waved this away. 'These are words.'

'Yes, but—'

'Listen, El, this is not a choice like going to school or wearing pants or some other bullshit. This is essential. Our very lives are at stake.'

'It just seems wrong paying for it. It should be natural.'

'Christ, you are such a hipster.'

'I'm not a hipster.'

Vincent was always trying to troll him saying *hipster, vegan, twee motherfucker*.

'That's right. Total hipster.'

The street knuckled and twisted between the houses. A man with a hook for a hand watered flowers in his little square of yard. Children played games of Cops and Robbers where it was unclear who was who. The grubby pretenders' faces turned after them. Ellis considered Newtown a sketchy area like that part of London where the Cockneys hung out. 'Outside the catchment,' his father said of it.

At last they came to a residence of particular shabbiness, a yawning door.

'This is it,' Vincent said.

'Right.'

'And don't worry, they're not . . . You know.'

'What?'

'You know, foreigners.'

Why would Ellis be worried about that? The only thing worrying about that was Vincent telling him not to worry. Vincent didn't talk like this. But no time to think about it now, they were in the gloomy hallway and climbing the single flight of stairs to a candlelit landing where two residents stood in adjacent doorways watching their approach. One was plainer around the face but heavier in the chest and here Vincent stopped, leaving Ellis with the other in the far room . . .

With the editor lost, a teenager was on the story, and this was what he had chosen to cover.

By the dim light he made out wide eyes and long dark hair and bright red lipstick, film-star red, drawn around a mouth pursed shut. Pretty, he thought. Only the mouth was slightly odd – sort of pinched, like it was wrestling with its owner. For some reason he couldn't tell her age. Some of her mannerisms were girlish, others much older.

She backed away into the room as he approached. With one

foot she shifted the thin mattress towards the wall. That and a tarnished dresser were the only furniture. Another stub of candle guttered on the floor. He paused at the threshold for fear of seeming – how to say it? – presumptuous.

Remember the instructions.

Three dollars was the ticket for the ride. He stepped forward, money held out. She examined the greenish faces on the bills, then his own.

'How old are you?'

He hadn't expected speech. Vincent hadn't warned him about this. Talking was not part of the deal. Words would only complicate the matter – no good could come of them.

'Old enough,' he mumbled.

Now besides he saw the reason for the struggle between mouth and owner. Her speaking had revealed a set of small and pointed teeth jutting crooked in her gums. She seemed to know and be ashamed for she barely opened her mouth, allowing the words through awkwardly, contorting her mouth rather than reveal its contents. Once he noted these contortions he saw others in play throughout her body. Her back, her chest, her shoulders ... Nothing was quite straight. Nothing existed without tremendous effort. She was holding herself in beauty, it was not a natural state for her. But these little lopsided details were only observable up close when she was forced to interact, and it seemed she knew that also and bore some deep resentment to any person whose interest made her betray her nature. Or perhaps it was the resentment of having to be beautiful, in this way or any other.

'You've got five minutes,' she said.

'Will that be enough time?'

A curl of lip. 'For you it will be plenty.'

Seeing himself talking sideways to this girl or woman, the whole thing felt to Ellis like a dream, where the details were not fixed on the page but sat like ink in water.

She put the bills in the dresser with all the others. Then she began unbuttoning. Unsure whether he should be watching, whether this too might be presumptuous, he turned his attention to the window. They had really climbed high. The whole city lay below. A few rich lights still glittered. In the darkness it looked a pretty nice place.

'Hey, El!' Vincent shouted through the wall. 'See us in the VIP!'

Was it true? Could it be? Had their hopeless asses reached the promised land at last? Ellis wasn't sure. It still didn't look like much, this VIP. As a place to sip the Henny and live like a boss it left much to be desired. He didn't know how he could be certain he was in the right place. Maybe it was like heaven, which his mother said was actually not a place you went to but a state inside yourself. Maybe there was a VIP area in each of them and only through true belief and careful seeking could they attain it. Maybe it was next to heaven, like a rival club.

Creaks from the mattress implied the clock was ticking and he was wasting time. Yet he couldn't bring himself to look into the room and remained looking out of it, trying to get himself ready, as Vincent put it. It felt odd, treacherous even, to have the grand prize laid out and pluckable before him. His lower half didn't trust or recognise the situation, while his mind kept drifting to the contorted mouth and tiny teeth, to the dirty mattress and the bills in the dresser, the sheer number of bills. His suspicion was this currency-based approach was all wrong. It yielded results which looked like the thing and sounded like the thing but were not quite the thing. It took the personal from the person. He wondered who this girl was and if someone else was making her do this. Perhaps that someone was watching right now through a hole in the wall. Parent, guardian, pimp – whoever might be watching, how did they feel?

Miserably he considered his own parents. His mother that afternoon when she finally broke her silence . . . Not good, not good. *How could the man have been so stupid? What was he thinking? And then this? News to no one except your father. Always the last to know. Some journalist!* All of which was a big surprise to Ellis. Recently she'd sometimes spoken more harshly to Cornelius, but never about him. Maybe Ellis's shock had showed because she broke off her ranting and said in a lighter voice, 'But we mustn't worry, I'm sure he'll be fine,' before attempting a smile which made her face look like a broken vase. It was a look she wore the rest of the evening, slumped at the living room table, staring at some point on the wall, smoking glumly, eating nothing. Where was the woman who rescued the bird, who carried everywhere those little songs?

And his father, who knew how he was ... Ellis imagined some gruff guard leading Cornelius down into the bowels of the police station after hours of questions to which there were no right answers. The beam of the guard's torch picking out the packed and watching faces who were to be his neighbours. Some alive with schemes and threats; others sunk into a lower realm, that level of blank inevitability inhabited by trees and moss, a vegetable state. Their hands grasping at the bars or bound together by cord or shackles giving the impression of prayer. He saw his father absorbing all this bad information. He hoped the man was alone in whatever cell they put him. Recently Urvin had covered a story about an inmate, an author, killed after allegedly making a pass at a fellow prisoner. *Tragedy behind bars: writer ends sentence with proposition* was the strap. (Not the most sensitive of souls, dear Urvin.) Ellis didn't expect his father to make any passes, all the same he was not the type to thrive in such conditions.

He felt powerless to help either parent. And they were powerless to help him, or to control him.

Of course these were not the thoughts he was meant to be having. Considering his mother and father while waiting for the mood to take him in a knocking shop? Old Peabody would have a field day. But Ellis hadn't chosen this timing or this plan, not really. Vincent had cooked it up mainly – Ellis did not have the cook's blind enthusiasm. Some part of him hoped the moment would fall through, that this girl might call it off and give him back his money. Wasn't that strange? If he'd been asked on the way up the hill whether he'd take the girl or the dollars, his answer would have been unfaltering.

But sometimes fate smiles its sharp-toothed smile only once and a person must grab it or be left behind. So here he was, grabbing it. Persevering in spite of himself. Certain things were expected of him. From the girl on the bed, from Vincent next door, from the whole city beyond. He just needed one good thought, one moment of inspiration . . .

And right then, with one hand coaxing history forward, it came to him: he would think of Joan.

He fumbled for the bed. Almost kicked the candle over in his hurry.

'Careful,' said the girl. 'That's how fires start.'

How right you are.

'Should I take off my flip-flops?' he asked.

'What do you think?'

Not much in that tone, no suggestion she was pleased about this arrangement or not. He decided to read it as playful. The flip-flops came off. His father's old evening jacket followed. Didn't want to mess that up, he'd begged to have it. On his knees, crawling forward, he found a leg sticky with sweat and followed it up.

Think of Joan . . .

Her hand found his and guided it forward. He felt her thigh muscles tighten. This was it. He would show her there was more to him, more to love, than flip-flops and dollars. He shifted closer, aware of the heat of her skin, closing in on the source of that heat, the true VIP area, the V of the VIP . . .

'Hey, universe!' Vincent cried into the night three minutes later. 'We're men!'

'Bully for you!' a woman's voice shouted back the other side of the street. 'Now shut up, we're sleeping here!'

IN A TRANCE she guided the supermarket trolley through the candlelit aisles. The parrot played figurehead on the prow, eyes open wide to take in the wonders of this new world. At home, hoping for news of Cornelius, for Ellis to drag himself back, the doom had been a living thing, holding Stella tight. So she slipped the bird from the cage and hit the streets. She didn't want to talk about it with anyone; she didn't want to sit in silence. She didn't want to be 'here' or 'there'. She wanted a hole in the ground she could scream into.

At the supermarket the doom was fainter. The blackout had killed the piped muzak and the strip lighting, and in the quiet candlelight she felt almost fond of the place. God bless the places of communal suffering, she thought. Supermarket doom was everyone's doom. The horrors no longer felt so dangerous, so specifically pursuing her, though they had not abated entirely. She was dimly aware of demons amid the discounts, and torture devices behind the empty meat counter. Of ghosts in the powerless fridge units. Of some terrible crime recently occurred, the few remaining items on the shelves left as tributes in the flickering vigil light.

'What do you think?' she asked the bird. 'Is that better?'

The parrot was busy bunching its claws and did not reply.

'Excuse me, madame?' A sorry-looking vampire stood beside a table of promotional blood. 'Would you like to try some delicious tomato juice?'

Her mistake: it was a shop assistant, not a vampire. Practically the same age as Ellis. With the same surly and hopeful look too.

'Does it have alcohol in it?' she asked.

'It does.'

She scrutinised the juice promoter.

'All right,' she said. 'Hit me.'

'The tomatoes are only plucked when fully ripe,' the young man intoned. 'They are hand-selected for freshness and flavour.'

Stella downed the sample offered.

'For freshness and—'

She took another from the line-up and downed that.

'Er, madame, it's one sample per—'

He was silenced with a look. Stella helped herself to a third cup.

'I should check this with my manager,' said the server. He headed off down the aisle, glancing nervously over his shoulder.

'He's going to check it with his manager,' she told the bird.

The bird turned one dark eye towards her.

'He's worried it's against the rules,' she said.

Always the rules. As a child she watched her own parents tear down and eat the anti-government posters pasted near their home for fear they would be found guilty by association. She remembered her mother's mouth, gummy with mulch.

Alone at the promotional stall, she leaned on the handlebar of the trolley and reached for another cup.

'He wants to help,' she muttered.

Everyone wanted to help. They couldn't resist. Another memory came to her from childhood, of men and women in blue jackets distributing fishing nets of strong synthetic rope, a wonderful gesture that moved many present to tears: the Westerners crying at the kindness of their act, the villagers weeping because the nearest body of water was a hundred miles away.

The dim supermarket brought back these bungled gestures. Like memory, it was a world neither living nor dead.

'Do you remember that storm,' she asked the parrot, 'when the wall fell over at the northern market and crushed that little boy?'

If the bird remembered he was not saying.

'A couple of years ago . . . No?'

The parrot opened its beak and watched her with one eye.

'Well, he went crazy trying to speak to the family of that little boy.'

By 'he' she meant Cornelius.

'Had people knocking on their door every hour. The *Gazette* had someone camped outside too. "I'm not about to get scooped by those cowboys," he kept saying. And I just ... I decided to leave.'

She'd never told anyone this. But here in the purgatory of the all-night supermarket, encouraged by the grain spirit and the bird's silence, she was filled with the urge to confess.

'I packed a bag and went to the train station and sat there, watching the departure board, wondering which train to get on. Sat there for hours. All the names on the board were these little places I'd never been to or big places I didn't want to visit. I thought, "Will I be better off there?" It was a Saturday, and there were all these families and friends going off on day trips or meeting relatives at the station with open arms. Everyone seemed to know where they were going and what they were doing except me.'

She stroked the parrot's chest. 'Apart from clothes, toiletries, all that stuff, I'd taken one book. Grabbed it as I was leaving. Didn't look. Now at the station I looked. You know what it was?'

The parrot did not.

'A book on the history of European roads ... I was going to go and live in a place where I didn't know anybody, where I'd be sick worrying about my husband and son – and you – and all I'd have for company was the most boring book in the world. I know I could have bought other books when I got there, but I wasn't thinking like that. I just thought, "This is going to be my life." And I couldn't do it. Couldn't bring myself to get on the train. I'd made that my future, that one thing. And I saw I'd done the same with this wall business, making it stand for my life at that moment. It was just one thing. Not nothing, but not everything. So I headed home. All the way back I was thinking, "You'll tell them you've had a change of heart. They'll understand. They'll be more relieved than upset." But you know what? No one even realised I'd gone. I walked through the door and the first thing they asked me was how long dinner would be.'

She downed her glass and reached for another cup, watched all the while by the bird's dark eyes. Now it puffed its feathers and with a preliminary, throat-clearing squawk cried, '*I saw it! I saw it! Balls to this!*'

'Yeah,' she said. 'Cheers.'

HE WOKE, travelling nowhere with weightless limbs, the sun gently warming through the blinds. Outside the sky was a glorious blue, a deep and heavenly blue. No doubt about it, someone in senior management picked that sky. It spoke of higher considerations, of hidden depths. Of magnificent heat too, another scorcher on the cards. But that was to come. Right now the air was relaxed and pleasant and the open window brought little chipper winds, a happy mob, to play about the face.

Yes, he thought, lying in his pomp and haze. *A fresh start. A clean slate. That's the best course for everyone in the best of all possible worlds . . . Have a yawn. Give it a stretch. The other one too. Another five minutes? Why not. No need to rush these things.* 'Please, after you,' said the body. 'Oh no, I insist,' the spirit replied. All the elements were getting along famously. Then, when he'd lazed all he could and he couldn't laze no more, he raised himself from the mattress and lifted himself onto his legs and the day went rapidly, tragically, downhill from there.

'You're up.'

Flat-footing it to the kitchen to check the cereal situation, his mother's voice stopped him short. She sat in the same position he'd left her in last night. Her face was pale, unfocused. The sunlight pouring through the window behind her didn't help. Nor did the smoke – she was smoking, of course.

'I thought you'd run away.'

Ah yes, now all the lousiness came flooding back. Because, by the way, what sort of behaviour was that? You didn't leave your mother alone in these circumstances. You didn't deliver the bad news and nip out to the brothel. It just wasn't on. Even he could see that – and he was the lowlife who'd done it. Sometimes in books and films people were said to betray their character, but in life he had found the opposite was true: you didn't betray your character, your character betrayed you.

'I wouldn't do that.' The loyal and noble son.

She took a last drag of her cigarette and killed it with three good stubs.

'You wouldn't be the only one thinking it,' she said.

Regardless of what they were thinking they were going to show support, she told him as they trudged the six flights down to the street. (He never thought he'd miss that vertical coffin of an elevator, but these cuts made a person sentimental for the crummiest things.) On the steps she fixed him with one of her quizzical looks and brushed his hair. He hadn't washed since his little adventure and was somewhat uncomfortable with this proximity. But he didn't want to hurt her feelings so he let her fuss. *Mothers*, he thought. They were always stroking their children's hair or rubbing their cheek or getting a bit of dirt off their lip. Personally he didn't care for all that stuff, but you had to let them get the mothering out sometimes. If they couldn't turn the tap on once in a while who knew what might happen. Maybe it got rusted shut.

Yet if he expected her to be in softly softly mode this morning he was mistaken. Some wild energy possessed her. She strode through the streets, ranting as he half ran along beside her.

'He's a proud man, Ellis. You must understand that . . . These stories he pursues – he doesn't do it out of some lofty sense of right and wrong. But tell him he's going to be beaten to a story, tell him he can't print a paper, tell him things are tense and conflict should be avoided, *then* he'll want to run something.'

'Okay, but—'

'Look, I didn't want him to get arrested. I don't want to see him hurt.'

'Right, of course—'

'I wish it was me in that cell, not him.'

'No . . .'

'But he needs to learn!'

Five snapped toothpicks sat on the sergeant's desk. Now he reached for a sixth. It was all go in the central police station this morning.

'The nature of your enquiry?' Death itself could not have lowered this bozo's enthusiasm further.

'It's my husband.'

'What about him?'

'He was brought in yesterday. For questioning.'

'That could mean anything.'

'Could you check the status or something?'

The desk sergeant exhaled deeply. 'Sure, I'll just tap it into my computer.' He played a prim little rhythm on his dead keyboard. 'Pulling up the database for you now. Why don't you take a seat? Might be a while.'

Ellis thought making jokes with his mother, in the mood she was in, extremely unwise. He wanted to warn the sergeant. Really, he almost felt sorry for the poor stooge.

'All right,' she said. 'I get it. But don't you keep a book, some sort of log? Dau is the name. An Officer Fedor brought him in . . .'

She provided the sergeant with the particulars.

'Oh,' he replied. 'You mean our new writer in residence.'

A good long chortle followed this remark. Long enough that Ellis began to wonder who this moron was and if this was still the police station. Adults had a certain type of humour which was lost on him – they would say they were going to eat more cake or drink a glass of wine or three, they would make a statement like that then laugh uproariously. He wondered if this were one of those jokes but it didn't seem to be. His mother wasn't laughing.

'Can we see him?'

'You need clearance from the duty officer.' Toothpick number six met the moronic mouth.

'How do I get that?'

'You need to speak to him, explain your request.'

'Can I do that?'

'Can you do what?' The toothpick went up.

'Speak to the duty officer.'

'He's not in.'

'Can I speak to someone else?'

'Who?'

'Someone who can give me clearance.'

'Er . . . No.' The toothpick went down.

'Why not?'

'They're not in. No one's in.'

'No one?'

The toothpick did a circular wiggle, the meaning of which was unclear.

'So . . .' The look she was giving this sergeant now, Ellis thought she was going to reach over the desk and pull his head off any minute.

'You can fill out a form if you like.'

'What will that do?'

'Couldn't tell you. I just give out the forms.'

'All right. Fine. Give me a form.'

Hastily she scribbled the details. Ellis had a sneaking feeling their lives were draining out of their bodies every minute they stayed here and he thought his mother felt it too.

'You're left-handed,' the sergeant observed.

'Yes,' she said.

'Like Hitler.'

'What the hell is that supposed to mean?' she said.

'Lots of people are left-handed,' Ellis interjected before Stella extracted the man's spine. He was aware that he was partly following her lead and partly looking after her.

'People like Hitler.' Contempt on the sergeant's face.

'Please,' said Ellis. 'The form. You'll make sure they get it, whoever deals with it?'

'When they get back I'll give them the form,' the sergeant said doubtfully.

'When will they be back?'

'Who?'

'The person we've been talking about!' Stella was shouting now. Her fingers gripped the desk. 'The one who handles the forms!'

'I've not been told. Not my department.'

Ellis dragged her away before she committed murder.

Not far from the station they paused to buy milk powder and other pieces at a minimarket. One of those little cave places where the shopkeeper was so packed in amongst the goods it was a mystery how they ever got in or if they could ever get out. In a cage on the counter, a little panting dog ran on a large hamster wheel. The wheel, hooked up to a dynamo, powered a fan pointing at the woman who ran the place.

'What's the dog's name?' asked Stella.

She was staring at the contraption in a way that made Ellis nervous. Again he felt he was both following her actions and trying to protect her from them.

'His name?' The woman looked confused. 'He doesn't have a name.'

'He must have a name.'

'Okay, his name's Battery.'

The dog stopped, tail wagging, to greet the newcomers. The woman picked up a stick and prodded the creature through the bars.

'Giddy up,' she said.

'You shouldn't do that,' said Stella.

'He needs encouragement.'

'It's not a nice thing to do.'

'What's it to you?'

'He shouldn't be in there!' Stella shouted.

'You shouldn't be in here!' the shopkeeper shouted back. 'Get out!'

'Doing that to a dog . . .' Stella was still going on as Ellis led her away to a bench in the main square.

'Mum, please, will you sit?'

'What's wrong with people?'

'I'll go back and buy the groceries. You stay here.'

Sometimes, he thought, you lived with a person for years and years, questioning nothing, and one day you realised you'd been living with a different person all along. They hadn't changed, you were just wrong the first time. His mother could be impetuous, but this . . . He didn't know what the hell she was going to do next. It wasn't necessarily bad – he sort of liked this new dynamic mother he'd got. In a funny way not completely trusting her made him trust her more. He only half trusted himself most of the time.

He left her sitting there and went back.

'I'm sorry about my mother,' he told the shopkeeper.

'Very rude.' The panting dog stopped for a breather and got the stick.

'I'm sorry.'

'She's totally cracked, that woman.'

'She's a little stressed. My father's been arrested.'

'She should be dancing in the street.'

'I'm not sure she sees it like that.'

'Very rude.'

When he got back to the square his mother was gone. He paced the block, he eyed the crowds, he retraced his steps, he worried. Perhaps she had gone to another shop or back to the police station to shout at the desk sergeant. Perhaps . . . But morning became afternoon and she did not return.

He lingered in the central square, waiting, not sure what to do. No one noticed him: many descended on this square every day for the specific purpose of lingering. The place was

Mecca for lingerers. Out-of-town families ate boiled eggs on the steps. Old men, several in goatherd hats, sat squinting in the shade. The city's bored youth milled about, some looking to fool and play, others graduated to young bucks. Which was he? He knew which one he would look like to the outside observer.

His eyes kept wandering to what remained of their former leader's statue, the stumps that were his legs. At school they were instructed to think of this Nestor like the sun: silent but watchful, as much a part of their country as the mountains and the crows. They learned songs his mother banned him from singing at home about Nestor's love forever shining down on them, how even when they couldn't see it they could feel its heat. (It struck him now there were different meanings in this comparison, for the sun's destructive power was everywhere in evidence about their land.) When one classmate, faint in the swelter of afternoon spelling, expressed a wish the sun might not rise tomorrow, he was removed from his seat and beaten for sedition. This was the climate. What that Nestor saw through the tinted windows of the presidential Mercedes could seal the fate of a bystander or a district, what he decreed was made gospel, what he disliked ceased to be. 'It was an inconvenience,' Cornelius suggested over dinner one night.

'An inconvenience?' said Stella. 'You make it sound like a little stone in your shoe.'

'Right.'

'Okay, Ellis,' she said, turning to him. 'It was like having a stone in your shoe *for five years.*'

One story of Dau family legend was that, out shopping with his mother during that era, Ellis had approached this statue of Nestor, raised one middle finger and asked, 'If you're always watching, how many fingers am I holding up?' He flipped their hallowed leader the finger, *the finger*, in front of the police headquarters. It was all his mother could do to rush him away, and all she could do to stop his father murdering him – out of love, always out of love – when he heard. 'You did *what*? Are you *mad*?' With each stress his fist fell on the bathroom door behind which Ellis had barricaded himself. At Cornelius's shoulder Stella tried to shush him as if he were the crazy one. And who was crazier: the boy who didn't fear the statue or the man who did?

AT THAT MOMENT on the other side of the square, a rehearsal was starting in the Grand Theatre. Torches did the lightning. Buckling cardboard stood in for thunder. The city skyline wobbled slightly as the priest appeared. Hoiking his dog collar and slicking his hair, he advanced on the trembling woman in the four-poster.

'Is that ... Is that you, Father?'

'Yes, dear lady, it's me.'

'Come closer, come closer ... Oh, but you are not the priest.'

'The other priest is sick.'

'But I don't know you.'

'It's all right, dear lady, you must not be afraid.' The priest's eyes burned in their hollows. 'You know my collar—'

'No!' cried a voice from the stalls. 'Stop!'

A figure rose up below the players. That thick-shouldered silhouette, that voice – they didn't belong to Romanov and yet they were familiar.

'I'm not getting the right vibe here,' said the shadow, moving along the row and out into the aisle. 'What's with the brooding and dagger-eyes?'

'I'm being threatening,' explained the priest. 'Imposing.'

'That's all wrong,' said the figure, climbing the stairs to the stage. The candlelight and torch beams revealed a military jacket with many tattered medals pinned to the chest. On the figure's head sat a pointed white hat.

'You should be nicer,' said Grotz (for it was he). 'That's how they do it.'

'Who?' asked the priest.

'Well, this is my theory. We should ask the writer, I suppose. Mr Romanov?'

'Yes?' said a small voice from the midst of the figures in the stalls.

'What does the priest represent, Mr Romanov?'

'Represent?'

'Yes.'

'He doesn't represent anything.'

'Come on.' Grotz wagged his finger. 'You writers are too clever for that. Everything means something else with you lot.'

'No, it's like I tried to tell Mr Blum. It's just a story.'

'What?' Grotz marvelled at this fantastical suggestion. 'Get out of town!'

'That's it. Nothing more.'

'Of course you know best . . . But talk to us on the level here, Mr Romanov. What does he stand for?'

'I am talking to you on the level.'

'Now Mr Romanov, you mustn't be so coy. You'll make me get upset.'

'All right, all right. He . . . I suppose you could say he represents a liar. A bad person.'

'I'll tell you how I see it,' said Grotz. 'The priest represents the immigrant. All smiling and humble and "let me help you", but in actual fact he's scheming, looking to take whatever he can get . . . And our country is the sick old lady, only she's not that sick, and soon she's going to start fighting back. Am I right, Mr Romanov? Is that what your play's about?'

Grotz waited for a reply. It seemed highly likely that every medal on his chest had been awarded for leaping to conclusions.

'Well I didn't—' Romanov began.

'Is it?'

'I suppose you could read—'

'Is it?'

'. . . Yes.'

'Yes what?'

'Yes, that's what my play is about.'

'I knew it,' said Grotz. 'I can sense these things. I'm a very deep reader actually. A lot of people say that about me. I can see all these layers . . .' He came towards the priest. 'So when you play the scene, it needs to be more like this.' He knelt down in front of the woman in the bed. 'Get closer. Invade her space, like an immigrant. But be really nice about it . . .'

He reached his hand towards the woman's face to smother her – no, to stroke her cheek.

'It's all right, dear lady,' he said softly. 'You must not be afraid.'

He held his hand against her cheek a long time. One finger played with a strand of her hair. No one spoke. The woman in the bed looked about to cry. Real fear was seeping into the play and players.

Eyes glistened in the shadows at the back of the auditorium. Young bucks and other rubberneckers, drawn to this hateful display, unable to look away. *Let's not feed them*, Stella had warned of the Horsemen the night the power went. She believed these goons grew strong through people's thoughts and fears. But that was only half the story. The Horsemen were also feeding people, nourishing some dark part of their nature. They were the latest delivery device for a universal habit, an all-ages addiction. The adult drank the evil and tragic stories in the news or hunted for them by lamplight in the pages of books. The child hid beneath the bedcovers and said 'Frighten me' and when the tale was finished said, 'Again, again.'

'You see?' Grotz said finally, getting to his feet. 'That's power.'

In the unlit stalls his fellow Horsemen whooped and clapped.

'Major league realness!'

'Some masterpiece theatre right there!'

'Thank you, Mr Grotz,' said the priest, eyes downcast.

'Quite all right, Peter.' Grotz put his arm around the actor in a chummy or forceful way. 'Glad to be of service . . . No disrespect, but you arty types don't always know much about life. You're a bit removed from it in your little libraries and playhouses. Is that fair, Peter? Would that be fair to say?'

'I suppose so, Mr Grotz.' The priest's head was low on his neck as if under a great thing.

'Sometimes I see these movies and I think, "Whoa, hold your horses, that is not correct." My wife says I shouldn't watch them, she thinks they cause my leg cramps. "Cartoons only, Anders," she says. It's true I do get angry. Sure, it's art perhaps, but it's not life. So I'm very happy to help you guys out, to bring you closer ...'

He looked down at the actor he was embracing and shook him gently from side to side.

'Do you see, Peter?'

Peter might have mumbled something. He was so stooped now it was hard to tell.

'Head up, Peter,' said Grotz. 'You know, I think your posture is holding you back. You look stressed. People don't realise this, but a lot of negativity can be resolved through a simple altera-tion of the spine.'

Casting a look around he addressed the cast and other hangers-on.

'Everyone! Can I have your attention, please?'

This one was always asking for attention.

'That's right. Come out here on the stage. You too, Mr Romanov ...'

Various actors and thuggish Horsemen types drifted forward. White Hair mounted the stage holding a sheet of cardboard.

'Look,' he said. 'I stole the sound guy's thunder. Ha ha.'

'I just want to say I am hugely enjoying my time in the theatre,' Grotz announced. 'Honestly, the fight for purity can really exhaust a body. I can't tell you how good it is to have a break from the homosexuals.'

Most of the cast, including the priest, looked elsewhere.

'This is an exciting time,' he went on. 'Things are changing fast. It's not just the political parties and the police any more. There's a third person in this marriage, and it's the streets. We are giving people hope. So it touches me to see you all here, on a national holiday no less. It's lovely to know you understand . . .'

Grotz paused, working the crowd. He was enjoying this.

'Not everyone does,' he said.

'Like yesterday at the museum,' said White Hair.

'Oh, that was sad,' said Grotz. 'You know the National Museum? Grand place. Lots of nice things. Did you know time used to go the other way? Down to zero! Really!'

'They had a pot from 10,000 Before Clocks,' said White Hair.

'Imagine!' said Grotz. '10,000 years!'

'I liked the liver of bronze,' said a goon in a child's baseball jacket.

'Oh yes,' said Grotz. 'Wasn't that nice? Because once upon a time they read livers to see the will of the gods and the liver was a sacred thing. The man told us that. What do you call him? The man in the museum?'

'The curator?' said Romanov. He looked even more miserable than the priest. Any bat or ghost would have thought that face a home.

'Yes! *The curator*. Nice man, very helpful . . . Although between you and me, I do not think he was working so hard in that place. Many times I asked him how much for this thing or that thing and he said, "It's priceless." "Well put a price on it then," I said, but he did not understand. Twenty years he'd been there and he hadn't put a price on anything! I tell you, he was lazy as a stone! Still, he was a nice man and we talked a long time. We both agreed these treasures must be saved. Imagine if those extremists got their hands on them! Or the gays! What do they know about culture or antiques? They could not appreciate such goodness!'

Grotz laughed at this thought.

'Yes, we agreed on many things, me and this man, this *curator*, and I was thinking how we had become friends. This is why I asked him about the beautiful thing.'

'A reasonable request,' said White Hair.

'I thought so,' said Grotz. '"Sir," I said, "as we are getting on so pleasant, will you show me where you keep the beautiful thing in this museum?" "I don't know what you mean," he told me. "Come on now, sir," I said. "Do you take me for a fool? Do I have the look of the baby born not so long ago? It is well known that every museum has a beautiful thing. I am asking very politely that you let me see the one you have here." "But everything here is beautiful," he said. I realised I would have to be firm with him. "Sir," I said, "you are trying to pacify me and I am insulted. I thought we were friends. Will you or will you not show me the beautiful thing? You know, the thing that is not spoiled or compromised in any way. The pure thing from the perfect past. That's what me and my boys are after." The man said again he did not know what I meant. I was so disappointed, you know. It's such a bad feeling, knowing someone is lying to you. What do they say? Truth is the first victim of war? So sad when you see it. Life can be so sad . . .'

Grotz let his words fade. A clear divide had formed among the group. The Horsemen stood in rapt attention, all eyes on their marvellous leader who wanted this one beautiful thing, who had suffered so much for the sins of the world. The others had their eyes on the rafters, on the floor, anywhere except Grotz. A variety of strickened faces trying to find interest in their shoes and the general molecules of air. They were not taking this story well. Like the circus boy in the wheelchair, they were ignoring the peril so carefully as to fool no one.

'Anyway,' said Grotz, 'point is, you're either with us or against us. Which is why it's wonderful to see everyone here thinking with their heads.'

'Use it or lose it,' said White Hair.

'Yes,' said Grotz. 'And let me tell you, no one is more upset about that than me . . . I thought we were friends. People are so stupid sometimes! All he had to do was show me!'

Romanov, sandwiched between two best-in-show bruisers, stifled a sob.

'Mr Romanov,' said Grotz. 'Are you crying?'

'I'm just ... so happy.'

'Oh? Why?'

'For what you've done to my play ...' Here he broke down into violent sobbing.

'There, there,' said Grotz. 'Get it all out. Let the healing begin.'

SHE DIDN'T come home that afternoon.

To lose your mother and *father? Oh boy.*

But his mother could be impetuous. Every autumn when the temperature dropped there'd be a day when she disappeared out and returned with tonnes of oranges which she sat for hours cutting and squeezing, forcing the juice on him and his father. *Drink more! You're not getting sick!* Another time, middle of the night, he was probably nine or ten, she burst into his room with a rope 'in case of fire' which she absolutely had to secure that minute. When a thought got into her head it could be damn near impossible to throw her off.

Yes, but the timing. That talk of leaving. 'You wouldn't be the only one thinking it,' she said.

Ellis tried to silence these voices. Was this how it would be from now on? Every time she popped to the shops he'd be contacting the milk carton people with a picture he wanted them to run. How silly, how ridiculous. Everyone had moments when the thought of leaving home crossed their mind – families could be a total drag. But most people didn't actually up and leave. For one thing you were kind of stuck with your family. It was like wanting a new brain. For another, what were you going to do, throw in the towel every time something irritated you? You'd be throwing in a lot of towels. Like actually that would be your main occupation.

All the same, he couldn't shake the feeling.

The paper was closed, no one else was home, he was left to his own devices. Yet all he wanted was to find his parents. Now there was a punch in the gut – that after this whole struggle his hopes and dreams were simply to have what he once had, to have his old life returned to him no questions asked.

*

What he wouldn't do for a distraction, a bit of power. Just enough to light the console, get the zombies up and running . . .

Whenever I smell rotting flesh I think of Amy.

An intro guaranteed to bring a tear to the eye. Adam Steele was a regular guy, he never asked for any of this. But when a mysterious infection turned the woman he loved into a cannibal corpse, he had to kick ass. He had to arm himself with high-powered weaponry and blast seven shades out of the zombie hordes, and if he ran out of ammo he had to strangle them with their own guts or devise some other workaround. When Cornelius and Stella complained about these games they ignored the valuable lessons being imparted. Yet how he missed their complaints – the game was much improved by their shock and disgust. He hoped they would return to complain soon.

He sat in the living room with the other unattended baggage. The flowers his mother had recently bought. Shoe polish on the table awaiting his father's return. In the apartment across, an old man watched a dead television: over the screen someone had pasted a picture of mountains running down to water.

On its perch the parrot croaked and hawhawed and puffed pompously. With occasional wary glances they measured the degree of their hatred. Was it his imagination or did the bird sense his misery? Was that a note of glee in its cries? He looked into the eyes of that secretive, sarcastic animal. He stared and the beast stared back. It blinked and cackled and blinked again.

In the bathroom he found his father's hair pomade and treated himself to a sniff and dab of that luxurious gloop. Bogus pineapple, his mother called that smell, Cornelius's smell, the thing both true and false.

He felt melancholy, weird. After pissing he actually put the toilet seat down. She always used to nag him about that and he figured it might bring her back, as a restless spirit might be appeased. A few hours ago every decision in his life was made according to their approval (or secretly, knowing of their disapproval). Now the world seemed huge, but not fantastic or exciting as he had expected. His freedom was simply endless undefined space. Nothing seemed more worthless. For a moment he glimpsed how the rest of his life might be.

Clinking bottles and kicks of homebrew announced a carnival afoot as the day wore on. This national holiday, this 'Live Long Day', celebrated the national life expectancy overtaking the percentage unemployed. On this glorious date, citizens commemorated life by drinking such quantities as to make death seem preferable. *A duty . . . A way of recognising our successes . . . A proud moment . . .* This nonsense was heard everywhere, people legless on the ground would quote it. It was embarrassing was what it was, Ellis thought. They should be more honest about the names of these holidays. No one could remember what half of them were anyway. People didn't even know what they were celebrating. Maybe he was not old enough to grasp the subtleties of adult parties, but they seemed seriously taxing for many. A person set out into the city, all prim and proper, with his hair done and a little flag in his hand and a vague but undeniable sense of occasion, only to end up in a pool of puke, shirt torn, perm frazzled. Why not lose the decoration and just call it 'Get Drunk Day' or 'National Liver Damage Day'? Something along those lines. 'Obliteration Day' had a nice ring to it. 'You Will Live to Regret This Day' was clear and to the point. Give people a cause they could believe in. Give them a festivity they could nail.

Now he could hear the holiday beginning. With one body and one brain the good citizens were moving through the gears. As evening fell, with nothing better to do, he joined them.

Uniforms and horn blare choked the streets. Pennants of the national red and white hung from the useless streetlights and there were huge painted posters of the President shaking hands with various kindly old men who on closer inspection were their neighbouring dictators: the one who renamed the days of the week, the one who patented breakfast, the one who killed those unarmed people that time (like that narrowed it down). All parties in all pictures in the very best of moods. Also a big painting of the President standing with a gun over a line of twelve dead bears, even the dead bears looking happy, because they had been killed by the President and there could be no higher honour, no better way to go.

Around these statements the revellers lurched and lilted, clutching bottles of fiery brew. *Holy mother, the zombie apocalypse was real.* Sweating men pawed after the womenfolk or occupied themselves in low alleys where the animal game was played or nostrils whitened with snorts. Customers vomited with the utmost respect outside that illustrious hole known as Chicago Pub. Stray hounds watched the proceedings with sly eyes and talked dog to one another. Children rushed pell-mell. A clown was led away. Vendors of anonymous meats festooned their greasy aprons with garlands of bright plastic and their faces were scowling as they worked the flaming spits and cried encouragements to the drunken appetite.

You wouldn't get this sort of behaviour in better countries, Ellis felt. In his mind he saw the exquisite civilisation of an English city centre on a Saturday night. The calm Tudor pubs, with their motherly barmaids and folded newspapers on the counter, library-quiet save for the occasional clink as halves of ale met. Did such countries ever think about here? What did they see? What did their satellites among the stars report when looking down at this powerless little mess? Was it all just darkness to them?

Here and there amongst the revelry: placards requesting *HOMOSEXALS BURN IN HELL* or *LETS LIVE ARE OWN WAY*. Many of these signs terribly spelled, as if written by a foreign hand. Here and there a white hat.

A group of rough-looking boys ran up, hands in their pockets. Ellis flinched and braced for trouble. They pulled out little fuzzy apricots which they offered as a gift. He took one and thanked them. They ran on.

In the fourth microdistrict a young man recounted Internet animal videos to a crowd crying out for 'Cat on office chair' and 'Dog dinner party' and other classics of the genre. The truth was they had never been so big on literature here. In some countries the written word was so advanced that people published books about *trying* to write books or loved books so much they converted bits of Internet into print. Even some blogs and accounts of people who couldn't write at all – that was how important books were to those countries. Here they enjoyed no such progress. The citizens preferred the nourishment of screens. They didn't want to hear the echoes of their imaginations in the silence of a book. Even with the screens dead they would rather not negotiate a novel. Why? Possibly their lives were already literary enough. Possibly they knew or wished to know so little of what was happening that each citizen invented, dreamed, lied, hid in fictions. Looking at it that way it was a nation of writers, writers who didn't read, writers who never marked a page.

Ellis watched this story-boy a while. Money was demanded up front but seldom earned: frequently the teller forgot the tale halfway through or made excuses about 'buffering' or droned on about a different story people had not paid to hear. Even when the right story was told it was often vague or misremembered. When complaints were made the rogue blamed the listeners, saying they were the ones skewing things, wanting it to be as they alone remembered it, taking everything so personal all the time. Refunds were refused. The audience griped and grumbled. *These unreliable tellers. There should be a law.* They looked about ready to fracture the boy's narrative.

Folk were edgy. As a solar eclipse made animals act up, this blackout had the people spooked. A pitiful nostalgia gripped them. Soon they would be turning to one another saying, 'Do you remember emails?' As if they had grown too attached to these computers and phones appointed mirrors to their nature. As if they had betrayed their hopes and lives and secrets so fully that even in death these machines held these confidences over them.

A little further on, at an upright piano, a bald and sombre man played accompaniment for a girl in bubblegum blue. With a reedy voice that strained to be heard, she sang:

If you lie to me,
You know I'll let it slide
The girl wasted and morose.
Is it so very odd
That I'm in love with you?

'My turn!' A woman pushed the girl away. Her thickly daubed face turned and a fug of cheap perfume descended over the crowd, causing the air to swim as if in great heat, which in turn asked questions of reality, of the soundness of things. Behind her the girl in blue stroppily smoothed the wrinkles from her micro-dress.

'Evening everyone, enjoying the show? Gents, come see me later if you want another sort of show. I am the best in town. And, special holiday deal for white hats, before midnight it's fifty per cent off.'

'Which fifty percent?' someone shouted.

Everybody laughed.

'Only two rules,' she said. 'No immigrants and no ignorants . . . Now if you'll excuse me, I must show these amateurs how this is done.'

A brief conference with the pianist followed. A tune started up.

We're trapped in the maze
There's no getting away.

Hidden in that woman was a foghorn. The punters gasped and goggled like fish on dry land.

Why can't you see?

The words of the old song brought forward through the years without a scratch on them. The whore engaged in faithful reproduction.

Because I love you so much, darling.

Everything was falling apart and no one seemed to care. Sometimes, sometimes, Ellis felt that as a people they did not have an inner core, an identity to hold onto in turbulent times.

Towards Independence Square a soldier grabbed him.

'Hey! Boy! Where's your smile?'

Ellis didn't feel much like smiling and told him so.

'What's that got to do with anything?' A little baggy was produced. 'Come on, try this white.'

'No thanks.' Ellis was too gloomy to even ask what the powder was or how it might turn him inside out.

'What, you can't snort with me? You think you're better than the rest of us? This is a national celebration!'

The soldier tried to grab his collar. Ellis ducked his grasp and ran.

'Hey!' he cried. 'Arrest that boy! He's a traitor!'

'Shut up, Bronco,' someone else shouted. 'Let's get chips!'

Ellis let the crowd swallow him. Drums joined the horns and the tattered streets surged. Shoulders shook. Rumps metronomed from side to side. Even the old and lame were moved to dancing, so jovial was the occasion and so mandatory also. Perhaps it does not sound genuine, this dancing. Perhaps it does not sound like it could not be both.

On a float in front a swaying boy with his face painted like the girls outside the barracks dropped his head onto his chest and gasped and stomped and rolled his eyes in their sockets as his body rocked and juddered with insistence, taking him one way and then the other but never so a person could tell what he might do next for he followed his limbs mysteriously like the tune he heard was his and his alone. He looked like no human being but a machine possessed of pistons and automated parts.

He was the one electric thing in this dim and wayzgoose city.

The people and soldiers howled, hooted, clapped like mad.

Now another boy joined him, this one topless, writhing and twisting his body like a rat in a trap. Crude and forceful were his movements, without the mystery of the other boy's. They danced around each other as the crowd hollered. The first boy paid the second no attention and kept moving in his obscure and electric manner but after a time this seemed to anger or unsettle the second boy for he grabbed his companion roughly and looked ready to abuse him in some way. The watching crowd cried out at this, half of them delighted by the turn of events, the other half displeased the first boy's dance had been so concluded, and there were scuffles and threats and bodies pulled off bodies, all watched in glee and majesty by the soldiers at the perimeters.

Here is what Ellis thought: *All these people were asleep. They were sleepwalking to their doom.*

But here was another thought: *Perhaps, like him, they were unhappy and chose to say nothing. Perhaps of him too someone was saying, 'He is sleeping.'*

'Ellis Island! Give us your tired and weary!'

Who should it be now but Vincent, chewing something like gum, grinding in a manner most appalling with three bored and slinky girls. *UNIVERSITY OF SALZBURG ALUMNI,* his faded T-shirt claimed.

'Come join us!' he cried, eyes wild.

Someone cracked a flare nearby. Harsh smoke filled the street to wails of misery and delight. For a moment Ellis lost sight of Vincent and the girls. When he saw them again the dancing girls wore gas masks and Vincent had tears running down his cheeks.

'Vincent!' he shouted over the din, pushing closer. 'I need to talk.'

'Yeah! Let's dance!'

'No, Vincent . . . Can we talk?'

'Sure. Ellis, this is Vera and—'

'Alone?'

'Oh, right. Ladies, you'll stay here, won't you? I'll just be a minute. I've got more moves to show you.'

The gas-masked girls danced on.

'One minute,' said Vincent.

They pushed through the crowd and ducked into the alcove of a bank selling fireworks while Vincent prattled on. 'I think I'm in there, you know. Maybe with the Vera girl. Maybe with all three. Maybe we'll do an orgy . . . I'll ask if you can join us but I can't make any promises, you know how it is . . .'

'Vincent . . .'

'I'm sort of itchy after last night. Are you itchy? I reckon I could still do it though . . . Hey, look, they've got the big blasters. Those things are loud! You wanna get some?'

'Vincent, please, would you listen?'

He described his father's arrest, his mother's disappearance. He tried to put into words this horrible feeling he had, how he didn't know what to do.

'That sucks,' said Vincent, looking past Ellis towards the three dancing girls. 'That really sucks.'

Ellis blocked his line of sight.

'What should I do?'

Vincent put his hands on Ellis's shoulders and looked him in the eye, his face all puckered and serious.

'It's going to be okay, El.' He had to shout over the band that had just started up. 'I know it is.'

'How do you know?'

'Because you're smart. You're going to figure it out . . . And I'm going to help you. You're like my brother, you know that? Maybe you didn't get the looks or charm but all the same you're my brother and things will be okay.'

Ellis thought that was sweet of Vincent, even if he were

drunk or stoned. He wasn't normally in the market for comments like that. In fact he did all his shopping for conversation in the opposite market. So Ellis appreciated it. He felt really buoyed up just then. Two seconds ago he'd been majorly down in the mouth, but maybe it wasn't so bad. He should have said something nice back – it might not have changed anything that happened after, but all the same.

'Also,' Vincent went on, 'you got to have a little faith. I mean, look at this! These people know how to throw a party! Big time! And they're not giving us any shit about being underage or anything. We're good enough. You know? We're good enough for them. We're free to do what we want. That's why you shouldn't worry. That's why you should come and dance and maybe have sex with these girls and it will all work out.'

That took the edge off Ellis's feeling better. Took the edge off and swapped it for a sinking feeling. This was not good reasoning, he felt. But whose fault was that? Vincent's? If you wanted your shoes mended you didn't go to the butcher. Only he didn't feel he had any other options. It sounded hokey but Vincent was the one friend he had.

'I can't . . . I can't do that.' Something else was rising up with this new wild atmosphere, something worse than anything that had gone before. 'My parents are missing.'

'That's exactly my point. They're missing and there's a huge party with crazy drunk girls. That's fate. That's like a sign from god. It's all happening, just there! When was the last time you saw this? Everyone on the same page!' He gestured to the seething chaos. 'We always complain about how much life here sucks. And now it's here! This is life, El! Right here! Let's go get it!'

But Ellis didn't want any more life. He felt if he had any more life he would die.

'Come on!' Vincent was pushing back towards the girls. He stopped to look back. 'El?'

Ellis waved to him and smiled but did not follow. He watched the crowd take his friend. Everything was pulling away from him or he was pulling away from it, he couldn't say which, like when two trains going different directions pull into a station at the same time and when things move the passenger is not sure whether it is his train or the other and for a while all he knows is the separation.

He didn't want to go where the others were going, but at the same time he didn't want to be left behind, not in his weakened state. Who was he against all this? So he considered it, as one would a business decision. He weighed the investment against the return. What would it cost to join the party? Even to put on that white hat? It wasn't easy to say . . . Certain obscure components of the spirit. Components whose value was vague at best. And what would that little hat give in return? Safe passage through this cannibal city, with a thousand Horsemen, a hundred thousand Horsemen, at his back. That sounded pretty good to lonely little him.

And Vincent talked of freedom! Forget it, freedom was not for the likes of them. It was too rich for their weak stomachs. The whole country was in the same state as him – adolescent, grounded, with a straining hard-on for things it would never have. Life here was against the idea of freedom. It was written in the laws of the earth itself. All energy and light existed to subdue them, all water and rock to contain them. The unflinching mountains and sprawling deserts had been their gaolers since time began. Past and future encircled them, the city encircled them. Down to the atoms of their flesh, shackled one to the next, they were encircled.

Of course this was very negative thinking. There were plenty of ways to live a happy life here, a life without abuse or discrimination. So long as one was not gay, female, poor, ill, foreign, Muslim, a pedestrian, or interested in truth, such a life was quite possible.

Once a person had these thoughts, was the mind already made up? Once it seeped into the soft and delicate brain tissue, was it as good as done? Everyone was asleep. Of him too, someone was saying, 'He is sleeping.'

Wait though. Hold on. Stumbling as he was, he wasn't completely clueless. As the newspaper's intern or dogsbody, immersed for the last month in a cauldron of cynicism, he had an education not many his age had. Even if he hadn't personally done much he had learned a lot by watching and listening. When everything was fresh and uncertain a journalist had to ask his brain certain questions like, 'What do you know and what do you assume you know?' and 'Are you choosing the story you want instead of the story it is?' He was accepting sleepwalking as his only option. He had been told the newspaper was closed and had chosen to believe it. What a chump he was! If Mr Anton were here he'd have laughed in his pupil's face. Old Anton was always complaining about how much people accepted. He used to say the evolutionary effect of years of disappointment and mismanagement could be seen in the smallness of the country's outlook – with every generation the questioning part of people's brains shrank further. *Were they just going to accept that?* In the calm of the classroom Ellis had winced and brooded at this question. When Mr Anton was removed, he had tried to answer it. Clumsily, as it turned out. At that time he had lacked the correct vernacular, the right means of expression. Now this question was once more being asked, and this time he knew where he had to go.

'HEY!' cries a voice off-camera. 'Look what we got!'

A torch shines into the blinking face of a man in pyjamas. A chubby skinhead stands beside him, one thickly tattooed arm resting around the man's neck.

'What you sleeping for, Mr Zookeeper? We wanna go to the zoo!'

The skinhead shoves the zookeeper towards a pair of wrought-iron gates. The man fumbles nervously with a bunch of keys and eventually gets the lock open. The camera pushes after him, into the deserted entrance yard of the city zoo. Bodies rush the turnstiles.

'Wake up, animals!' someone shouts.

The zookeeper pleads with them to leave the animals alone. Many are unwell, he says. (Recent online reviews give weight to these claims: 'bear actually did have a sore head', 'worst zoo ever', 'python gave me fleas'.)

Undeterred, the hoodlums go from cage to cage. Various zoological observations and opinions are offered. They are angry about the Bengal tiger – were no local tigers available? They think the giraffe's neck is too long, the bisons' hooves inferior to the human hand. Two male donkeys in the same enclosure are denounced as homosexual criminals.

'Which would win in a fight,' someone asks, 'a gorilla or a crocodile?'

The zookeeper looks horrified. He is mumbling a response when the voice behind the camera interjects.

'Who cares what he thinks? Let's find out.'

NOT SO LONG ago Miss Armitage had a story about a dog that refused to leave his master's grave. Every time the family tried to take him home this Buster or Banjo or Boudro ran back to the cemetery and sat beside the headstone. Loyal panting Banjo kept watch through wind and rain and mortifying heat. He growled when strangers came close. At night he slept on top of it. For all anyone knows he might still be there. The cold hard truth is that things most likely won't turn out well for Banjo. They never do, do they?

Did Ellis ever think about how things would end for him, for all of them? Certainly. Yesterday, watching them lead his father away, he had assumed (that word again) it was a matter of protocol, dotting the *is* and so forth. The interviewing officers would soon see there was no reason to detain a man so clearly innocent and let him go. But everything felt more serious today. Anything seemed possible. Not in that happy spangled way people say it on TV – this was very much a downward sort of possible. The lofty heights remained the same as ever, it was the depths that had been refurbished, the depths that were newly extended.

A few strips of *POLICE DO NOT CROSS* – or *DO NOT CROSS POLICE* – taped over the door, that was it. Spare key in the usual place. He found the candles and matches and there it was, all the same. Yellowing and dust-bound papers lay about the abandoned desks, the scribbled shorthand on their pages already hieroglyphic. Theories, plots, conjectures. *THE TRUTH ABOUT THE BLACKOUT*, said the top page of Jonquil's notepad. No words followed the claim. The story was never finished.

Little things he noticed for the first time. A lakeside scene beside Armitage's keyboard. Jonquil's collection of press releases spelling his name wrong. A copy of *One Hundred Baking Secrets* Mr Geffen had used to raise his computer screen. The smiley face drawn on the bottom of the editor's door. This evening he had on special awareness goggles, the awareness of knowing these details might soon be gone.

Was he forgetting the task in hand? Was he getting distracted by the spider in the corner, so to speak? No, but he wasn't going to rush into anything either. Not this time.

For a while he read his father's book on Gutenberg. Yesterday they had been about to start printing again in the old way; Cornelius wanted to teach him how. Now he had to make do with a book on the subject. A chapter called *The Holy Mirrors Scandal* caught his eye. Only it seemed their friend Gutenberg was doing the scandalising. These mirrors were a scam he hoped to flog to pilgrims, claiming they could hold the powers of a sacred relic. Customers might take them home to heal their sick families or livestock. Many mirrors were produced for this purpose and great wealth anticipated – except Gutenberg miscalculated the year the pilgrimage took place. No pilgrims on the roads. A misreading, a typo – who knew how it happened. From that one error a long streak of misfortune followed. A key investor died of plague while Gutenberg waited to sell his mirrors. The investor's brother asked to take his place and was refused. Gutenberg would not share the mirror formula. The brother sued and won. Penniless Gutenberg faced a prison sentence. In desperation he revealed another secret: his design for printing . . .

So it wasn't a gift to the world, as his father told it, but a byproduct of shady deeds. That was how printing began – with lies. That was the moment the noble art of literature took off, when a great fibber was backed into a corner. He put the book down. This was why people didn't read around here. Words were so problematic.

Behind Mr Urvin's chair someone had pinned a sheet of banned phrases. *Embarrassing U-turn, extraordinary scenes, crime of passion, needless to say, at the end of the day, troubled* (as in country), *unsung hero* (because who sang of heroes any more?) and *mystery surrounds*, that phrase beloved of journalists without hard facts. All the classics. Also those shorter, punchier words favoured by the *Gazette*, the *slam* and *snub* and *row*. These words were against the rules. Except there were no longer any rules in this office. The *Chronicle* was officially dead. It felt so inevitable, that death, as if it had been waiting in the wings all along. How sickening that inevitability was. That lies and injustice and aggression were the natural order. That a person couldn't do one thing in this town, not one measly thing, without someone smashing it to pieces. That everyone else just shrugged their shoulders and walked on by. As a boy who had burned down his school and abandoned his mother to visit a house of emergency women, he was aware this was rich coming from him.

He slumped at Jonquil's desk. How to improve their chances, spring their prisoners, return to better times? How to make their sick country well again? What to say and how best to say it? Making ink meet paper was not as simple as it sounded.

His tired mind wandered to a legend his mother used to tell. Of an underwater kingdom from where the dead watched the living and waited for a time they might return to be amongst them. Closing his eyes now, he saw a river with hopeful faces beneath the rushing current, gazing upward. In the long rushes on the river's banks a lurking serpent watched with darting eyes the souls beneath, hissing at the prey beyond its reach, scheming on some way to lure them forth and enact new deaths upon them. In its whitely glistening coils he knew it beneath its scaly form to be the true enemy of their land. The jaws of that flat and arrowed head would one day open wide enough to swallow both the living and the dead. Or perhaps, perhaps this was not a vision of the future but of the past and they were already swallowed in the bloated belly of the beast . . . How to escape? What words would open the serpent's stomach and deliver them screaming, spilling, newborn into light?

A noise disturbed him. Outside. Nearby. A thud too heavy to be the dogs that ran in stringy packs about the city. He must have dozed off . . . Night was at the window with its caravan of sounds and silences. No moon could be seen. He was obliged to take as written the trees and houses and faded street furnishings he knew to be there. Darkness drew strange codes before his eyes. Odd to wake and find it dark, as if the world had been plotting things in his absence. The night seemed big and unknowable. Times like this he felt there should be a night school that taught people specifically about night. It was something they didn't know enough about.

He was mustering the courage to leave and make a path for home when things took an unpleasant turn.

A knock sounded at the door.

In his head the usual troupe of restaurant musicians began to wail.

It's the police and you've got no business here . . .

Worse than that, it's the Horsemen. Won't they be happy to see you . . .

Whoever it is, they hate your guts. This paper's got no friends left . . .

Another knock. Fearing he'd be seen through the one good window he crouched beneath Jonquil's desk. He hoped if he were quiet whoever it was would leave.

'We know you're in there,' said a man's voice. 'You left the candle burning.'

Damn it. Damn and blast. Would it be too much to ask for a break from this constant crisis and peril, this fear and shame and history and condescension, this always being on the verge of losing everything? Just a few minutes where no one threatened to burst his brains or rearrange his face, that was all he asked. Once in a while. For a change. It was so tiring trying not to die all the time. One day he would croak of sheer exhaustion and wouldn't that be ironic.

Now the lock on the door began to rattle. Softly at first, as if the trade winds whispered against it. Sometimes night had its own way of speaking, it was true, but this was no wind or midnight murmur.

'Open up,' said another voice. 'We promise we won't hurt you.'

Beneath Jonquil's desk he made no movement or sound. Promises weren't what they were cracked up to be, he was starting to think.

The rattling began again, real force behind it now. The bolt was jumping and squealing in its chamber and the frame was making to run away with the hinges. He listened in terror. Was this really happening? It was as if his dream still clung to him. Some taint of nightmare had passed through the veil, trailing its horror across the waking life.

'This door won't hold much longer,' said the first voice. 'Last chance. Then we're coming in.'

'All right,' he cried. 'All right. I'm here. I'll open it.'

Say you're with the paper, whispered his backing band. *No, the Horsemen, that's safer.*

Ignoring the advice, he crawled out of his hiding spot and ransacked his pockets for the key. The voices behind the door kept on with their encouragements. They suspected he was wasting time, that he wanted his head smashed like a melon. He assured them honestly he did not, it was just his hands wouldn't stop shaking. When he thought of taking a holiday from the threats, he didn't mean only him and the other abused. Surely the abusers could do with a break too. Even in a dog eat dog world, the dogs doing the eating must get tired of the taste of dog.

At last he got the door unlocked and edged it open. Two huge shadows loomed. The spilling candlelight revealed hard faces, unfriendly faces, faces that didn't know friendly from a kick in the teeth.

'What are you doing here?' snarled one. 'This place is shut.'

These blocks of granite wore no uniform so far as he could see. Perhaps they were some new threat. It wasn't easy to keep tabs on who was trying to beat you up or shut you down these days. He didn't know what to say and could only stammer dumbly. Right then he would have said anything, pledged allegiance to anyone if he thought it would save his skin. A horrible state to be in. Wherever he went, whatever he did, there they were. It was time to admit defeat: the zombies and meatheads had won and this was game over. His lives were all used up.

'It's okay, boys,' said a girl's voice. 'I know him.'

Out of the deep, out of the darkness, his pin-up and saviour appeared. Yes, that's the one. Her. Beyond that, he didn't have the words, they were not sufficiently his. He was a poor fool born outside language. He didn't possess it as a bird possessed its song or as Joan possessed her beauty. Instead of owning absolutely, he begged, borrowed and stole. He was not normally so down on words, but faced with her image, *zip*. Again it was the problem of language as a blunt instrument. As a general observation, however, a woman was rarely more beautiful to a man than when she was calling off the gorillas about to smash his head.

'LIKE A MELON, they said. I thought it was the end of my life.'

'So this is what a newspaper's brain looks like.'

'Decent people don't say that sort of thing.'

'It's much smaller than I imagined.'

'Why are they even here?'

'I asked them to drive past. Then we saw the light on and we thought . . .' As she talked she wandered around the room examining various objects and trinkets, pausing to read the hacks' rude little signs and Post-it notes like they were placards explaining some high-brow art installation. 'Last night, my dad was at this party in Geneva, and this Hollywood producer had heard what happened to your paper . . .' Softly, needily, with no small amount of fawning, the candlelight followed her. 'The movie producer's going to post a photo of himself holding a piece of a paper saying it's bad.'

Could Ellis say this news made him feel any better? He could not.

'Why are you here?' she asked.

He shrugged, a little defensively, uncertain how much to tell her.

She smiled. Not having the greatest knowledge of girls, un-familiar with their moods and signals, he couldn't say exactly what sort of smile it was and what it meant.

'Ellis against the world,' she said.

'Something like that.'

'What happened to your window?'

'It got broken.'

'I can see that. If it wasn't broken I wouldn't have asked.'

'The Forty-four Horsemen happened to it.'

'Those shits.'

'I thought it was them again tonight.'

'Ivan and Igor are actually quite sweet.'

'I bet.' Sweet like their victims spoke highly of them. Sweet like they took their rings off first. He looked through the window at the darkened Range Rover across the street where Igor and Ivan, relieved of their immediate duties, denied their skull-crushing opportunity, sat humming lullabies or discussing crocheting or whatever filled their sweet cherub heads.

'All right, they're not sweet,' said Joan. 'But they're not my idea. My dad, you know . . . He's a big believer in brute force. Him and those Horsemen have that in common. They have lots in common. He's always badmouthing the Chinese and the Turks. And the immigrants on his sites. Pays them nothing and works them half to death – some of them *do* die, and even then he complains . . . He curses the West, says they know nothing, but insists on sending me to school there. Thinks it raises my stock. Or his. If he saw a profit margin in attacking gays he'd probably do that too.'

Drunk and disembodied screams drifted from the street. Joan examined a picture on Geffen's desk of a woman Ellis assumed was his wife. It felt wrong, this girl being here, rooting through their stuff. Partly because of who she was, and partly because of what this place was now: a museum, an archive of a struggling newspaper in the twenty-first century whose exhibits were fragile and not to be touched. She returned the picture and picked up a Dictaphone.

'*Chronicle* Exclusive,' she whined. '*Rich person has money.*'

'Please put that down.'

'Your paper wrote some shitty things about my dad.'

'I'm sorry about that.'

'He probably deserved it.'

She swapped the Dictaphone for a crumpled black tie Geffen kept in case of a function or funeral at short notice.

'The boys at my school have to wear ties like this,' she said.

That seemed irresponsible, allowing boys near her.

'Maybe don't touch that . . .'

Ignoring him, she draped it loose around her neck and walked on. He followed like some bumbling anxious servant.

'You should see this English school.' She lifted up the plastic figurine of Snoopy to which Urvin appealed in times of editorial distress. 'All these funny old laws and traditions. Assembly in Latin. Meals in this medieval oak hall. And every year, they play a game where they throw a pancake over a bar and everyone tries to get a piece and it turns into a big fight.'

'They don't give you enough food?' He had seen that happen once near Newtown, when these bread rolls fell off someone's bike.

She looked at him and smiled again. An amused or patronising smile. Maybe both. The jury was still out on what she thought of him.

'No, it's not like that.'

She gave Snoopy a wobble. The dog nodded vigorously.

'I don't think Mr Urvin likes his stuff being . . .'

'And there's lots of statues of old men with moustaches . . .'

That sounded familiar.

'And apparently the scholars are protected by the Queen, and one time they killed some random guy in the street and the Queen pardoned them because they were from the school.'

Getting away with murder? That too could happen here. A few years back a politician's pissed-up son drove his BMW into a shop front where the homeless were sleeping. Crushed a woman beneath the wheels. Cue lots of outrage and everyone agreeing it was absolutely not on and something must be done. And it was: rough sleeping was made illegal in the capital.

'Sounds nice,' Ellis said weakly.

'It's okay.' She put down the figurine and met his eyes. 'I don't plan on burning it down, if that's what you mean.'

That was not what he meant.

'What's through here?' She moved towards the back room. Geffen's tie slid from her shoulders and spooled on the floor.

'That's the tech room.' He picked up the tie as he followed. 'There's nothing really in there ...'

'Look at this!' She'd found the old proofing press and was running a hand across its monstrous sleeping sides, admiring its bulk and mass, pausing occasionally to examine some resolute meeting of parts.

'Does it work?'

'Sort of.'

'What's this weird bin?'

'A hell box,' he said, trying not to sound like he had learned it yesterday. 'For the broken type.'

'Oh.'

'Before you melt them down and remould them into new letters. It's useless now. My dad likes all this old stuff.'

'Hey,' she said. 'We should print something.'

Whoa. Hang on a minute. It was true he had been planning on doing just that, but hearing it said was a different matter. Startled, he found himself arguing against his own position, playing the sceptic.

'We shouldn't even be in here,' he said.

'I know. But we are.'

'We're not allowed.'

'That's why we should.'

Yes, he thought. Who were the police to close the paper, to tell them what to do? Yet still he feared the repercussions.

'They want you to be afraid,' said Joan, as if reading his mind. 'And you shouldn't give them the satisfaction ... That's why this country is screwed.'

He knew she was trying to be sympathetic, but that grated. Did other places have a word for this feeling? It was like a love of the hated thing, a terror of its existence and a fear of its loss. Instead of blaming the rod across the back, you resented any who spoke ill of it.

'We'd give them a reason to hit us,' he said.

'I'd say they already hit when they made the arrests.'

'One arrest.'

'Oh.' Her tone changed. 'You didn't hear? I thought you knew. They took your mother this morning.'

He sank at that. He forgot all about posture makes a gentleman and he sank. What sort of creep move was this? His mother was absolutely blameless. Not saying it was right to arrest his father but he could see how the man might rub people up wrong. His mother wasn't meek exactly, but he couldn't see how anyone could view her as a threat. They might as well arrest the goddamn parrot if they were going to arrest his mother.

'I'm sorry, Ellis.' She came over and put her hand on his arm. Contact, people. A lot of heartache, but also this. 'It stinks. And you shouldn't let them get away with it.'

In the end they settled on a headline of sorts. Joan wanted to push it further, to leave no element of doubt. He fought for a little vagueness.

'You're scared,' she said.

He preferred 'cautious'.

'You'll dilute the message,' she said.

He told her there were times when obscuring an idea made it clearer.

And when she saw the message printed it seemed she understood since she pushed her case no further.

Foolish boy, muttered the trolls in his head. *Still a child who does not understand the world.* But meanwhile the country was stiffening, whitening, sucking itself in . . . A blunt approach might stir something to life. A little madness paved the way for all new positions. It wasn't childish to think this, he felt, quite the opposite: he was refusing to follow the rules written for him. When a child, watching adults drinking wine and having fun, asked if he could have wine too and the adults told him no, this drink was just for them, the child accepted it without question, without even thinking to challenge their decision or wondering why this refusal might be the case. Well there came a time when the child no longer quietly accepted and that was when he was not a child any more. The adults might disapprove or they might raise a glass and say well done Ellis for sticking it to them.

You're making excuses for your actions.

You're nervous for what you've decided.

The trolls were not wrong. Perhaps he would soon join his parents in the cells. Perhaps he couldn't change the world or even make a dent in it, but if he failed he would like to fail in his own way. Everyone was owed that much, weren't they? This was him claiming something for himself, becoming the head honcho of his own life, gaining power over something bigger than him, something which had been roughly handling him. He'd felt this way before, as the first flames licked the textbooks in the school. Like he was aligning himself with a bigger force, a more powerful ally.

Oh yes, and we all remember how well that turned out.

The business of taking a pull from the press was a two person job, one inking while the other laid on the paper and operated the press and hung the printed sheets. A clean pair of hands and a dirty pair of hands. It fell to Joan to mix the ink about the scratchy glass and roll the blocks. Then he would pull and hang and she'd roll again. They printed a number of copies this way, interrupted only now and then by Ivan or Igor checking to see if Joan was all right.

Was she all right? More than. To see her in the candlelight, her hair tied up to stop it falling into her eyes, her smooth skin flecked with ink ... In spite of (or perhaps because of) all the bad news thrown his way, Ellis found himself unable to stop thinking what it would be like to kiss her. She'd catch him looking and would smile. *Ho ho, she didn't suspect a thing.* Or did she? Sometimes there was a flare of – how to describe it? – curiosity. A specific exciting dangerous brand of curiosity he hadn't encountered before. While he wanted to explore this, wanted it greatly, he felt a heaviness in his stomach at how serious his life would become by doing it. Of course his life was already serious in many unpalatable ways. He was referring to a different order of seriousness here – one, if possible, he knew even less about.

The printing continued. They fell into the motion and repetition of the task. A crackling and lively silence grew. He was aware of her tiniest movements, to the point he found himself wondering how to disrupt them, through blatant sabotage if need be.

'That's a few,' she said.

'Yes.'

He could hear her breathing beside him.

'Let's stop a while.'

'Okay.'

It wasn't clear what she wanted. But he hadn't got where he was (expelled, threatened, alone) playing it by the book. So he did a stupid thing. He tried to kiss her.

She pulled back.

'Hold on.'

'Of course, yes.'

'I'm not some easy—'

'No, no.'

'I don't just—'

'Right, that would be—'

'I'm not like those Newtown girls.'

'What?' Why that word out of all the words she could have chosen?

'I wouldn't even—'

'Did you say Newtown?'

Silence.

'Have you been following me?'

'What are you talking about?'

'You said Newtown.'

'I don't know what you mean.'

'You've been spying on me!'

'Oh, please,' she spat back. 'You spied on me!'

He froze.

'You think I didn't notice? With your stupid flip-flops slapping along behind me? I could hear you a mile off. Plus about a dozen different people shouted at you. You're a terrible spy.'

'That was ... Don't dodge this. You were following me, or having me followed.'

'It was a lucky guess. You look like the type who'd visit a Newtown whore.'

'I didn't visit ... Well, I did. But I didn't do anything.'

'Right. Just held hands.'

'No ...' He couldn't believe he was telling her this. He had a private rule that this information and other people would be kept forever apart. 'I tried. But I couldn't.'

That was the truth, if it must be told. He had made every effort, but his heart wasn't in it. How was this possible, a person of his evident libido? Ordinarily he was up and ready at a smile, a blush, a suggestion, a gentle breath of wind, a sudden change of traffic lights. He had heard and heeded the call of romance in the grubbiest toilet cubicles, in the deathliest library reading rooms. The merest glimpse of a beachwear poster or fitness video and the launch codes were keyed in, the warhead primed. He could scramble the jets in seconds. He was immediately at DEFCON 4. He was trigger-happy to the point of goddamn reckless. So imagine his concern in the fleshy stew of the brothel, with the equivalent of World War III breaking out, to find his trusty nuke unresponsive. After an excruciating minute or so he had to make his apologies and crawl out from between the girl's legs. A mortifying minute. Though if anything the minutes after that were worse, as they waited out the clock in silence, serenaded by the groans of Vincent through the wall.

'I thought of you and I couldn't go through with it.'

Was that a smart or dumb thing to say? Was it even true? He had thought of Joan so he *could* go through with it, but this prospect had twisted and grown grubby as he and the crooked girl fumbled. Like he was thinking of Joan in order to cheat on Joan, which was all sorts of wrong. And somewhere along the way he realised the moment had passed, and the mood, such as it had been, had soured.

'Am I supposed to be happy about that?' said Joan. 'That you visited a whorehouse and thought of me? Do me a favour, don't think about me. Remove me from your filthy mind.'

'But nothing happened.'

'No, it sounds totally innocent. And when you spent half the day stalking me, I suppose that was innocent too.'

Some of this was pretty much shouted. He tried to shush her before Ivan and Igor ran in and stomped him, but that only made her more angry. She grabbed a wrench hanging off the back of the proofing press and made to strike him with it.

'Pig!'

Oh, she was furious. A terrifying spectacle. But also, he noticed, a spectacle that was not leaving.

'I'm so tired of the men in this city,' she said, jabbing the jaw of the wrench against his chest. 'All they ever do is talk and take.'

Now she let the wrench rest. Through his T-shirt he felt the cool steel sharpening his skin.

'And you're as bad as the rest of them.'

Slowly the wrench dragged down.

'Aren't you?'

'No,' he said.

'You just like to stalk girls. Is that it?'

What questions were these? And by the way, wasn't he meant to be questioning her? He had really lost control of this interrogation.

All the time the wrench went lower.

Forget that, he wanted to shout. *I endangered my life for you.*

I'm putting my life in danger right now for you! All for you! But no words would come out.

The wrench jabbed the underside of his belly. It was a kind of agony, though it would be untrue to say he suffered.

'Well?' she said. 'Is that what you like to do?'

He shook his head. The wrench got *close*. Her colour too was high. Things unmentioned trembled in the air.

'I don't,' he told her. 'I swear.'

'Liar.' This offered without flirtation or damnation. Her voice was harsh and she was breathing heavily as though in anger or another excitement like it. Truly he did not know what to make of this girl.

She stepped back without taking her eyes off him, the wrench still levelled in accusation. She kept her eyes fixed on his. The weapon fell to the floor with a clang. Her eyes still fixed on his. Swiftly she moved towards him and kissed his lips. He smelled the privilege and parties in Geneva, he tasted it on her, and it was not the only thing but it was a thing. He felt the delicate brushwork of her fingers, the play of muscle and flesh beneath her clothes, and her body against his both warmer and more sharpening than the steel before it.

That night a bed was made on the floor of the print room. Bundles of old *Chronicle*s formed a mattress between Mr Kozlov's desk and the cranky press. Type boxes became passable pillows when draped with older thicker editions. The elements of this bed were not much, but even the cruellest cops in the city (were they not otherwise engaged in boozing and carousing and shooting the smiles off statues), even the nastiest trolls, would have agreed the arrangement had a certain charm.

The details of what happened in that bed, while engrossing, have no business in this report. Nor is it certain that, put into words, they would survive the imprisonment. But it is worth noting that when people shed their clothes they lose certain trappings and conventions. A clothed body is always human or human-like, a naked body always animal or animal-like. Only at close quarters is the full extent of a body's wildness revealed, like when a bird gets trapped inside a house. One is moved to not entirely human thinking then. One goes towards its animalness.

No more on that—

The shadows on the wall can tell the story of their rise and fall.

The drying prints around them can whisper the finer points.

The dogs and other spirits outside can recount it in their howls and whines, a clamour growing louder and more raucous, threatening to reveal them in that place they were not meant to be.

Sometimes during he would think about where he was and feel a start of fright at doing this in his father's place of work – until he remembered his parents were in prison and couldn't catch him and this would fill him with relief. Then he'd feel ashamed and regret his relief. In some sense their arrests had made space for he and Joan to do these things – a fact he hated even as he took advantage of it.

At some point, however, his anxiety faded and the rest of the world retreated and their blanket kicked loose exposing old *Chronicle*s whose ink, never of the highest quality, left dark smudges and in some cases full words transferred on shoulders, thighs and other regions. Then the bed was their device, pressing the proof on their paper-thin skin.

Later, when calmer, he found above her left shoulder a sentence in single column which struck him as the work of Mr Geffen:

> *She has visited the country*
> *where she was born many*
> *times.*

Below this, another legend. A large welt of skin, melted more than scarred, smooth beneath his fingers.

'Don't touch that,' she said.

'What is it?'

'Leave it alone.' Her body had turned brittle beneath his hand.

'It's okay. You don't have to tell me.'

'I know I don't.'

In one swift move she pulled herself up and off the bed.

'It's late,' she said, slipping on her dress. 'I should go.'

Night fell away. He had woken early and seen the tail end of dawn before, but he'd never been up late enough to see the first suggestions of light warm the earth's sleeping brain. It was stealthier than he had imagined: if he kept his eyes on it he saw nothing, but if he looked away and back he was shocked to see it closer. Children here played a game called *Statues* where the sentry turned his back and the statues shuffled forward, trying to get the sentry without being seen moving. He felt like the day, and maybe other things besides, was playing this game with him.

Considering the drying pulls from a cooler position he wondered if they had still been too forthright, if he'd let himself get turned inside out and burgled like a tourist. He wanted to believe he wasn't choosing between her and his parents, that what was good for one was good for everyone. There was a great benefit in that being true. He told himself he was doing the right thing, though he couldn't swear it was for the right reason.

Nor could he deny his parents had been eclipsed. That didn't mean thrown out of the window or under the bus – only overtaken, overwritten, by a greater force. Now he saw why the marriage of *crime* and *passion* was banned in the newspaper: it was a doubling-down on meaning. Passion was a criminal, a terrible crook – it wanted to see order smashed and chaos reign so its grotesqueness went unnoticed and the object of its fascination was lost with it in the madness. It wished to carry the matter too far, to strain all decency, *to dance on the nose* as they said round here. It pushed people towards its own intentions until like characters in a dream or novel they were no longer in control of their choices, they lost any sense of what was reasonable or appropriate.

In short he didn't know whether his act was a strong one or a weak one, only that he'd set it in ink.

But enough hand-wringing about the why and how. In the name of Ignorance or Bravery or Passion or Justice or Freedom or Getting Some or Rebellion or Answering Critics or Tearing the Wallpaper or simply Cheering Himself Up, in one name or another it was done. He didn't know exactly what it would cause or where it would lead, and he didn't mind not knowing.

It was time to make his deliveries across the city. He would tack copies to walls and lampposts. He'd leave them in piles outside the bakeries and butchers. He'd slip them through the cold gilt letterboxes of the grand houses and press them into palms in the shanties. A thin paper this week, there had been cutbacks. Right back. Down to the *Chronicle* masthead and a headline. That's all, folks. Four little words. A friend to those with short attention spans. A very modern paper. But it hit, oh yes, absolutely, it was mud in the eye.

Extra! Extra! Get your paper!

The *Chronicle* had a new edition.

THESE WORDS ARE
FORBIDDEN

WITH SEVERAL HUNDRED of these pages he stepped out. Now here was a surprise: the sun was missing. It hadn't turned up for work. Grey grey was the colour of the limitless expanse. He knew that sky. A storm was on the way.

Weather standing in for real events? How pathetic, some might say. A cloud didn't wield the knife or pull the trigger. They might say it was dishonest to talk about weather at a time like this, that the talker was avoiding a more dangerous subject. Maybe in any country, at any time, people who talk about the weather are covering up something and should be treated with suspicion.

Yet it was true people responded to their surroundings, they found encouragement in the right conditions. And statistically they *were* more likely to die here in the build-up to a storm. Something in the atmosphere. A tension felt in the gut. To do with the ions, it was said, the ratio of positive to negative. This was the time friends fell out, pets turned on their owners, old quarrels reignited. Headaches were frequent. Talking to a neighbour, one's eye was drawn to the soft unguarded centre of his neck. There were no open questions, no casual observations, no harmless noises at night. Every fire was intentional, every party ended with the police. Children seemed to be masquerading as children. At root it was a problem with reality – reality no longer felt real. Superstition surged and there were long muggy afternoons of Hail Mary and Father where art thou and normally rational people queuing hours to touch the liquid that seeped from holy bones. Nothing seemed impossible in such an environment. Violence and madness became fair considerations and that was a simple fact.

Here was another thought: was Ellis, with his *Chronicles*, cutting through this madness or another victim of it?

The early streets held few living souls. Assorted waifs and strays. A handful of drunken soldiers deep in conversation.

Can't be doing with that negativity . . .

Totally, brother, not fair on you . . .

Tell you this, my next girl's gonna be optimistic . . .

Dropping off copies at the Hotel Excelsior he found the place in disarray. Bottles and banners and balding feather boas lay strewn about the floor. Confetti sunk in cocktails half drunk. The only sounds in the city's finest hotel were the snores of the desk clerk and the cries of urgent coupling in a nearby conference room. Next to the French restaurant, his gut facing outwards to the grandness of the atrium, a dull-eyed man in shirt tails and boxer shorts urinated with the poise of a water feature. To think what this place used to be. People used to do one round in the revolving door just to say they'd visited.

On he went, leaving copies wherever it was safe to do so. As he went his mind flitted to his parents – praying that no harm had come to them, that no dimwit had taken the initiative to cause them further grief – and to Joan, that beautiful billionairess, that provoker, that scarred object of his lust. What did the scar say? It spoke of hushing and huddling, of soldiers low like animals. Of screams and whites of eyes. Of fire, the unfriendly sort of fire, and her face blank, expressionless, given up. It spoke of things like that.

At Independence Square a group of young men were building a stage. With wires and planks of wood they hurried here and there. He made sure his *Chronicle*s were out of sight.

'Come on, people,' a bossman shouted. 'Show starts at noon. Let's pick up the pace!'

Did this national holiday never end or was it something else? Hard to tell from the skeleton stage. It might have been a fairground or a gallows.

For a while he fell in behind a procession on its way to a

funeral. Just the family and the first few mourners following a white pick-up truck full of flowers, the garlands large and bright and fake. He saw no body. In front of the truck walked the wreath-bearers and in front of them the band, slightly dishevelled, perhaps come straight from a party, clutching dented horns and scratchy fiddles. At the head, three old and earnest men marched with ancient banners aloft. On these faded tapestries the usual stories of life and death, joy and misery, backhanders and redemption.

In the street where yesterday the women sang, a soldier in a balaclava tinkled the ivories of the upright piano. A girl at his side looked like the crooked mistress with the sharp teeth. Who knew – that morning everything was strange. The strangeness felt when, alone at home, you noticed a door rarely opened was ajar and the sliver of the room beyond was not as you remembered, did not answer to what you knew of it, did not seem to be that room at all but another room in another house in another person's life and the back of your neck hackled with questions of how that could be and why that other version filled you with such dread and who, if not you, opened that door.

Around him the city groaned slowly back to life, blinking, hungover, glaring with thirst. Shaking hands found this latest *Chronicle*. Groggy readers rubbed their eyes, certain they were tripping from the booze. How would they feel, how would they react?

On a billboard not a hundred yards from home, on the little strip opposite the Autolux car hire and its resident streetwalker, a workman smoothed the last wrinkles from a new poster.

I, Cornelius Dau, am deeply sorry for my actions as editor of the Chronicle *newspaper.*

A free and open press should be a positive force in society. It should promote the value of decency and the rule of law.

In these regards the Chronicle *has failed.*

It has spread panic and incited violence, and for this it has rightly been closed until further notice.

Of course apologies are not enough. I only hope that you, the people, can forgive these crimes.

RUBBISH, Ellis thought as he stomped the six flights up. Total rubbish. A grab-bag of accusation and character assassination. No person with half a brain would fall for it. They'd gone too far this time, these keepers of the peace. This bending and twisting was a clumsy, greedy way for a body to move. Like rules could mean whatever they wanted them to mean, like they were right because they said so. This showed poor thinking on their part, a lack of discernment.

Yet wasn't the accusation enough? So what if it wasn't true, since when did a thing need to be true to exist in the mind? To read it, to hear it, that was enough to give it life. After all, it was not an unthinkable act. Even he, knowing what he did, could sense his brain *trying* to believe it. His own brain, letting this false account push against his knowledge, crowding out his own opinion. It didn't replace the proper version, but it existed in the same little system, a nasty little wart on the real thing.

If that weren't bad enough, he opened the door to find Officer Fedor in his father's chair.

'Why not?' he was saying. 'Make it two sugars.'

'Ellis!'

His parents rushed forward and squeezed the life out of him. The three of them hadn't been this close since the family photograph several years ago, when in a tiny second-floor studio they posed stiffly in front of the Eiffel Tower, the Coliseum, Big Ben and other painted backdrops. There were several locations to choose from, though their city was not one of them.

Cornelius and Stella didn't notice the slight crinkle and crumple – *thank god* – as beneath his T-shirt the last few *Chronicle*s were pressed up against him.

'We were so worried.'

'Where did you go?'

Whew, they just kept squeezing. Don't misunderstand, he'd been worried about them too, and would have told them if they'd just—

'You're safe.'

'You look tired.'

'Did you sleep?'

'Did you eat?'

He hadn't eaten for about a million years. His belly rumbled like murder.

'Anyway, you're okay.'

'Are you okay?'

'You're not talking.'

'How can he? You haven't let him.'

'Hello, Ellis,' said Fedor.

'Hello.' Although Fedor was the last person in the world Ellis wished to speak to, he seemed the person most important to answer.

'How've you been?'

'Oh, I've been.'

'Had to borrow your parents. Straighten a few things out.'

'But it's all right, darling,' said Stella.

'I will take that tea, Stella,' said Fedor.

'Right.' She brushed the palms of her hands against her sides. 'Of course.' She went into the kitchen and began filling the old stove-top kettle at the sink. Cornelius stayed where he was, one hand on Ellis's shoulder.

'Did you know, Ellis,' Fedor continued, 'your mother and I used to be an item?'

'What item?'

'You don't know that phrase? Kids today, eh, Cornelius?'

Cornelius said nothing.

'I mean your mother and I used to date,' said Fedor. 'Isn't that funny?'

At first Ellis thought Fedor was messing with him, trolling *a la* Vincent. *Your mum this, your mum that.* But this wasn't the officer's agenda. From where Ellis stood he could see his mother paused over the kitchen sink.

'Maybe they didn't tell you ... Long time ago, this was. I went off to fight and your father made his move.'

Neither parent spoke. Cornelius gripped Ellis's shoulder a little more tightly than was comfortable. The parrot on his perch made no sound. Even that graceless creature recognised the situation.

Right then Ellis pictured what this Fedor went home to every night: the drab furnishings, the conspiring appliances, the drinks coasters (without question a psycho like Fedor had drinks coasters), the half-hearted pictures on the walls, the coffee table pretending to be wood, the lampshades, the wallpaper. Oh, the wallpaper. He imagined no one could get over losing his mother and that without her love he'd gone bad, that things had festered in him. This other Fedor he now saw clearly. Night after night staring at a gaudy line of ducks migrating from kitchen to living room, the lonely hunter, police-issue revolver at his side. What did the hunter dream of? What did the hunter want? Coming home from war to an empty bed, how could he not be bitter? His parents might have put it to the back of their thoughts, but not Fedor.

Of course this was only guesswork or conjecture. It might not have been true.

'I never told you about my time in the war, did I, Cornelius?' said Fedor, settling back in his seat. 'You know, you remind me of a guy in my unit ... Please, why don't you both sit?' He laughed. 'Look at me, in your house, and I'm offering you a seat!'

Ha ha. Like they were all friends again. Cornelius took an edge of sofa and Ellis followed. Neither of them joined Fedor in his laughter, it hadn't exactly been an invitation.

'Wallace, his name was. We were trailing the God's Army through the bush, maybe a day behind. Slow going. Bastards had set these little IEDs along the path. One day Wallace got unlucky. Blast took off both legs from the knees down. Most wretched sight . . . Now we were a small unit, no vehicles, very basic first aid. Strict ban on taking casualties with us. But it was heartbreaking to see Wallace like this. We were heading to a town a day north and I begged the captain to make an exception. Captain told me, "Okay, but he's your responsibility."'

In the kitchen the kettle whistled. Fedor continued.

'I patched up Wallace best I could and got him on my back. The ground was a swamp from all the rain. If I stopped for a moment I'd start sinking. And Wallace was heavy. With all my kit and him I could hardly move. But he was whispering thanks and I was relieved we hadn't left him and I kept going, all that day I carried him. The unit pulled ahead and left me stumbling through the mud . . .'

Stella came in with Fedor's cup of tea. The spoon danced on the saucer's rim. In her other hand Ellis saw a plate of oat biscuits. Though his parents always said, 'Be polite, wait for your guests to start,' when she put down those biscuits he jumped at them. *Screw this guest anyway.*

'When we hit camp that evening I was done. My back was torn up, I was covered in blood, I'd spent hours listening to Wallace moaning and crying. I couldn't do it again in the morning. He'd lost too much blood anyway, he was going to die. I was dragging a corpse around out of sentimentality.'

Fedor paused to blow delicately on his tea. Cornelius and Stella watched in silence. What were their faces saying? Ellis, wolfing biscuits, couldn't read what was written there.

'I crawled beneath the shelter to sleep, but all I could hear was Wallace near the campfire, wailing and gibbering. He wouldn't shut up. And I thought maybe he *should* die, maybe death would be a kindness . . . Our unit had another policy: if a person's wound was particularly grave we'd put them out of their misery. The old pros would cut the throat, but can you imagine me doing that? Cornelius? Stella? You know how I was as a student.'

Ellis tried to imagine the university Fedor, stooped and sad, bringing his own cutlery to the cafeteria for fear theirs was not properly washed.

'But bullets were valuable,' Fedor went on. 'To use them for pain relief you needed special dispensation. So I went to the captain's tent. He knew what I was going to ask. 'One,' he said. 'No more.' I was so grateful. When I felt that, I knew it was the right decision . . . I walked over to the fire, coming round behind Wallace. I didn't say anything. The rest of the unit were watching from the shelter. Everyone knew I was going to shoot Wallace except Wallace. But I couldn't bring myself to shoot him in the head. He had such a big, innocent face. So I took aim at his back, aiming for the heart. "Rest in peace, friend," I said, and I shot him.'

Fedor paused and looked at their faces in turn, checking what they made of his story. But he wasn't finished.

'Except Wallace didn't die. Instead he screamed and tried to crawl away. I didn't know what to do . . . I ran back to the captain's tent. 'Captain, please, I need one more bullet for this!' Captain wasn't interested. Old tight ass told me to use a knife and make it quick. I ran back to Wallace, but he saw the knife in my hand and crawled too close to the fire and just went *up*. Heat coming off him was insane. I couldn't get close enough to cut his throat.

'My instinct was to put him out, but then he might not die. So I let him burn. I tried to soothe him. 'Keep calm,' I told him. 'Stay positive.' But Wallace wouldn't keep calm and he wouldn't die. He crawled right into the shelter, flames three foot off the back of him. The shelter caught fire. The soldiers panicked and threw themselves out. Some left their packs and ammo behind. Bullets started popping in the heat. One guy got shrapnel in the chest. We had to cut his throat later. All the while Wallace was screaming. I thought he was never going to die. But someone must have left their grenades in that tent because there was a huge bang and lumps of flesh and burning god knows what. A thigh knocked a guy out cold. Only then the screaming stopped. And the camp, you've never seen anything like it . . . '

Thoughtfully, Fedor raised the cup to his lips and drank.

'That's a lovely cup of tea, Stella,' he said. 'Thank you.'

The room was still. Ellis put the biscuit in his hand back on the plate.

'I often think about that day,' Fedor said at last. 'And it occurs to me I could have treated Wallace better.'

No one had anything to add to that statement.

'What I should have done,' Fedor went on, 'was shoot him in the head as soon as I saw him on the path. Instead I tried to help him and only caused him further suffering. Do you see?'

Ellis saw how a person might move away from black and white, light and dark. When they made a transition into shades, all they had for reference was other shades, mostly dark. The shade they wore looked light by comparison. It threw the standard off. A person might do darker deeds and think them not so dark, and that in turn darkened the waters a little more. The waters grew ever darker.

'Wallace fooled me and he fooled himself,' Fedor went on. 'He wouldn't admit he was finished. And I, being naïve, encouraged him. I thought he knew what was best for him. That was cruel to both of us . . . Sometimes things must be done for people that they don't like.'

Now Ellis saw the words in the spirit they were intended. He felt the crinkling *Chronicle*s pressed up against him, burning the flesh. When he printed those copies and made that two-fingered gesture he hadn't realised quite how serious things were. Once again he had underestimated life's capacity for shittiness and peril. Part of him wished he could rewind the tape on life and snatch back in double time every copy he had left across the city. But life didn't work like that. Despite its drama it was not a drama. Despite its games it was not a game. He crossed his arms tight, praying no slip of paper could be seen, and fixed his eyes on the rug at his feet. Not so long ago the most strenuous part of his existence had been rolling himself up in that rug and bowling himself at the furniture. He missed his former life as a bowling ball. He half wished to roll up in that rug and let the world forget him.

'Lovely to reminisce,' said Fedor, returning his cup to the saucer and getting to his feet, 'but I must dash. Cornelius, you take it easy now. Leave everything to us. Don't worry yourself. Keep calm. Stay positive.'

As soon as he was safely gone Ellis started in on him.

'That scumbag. That lowlife. How can he say those things?'

Cornelius just sat there rubbing his eyes like it was his only comfort.

'You've done nothing wrong.'

The sound his father made was more than a sigh and not quite a word.

'And the billboard outside ... They can't do that. Putting words into your mouth, they have no right.'

'Ellis,' his mother began.

'We should fight to clear your name. We must refuse to ... to suffer these injustices. Right, Dad?'

'Son,' said his father. 'Please. Right now I need an inspiring monologue like I need a hole in the head.'

'You sound like you're giving up.'

'Of course I'm giving up!' He was angry but in a pathetic way, like a toddler who'd dropped his ice cream on the floor.

'The country is making you talk this way. It's made you think like a victim,' Ellis told him. 'With a push from the paper ...'

'The paper?'

He looked at Ellis with a curiosity that might less generously be called disappointment. *Who was this boy?* the look said. *How did I end up with this disobedient child, where does he get it from, can he really be mine?* It was not the first time Ellis had seen this look.

'Let's leave all talk of the paper,' he said, 'until things calm down.'

Calm down? Why should it calm down? Ellis saw how his father had changed. His movements were heavier, his outline smaller. In the hazy daylight he seemed somehow turned in on himself. The spirit within was bashed and knocked about, cracked in small yet definite ways by the humiliation and uncertainty he'd suffered. An old person after a fall, that's what he was like. He remembered his grandmother on his mother's side, when she wasn't so steady on her feet any more and starting to skim over certain details like which one was her son-in-law and what day of the week it was. She still lived in her house, but there were eyes on her now, she wasn't trusted with anything herself, and mostly she sat in her chair or lay in her bed, waiting for the inevitable. And one day, a stormy day full of thunder and lightning, a priest came to take her confession, except he wasn't actually a priest and – wait, no, that was something else.

His father had lost his nerve. His appetite for this was all gone. He'd reinterpreted Urvin's 'happiness writes white' to mean happiness was being invisible. A blank page free of troublesome text. Well, they would have to agree to disagree on that one. With his *Chronicle*s Ellis was a paid-up member of the church of the headfirst, possibly heading for destruction and damnation, yes, but he knew what he could smell in his nostrils. It stank so bad it couldn't be ignored or waited out.

'Something terrible is about to happen,' he told his parents.

'That's your overactive imagination,' Cornelius replied. 'All those films you watch. Those violent games.'

In a way his father wasn't wrong: they were drifting into fiction territory, they were being smuggled out of reality. This nasty dream machine had been there all along, underneath the cafes and football matches and theatres, waiting to grab them.

Ellis was ready to argue but was beaten to it.

'Actually,' said Stella, 'I think the boy's right.'

'Your mother doesn't mean that,' Cornelius told him.

'Don't tell me what I mean,' she said.

'I'm only saying,' Cornelius began.

'I know what you're saying,' she said. 'For a long time now we've been hearing what you're saying.'

'Darling, I don't think this is exactly—'

'Can I speak? Please? You're always talking about freedom of speech. Giving people a voice. Well, that begins at home. And I think the boy is right. We can't just bury our heads and wait for this to pass.'

'Yes,' said Ellis. 'That's why we need to—'

'Hang on,' said Cornelius, talking over him. 'You make out I'm being pig-headed . . . I'm following your advice! You said I should butt out, and now when I agree you say I'm not listening! How can I be wrong on both counts?'

'Things aren't the same as before.'

'I know that. After the two days I've just had, believe me.'

'But I don't think you see how bad it could get. I don't think a low profile is going to be enough.'

'Then we'll deal with that when the times comes.'

'No,' she said, not meanly, but bluntly. 'You always let the situation lead you by the nose. We must get out in front of this.'

'Are you talking about running? You want us to run away?'

'We should fight,' said Ellis.

This boy, his mother's smile said.

'For the last time, Ellis,' said Cornelius, 'the paper is closed. It's not up to you.'

An editor who needed no regulation, who was perfectly capable of burying the lede without assistance. Horrible as it was to say, in this moment his father was all worn out as a forceful entity.

'Maybe it is,' said Ellis.

There it was: the white edge of *Chronicle* poking out. His father wasn't the only one who'd changed. While Cornelius had been warped by cell and chain, Ellis had been shaped by special components of curve and shadow, by a night in the VIP. That girl had formed him more powerfully than any historical event.

'What do you mean?'

'Maybe I reopened the paper already.'

'What? Stella, what's he talking about?'

'Let's not get worked up. Darling, when you say reopened . . .'

'Two days in a cell and I come out to this! Damn right I'm getting worked up! I want to know what you mean, Ellis.'

'Take a look.' Ellis pulled out the last copies and threw them on the floor. This was something – a statement, a refusal to go quietly – while his father's hopelessness was nothing. This said they were alive at least.

'Keep them,' he told his parents. 'There's plenty more out in the streets.'

Then he ran. What choice did he have? His father would have murdered him if he stayed. Out the door and down the stairs, all six flights. He heard Cornelius shouting, but the old man could do nothing.

THE SOUND of drums and horns announced it. In the main square a band was going at it, bashing out a wild countdown music. There was the old drummer frantically stroking the snare, the boss man in purple velvet pawing the synth, the trio of horn players blasting out their parps and swells. The sort of music everyone thinks they're better than but no one can resist . . .

Is any of this familiar?

In front was a huge crowd, drawn by this promise of peril. The sort of promise – of imminent injury or death, of blood about to be spilled – everyone thought they were better than but no one could resist.

What was the meaning of this threat music? What sort of threat hired a band? It was a circus of sorts, but not the same as previous. History was not playing by the book in this account. It was repeating itself, but how it wanted: it had done the farce first and saved the tragedy for last.

Ellis slipped into the crowd. So many people! Packed tight tight. Smell coming off them of many bodies in close prox-imity, of beasts penned and cautious. Peanut sellers elbowed through, an odd note of festival and celebration. Faces craned forward towards a spot unseen. Edging closer he saw at last the focus: a figure kneeling on the stage, head covered with a sack, hands bound. The bulk and clothes suggested a man in middle age. Around and about young men waited, not soldiers exactly – they had guns but no proper uniforms. A dread came over him then, for he had a sneaking suspicion what came next.

He might have left then and escaped what followed. No, some executive territory of his brain had already decided otherwise and pushed him forward, as near to the front as he could get, seeking more, looking to feed that part hungry for darkness.

Two players raised enormous trumpets to the crowd and burst into a doomy warning fanfare. The pinching dread around his vitals became a vice, for now a man he knew mounted the stage and with a showman's swagger strolled across it, a megaphone and a machine gun hanging from his neck, a gleam of power in his eyes.

'One two, one two!' cried Grotz. 'How about that for an intro? Give it up for the trumpeters!'

So this was the sort of threat that hired a band. The crowd gave a cursory clap.

'Good people, fellow citizens!' Grotz doffed his goatherd hat.

Poor hat, thought Ellis. *Bet it dreamed of escaping. How embarrassed it must be, living on top of such a brain.*

'How are we doing today?'

An uncertain murmur from the crowd. It was not at this moment an easy question to answer.

'We are the Forty-four Horsemen and we are delighted to see you all. We're delighted you have chosen to join us on our journey towards a better country and a brighter future . . . Now perhaps you don't know much about our group. That's okay! Don't worry! All you need to know is we're the same as you. Ordinary people who one day thought, "You know what? We're not going to take this any more!"'

Cheers from the assembled Horsemen.

'Why should we sit here while foreigners take our jobs? Why should we watch the rich get richer and the poor sink into the dirt? Why should our taxes pay to feed and house immigrants, when we can hardly feed and house ourselves? Why should we let the lazy bureaucrats and the out-of-touch elites tells us what to do – while they rob the gravy train! Why should we let the gays and other moral degenerates destroy the values of our beautiful country? Why should we let the West corrupt our children with its short skirts and hip-hop honeys, its heavy-metal music so loud it breaks the hymen and deflowers our virgin girls? Why should we allow this, I ask you? Why?'

Applause. Amid the kneejerk stuff were one or two things it was not unreasonable to feel anxious about, little grains of truth salting the hysteria. But who knew what the crowd believed. Some were there more for the public adventure the words offered; others cared less what was said than how. By dressing up easy slurs as hard truths, by claiming to tell it like it is, Grotz had become a prophet and champion in this uncertain age. Yet in all this speechifying, no mention of the hooded figure swaying in front.

'So we took up arms and fought back,' Grotz continued. 'We said, "If not us then who?" I don't mean to be rude, but do you see this government doing it? They can't even switch on the lights! In times like this you need a strong hand or evil runs riot. Just look at how gayness spreads in countries which tolerate it.'

The crowd absorbed these lessons in security from the wolf at the gate.

'So today we're going to show you how strong we are . . . Okay, let's have them up here. Bring out the new volunteers!'

More raggly militia types filed onto the stage. White Hair was there ushering the smaller cadets, other familiar faces in support. A gum-chewing phalanx was formed which Grotz turned to admire.

'Oh yes,' he said. 'Oh wow.'

One of the younger boys Ellis recognised from school. No question, it was spotty Pavel, a howler slap bang on the forehead as was his custom. Good old Pavel, conspicuous by his abscess. So he'd ended up with the Horsemen. That was no surprise: he had the right brain architecture for this knuckle-dragging enterprise. But who was this behind Pavel? Ellis thought he recognised him too . . . Now the dread gripped tighter, for he knew that shuffle, that flabby face which claimed it was irresistible to the female sex. Yes, he knew this individual well.

Vincent stood quite still and relaxed up there behind Grotz and the hooded kneeling figure, as if it were a natural position for him. Today he wore no slogan-bearing T-shirt, just a track-suit top, the same as all the others on the stage.

Vincent, you fool! Ellis wanted to shout. *This isn't a game! Get out of there!* It shouldn't have been Vincent up there. Anyone but him. Vincent was the optimist, the great believer, the one who always told Ellis, 'It'll get better.' Or was that why he was on the stage: he had all that hope and nothing to put it in. Wherever the party was, he was ready to go. Whatever the popular song he would have sung it. In another country he might have stood up for slow food or saving the whales. But these were the stars he was born under. This was the tone, so this was what he had chosen. Whereas Ellis, always the more cautious, had chosen doubt. Doubt about the game they were being asked to play, doubt about the rules and who was making them.

'Look at these fresh young faces,' said Grotz. 'Now I ask you, if our cause is not the true one, how come we have children fighting for us? Eh? Even the innocents know this is the right side and are prepared to die for it. What more proof do you want?'

He smiled his showman's smile, as if he did not quite believe these words himself.

'Even the children, when they join the cause, become strong. Look at these faces! Eh? Look at all our faces! We are afraid of nothing!'

Ellis looked at Vincent's big sloppy face and thought, *But that's not true.* He knew for a fact Vincent was afraid of lots of things. Undercooked chicken and cold beds and the fatal kidney slap which only certified black-belts could perform. The wibbly bit of skin under Mrs Kuper's chin when she bent over to correct classwork in Geography. Also ants, cracks in pavements, forthcoming super-hero movies that might be unfaithful to the comic book source material, and the creepy dude in Space Odyssey cafe who gave kids extra minutes if they showed him their ankles. Vincent was scared of tonnes of stuff. It would be shorter to list the stuff he wasn't scared of.

He didn't know the rest of them – except Pavel, who was afraid of 7 times 7 – but now, seeing Vincent with them, he thought maybe the whole mob was afraid. Of strangers. Of difference. Of answers that weren't simple and conclusions that couldn't be leapt at but had to be schlepped towards, slowly, painfully, with lots of head-scratching and hand-wringing. Of the unknown, which was most things for these meatheads.

Grotz looked again at his recruits. His face fell.

'What's this?' he said to one of the boys. 'You are wearing yellow shorts?'

The boy could not very well deny it.

'This is a poor choice,' said Grotz. 'I am disappointed.'

The boy hung his head.

Ellis scanned the scene for other familiars, running his eyes across the faces as the compositor checks the chase before proofing, searching for the error among the type that might throw everything off. Actually that was dressing up his intentions: he was looking for you-know-who.

Sometimes, muttered the trolls in his head, *it's like you're concerned about all the wrong things.*

With a start he saw her, shifty behind the shoulder of dear sweet Ivan or Igor or another of her cuddly hoods. Obscured but definitely her. Only she seemed different. When she was in his bed of paper and ink he knew who she was, but on the other side of this crowd, no longer with him, he couldn't see her as the girl whose every inch of skin he'd read last night. He couldn't be sure she and he were close or even friends. Now her eyes met his as if he were a stranger.

'I don't know if you've heard about it,' Grotz was telling the crowd. 'The *Chronicle*?'

Ellis's attention swung back.

'It's been promoting extremism, not to mention belittling the work of our organisation. These journalists, they portray us in a very bad light ... So the police went in, questioned a few people. But what are they going to do? This is the whole problem. They're toothless under this government. If you don't enforce anything, people are going to walk all over you. So we thought we'd show them how it's done.'

Grotz stepped forward to the kneeling figure and pulled off the hood. A gagged and blinking face squinted up into the sky, then down at the crude enquiring faces of the crowd. Despite the awfulness of his position, some sarcasm still lurked in Urvin's features. Their crime reporter was not lost after all.

'We happen to have one of these *Chronicle* lowlifes right here ...'

Ellis looked again at Joan and saw the muscles in her neck taut as wires in suspension. He looked from her to Vincent on the stage, hoping for some flicker, but no. He despised him for not standing up to this, for not being stronger than this. He had never cared about him more than in that moment when he hated him.

'Take a good look at this man,' said Grotz. 'Study this face. This is the face of a man who doesn't care about this country!'

The crowd murmured in shock. It was unclear whether they were troubled by the apprehension or the allegation.

'He and his kind are the rats in our sewers, spreading disease through our city. They poison your hearts against us. They want to ruin what we could accomplish together!'

'Scumbag!' cried a woman's voice nearby.

Who said that? Desperately, Ellis looked around.

'Punish him!' she cried.

Twenty bodies or so to his left he saw a little woman bobbing up and down as if on tiptoes.

'Hanging's too good for him!' she shouted.

Ellis knew her face too. Hadn't she been much older, much paler, last time he saw her? Yes, she was the old lady from the play. What was she doing here? This was not a play. An act perhaps, a performance, but not a play. Unless they were all actors and the whole thing was a tip-top simulation of a country losing its mind. Unless there were hidden cameras like they used for those fly-on-the-wall jobs, and this one playing Grotz would win best actor for his blistering portrayal of a cretin, and they would all laugh about this some time in the VIP. *If only.*

Grotz raised a hand for silence. Leaning in, he told Urvin, 'I'm going to take the gag off now. This is the part where you make your confession.'

He jerked the cloth from the man's mouth and held the megaphone in front, his own face fatly expecting like a child who had seen chocolate in his mother's grocery bag.

'Come on,' he said, looking up towards one of the grand buildings which faced the scene. 'Let's not keep people waiting.'

Ellis followed his look. In a first-floor window a shadow watched.

'I have nothing to confess,' said Urvin.

'We all have something to confess,' said Grotz.

Urvin stared straight ahead, breathing hard. Every so often he flinched and twisted his head like a spasm. Ellis didn't remember him having a tick. No, now he saw – Urvin was trying to shoo a fly. He had no other way to get rid of it with his hands tied behind his back. He kept shaking off the fly and it kept returning, oblivious to the situation. It didn't care whose face it was on. Grotz noticed the fly was bothering Urvin and waved it away. That gesture, no more than a flick of the wrist, threw Ellis. Those dark fingers seeming to brush the journalist's cheek, as though fondly and brimming with human warmth. Why this man would bother to care for a moment. How that care could live in the same place as all those blunter and nastier elements. It made no sense and yet it happened, it was true. People did say it was the little acts of kindness that stayed with you.

'Come on, Mr Urvin,' said Grotz. 'You're a writer. Time to let those words flow.'

'Okay,' said Urvin, looking at the crowd. 'I don't have a long speech or anything. Just this . . .'

He took a breath.

'Watch out for bullshit. That's all. Just watch out for bullshit.'

Bullshit was right, thought Ellis. It was as if language itself was sick.

'Now really,' said Grotz. 'Nasty toilet talk? Negativity? You're better than that, Mr Writer. Come on, try again.'

'You're right,' said Urvin. 'I'm sorry. I'll do better.'

He squinted at the crowd, took another breath. There were a lot of possible outcomes spanning from this moment – it was almost possible to see their fine threads in the air, entangling everyone. Urvin flinched and shook his head one final time.

'I mean to say . . .'

He paused.

'Watch out for horseshit.'

'You could have just gone along with it,' said Grotz. 'You didn't have to be so difficult about it.'

He raised the AK to the back of Urvin's head.

The gun clapped.

Just one little clap. Hardly a thing at all.

The bullet entered the back of Urvin's skull and announced itself through the forehead in a bloom of carnage as the brains and blood burst out completely. A sloppy spray hit the on-lookers in front and the boys behind and nearby. Someone screamed. Urvin remained kneeling a moment, eyes open, barely a fleck of gore upon the rest of him as if he alone had survived it, before he teetered and fell to one side.

All this Ellis witnessed. *He saw it.* Yet he did nothing to stop it.

Sometimes, his trolls reminded him, *it's the way a person does nothing that's the problem.*

Okay, true, but it was not so easy to—

How to put it—

While it was happening, he was not.

In the movies there was so much build-up, the strings going hell for leather and the camera cutting close to watch the sweat running from the doomed man's brow, the bad guy squinting like maybe he will maybe he won't. Whereas this was so quick. Nothing in his life had prepared him for it. He only understood in part, the bullet in the head part, which was both too much and not enough. But probably with a hundred more facts and a lifetime arranging them still no more sense could be made. It was the why that was the problem. (That was always Peabody's thing, the why. Did he used to bang on about *that*.) Maybe for the really bad stuff there was no answer, no why. Maybe the darkness at the centre was never known.

'Did you see that?' Grotz shouted. 'Wow!'

He looked around at his troops and saw the boy with the beach shorts now dark and bloodied.

'And *that's* why we don't wear yellow shorts to a killing,' he said.

The crowd had grown skittish. Stomping and murmuring and breathing fast and slow. This crackling mood persuaded Ellis of something: they didn't like what they'd seen. Whatever ground they had shared with these Horsemen had been overstepped. There was no cheering or celebrating or cries of encouragement – even the shouting woman was silent. They were not exactly happy about the bullet in the head. Great, fantastic, except shuffling and murmuring wasn't going to cut it. Would no one fight? At this moment the whole nightmarish occasion seemed less a demonstration of strength from these thugs than a show of weakness from the people. Like Cornelius, the crowd thought they could turn the other cheek and carry on. The assumption was they must accept their fate.

And Ellis, would he fight? Urvin would have: he was always looking to flam things up, to exaggerate the predicament. But he could no longer flam things up on account of a bullet in the head. Yes, thinking about that blossoming head, maybe Ellis would give fighting a rest.

In the clenched fist of a neighbour he saw a copy of this morning's *Chronicle*. Hard to imagine only a few hours ago he had set those words ... It seemed a different him. Standing on the cusp of this moment, with the air closing in, he felt no connection to that deed beyond the fact he'd done it.

Then a horrible thought struck him: was this partly his doing? Was he in some way to blame for Urvin's death? Had his guerilla printing, his little tin-hat rebellion, pushed these thugs to this? He had thrown a stone and they had blown a man's head off. He had written a headline and they had passed a death sentence. *They* had done it – but it wasn't enough somehow to blame thugs for being thuggish. Might as well blame the fire for burning down his school. It was up to the rest of them to navigate these murderous elements.

His insides felt wrung-out, ragged. Terror and guilt contended in him. He kept thinking about Urvin trying to get the fly out of his eyes. In need of an anchor, he searched the crowd for faces he knew ... Joan deathly pale. The shouting woman gone. And Vincent, his old pal Vincent, still on the stage behind Grotz. His expression blank. Unmoving save for the slightest nod of his head. No one else would have noticed it, they'd have just seen another boy with a gun, but Ellis knew that was Vincent's nervous nod, when he was trying to tell himself things were all right.

'He upset the peace and for that he was killed,' Grotz was saying. 'We are patient people, but do not push us. When we reach breaking point we are barbarians. It's in our genes ... Really I should have cut off his head, that would have been more traditional.'

The crowd's murmuring amplified to muttering and the space between the bodies was constantly contested by small and violent demonstrations of movement, of handwringing and gathering gestures and other signalling at once obvious and unknown. Some silent rising option was gradually pushing forward. The muttering was out in the open now and Ellis could hear the voices on all sides.

Who's in charge?

Animals!

No mercy.

At least Nestor paid you to show support.

This lot shoots you if you don't.

A woman cried, *Murder!*

This was joined by other cries for *liberty*, *justice* and *TV*.

'Hey,' Grotz told the crowd. 'We're on your side here. Who do you think we're doing this for? Do you want to be overrun by foreigners and lying journalists? Or those religious nut jobs? Because they're out there, oh yes, they're out there just waiting.'

One can only imagine the shock and anguish of the crowd, gathered at this all-ages execution, to hear their friendly local murderers were at threat from terrorist elements. To discover this way of life might soon be shattered by unsavoury types. To learn that somewhere beyond this peaceful bubble of slaughter, desperate and unpleasant views fermented.

'Yes,' said Grotz. 'We are the firm hand this country needs.'

'Screw you lot!' someone shouted.

'Who said that?' Nostrils quivering, Grotz angled his AK at the crowd. 'Who's using that language in front of children?' He gestured to Vincent and the other young recruits beside Urvin's corpse.

'You can't point that gun at all of us!' shouted someone else.

'Who said it?' Grotz asked again. 'I'll count to three. We will kill all the rats.'

And then what? After they had got rid of the foreigners and the people they didn't like and the country was still not well, what then? What would they eliminate next?

'One.'

It was like school when the teacher raised a hand and started the countdown to silence or punishment except the hand was a gun and the teacher was a psycho and the only lesson here was death because this school was hell.

Not that many, the voices gabbled.

We could take them.

How?

And what then?

'Two,' said Grotz. 'I will make a hat of treacherous ears and noses.'

Creativity was not dead in this country after all. The stunted imagination found new expression as these grunts sought to abuse them one by each. Every face in the crowd was tensed to bear the weight of what pressed down upon them. A small squall momentarily pierced the heat and raised a veil of dust. Grit was tasted on the tongue.

Who said it?

Pull them out.

No one gives them up.

Them today, us tomorrow.

'Three,' said Grotz.

He aimed at random and pulled the trigger. The first few bullets were swallowed in the crowd as if of little consequence. Then a woman fell and another figure slumped close by and the crowd panicked. Some people in their proximity to one another ran in all directions without moving from the spot and Grotz raised his gun and fired further shots and would have fired more but one of his party had the inspiration to restrain him.

The crowd fled without consideration or pause.

Amid the cacophony Ellis moved low, ducking through the frayed, careering mass. Now and then bodies spilled towards the Horsemen and the thugs opened fire. The young men tireless in their brutality, heroes in a terror of their own devising. Sometimes elements of the crowd rushed forward in an effort to snatch their guns and sometimes they were successful and more often they were not. Many fell and did not get up.

What were the cops and soldiers doing in all this? Nothing. Those present were trying to look the other way. They were so weak, so unsure, they couldn't even be sure a woman getting a bullet in her head was wrong.

And the zombie President, what was he doing? Sitting in the silent Palace only yards away, sinking his teeth into the flesh of some tender fruit.

Ellis wanted to look away too, more than anything. But he had to witness and record, for the paper, for what came next. He tried to think of the real living horror in front of him as words on a page, words he would one day write. In his mind he started composing a description of the scene: the young and old crumpled in the dust, the harsh cries, his flip-flops slipping in what might have been blood, and look there, Vincent, his friend, was he running or firing? Ellis couldn't tell, he was lost in the scrum.

People fled in the direction of less open streets. The swell of feeling so caught him that he was moving, following, before he knew his mind. They ran with one brain then, and cleared some distance from the bloodshed when they turned a corner straight into a gang of soldiers twitchy and tense.

'Join us!' the frontrunners shouted to the men with guns. But they were shot at. Perhaps the gunmen wrestled with it – who knew how hard it was for them, whether thin strands of compassion existed amid their cruelty.

The other runners twisted back behind another corner and on into the rich quarter. Some ran up to the grand houses to hammer on doors or push pleas through gates and letterboxes. In vain. The houses did not open. This richest of areas was also the coldest. How beautiful Ellis had thought these central avenues, these colonial houses. People compared the place to Paris.

A convoy of military trucks rolled past. The fugitives scattered before it might stop to deal with them. Ellis quit the road in favour of a narrow and reeking alley of which the city had no shortage. He threw himself down in a shaded gutter and there he stayed, listening to the gunfire wax and wane. Other people sprinted or sneaked past or walked in false calmness with the rush of recent running still on them. He did not call out to any of these people. All the faces looked like soldiers' faces.

It had been untrue, unfair, to think the Horsemen useless. While people grumbled about electricity, money, law and order, they were looking at the bigger picture. While the hacks dismissed them as idiots, they had remained committed to hate and destruction. Quietly going about their business, never saying never, proving the doubters wrong.

Regret pooled in Ellis. Oh doctor, it was a bad case, a chronic episode. Perhaps regret was just a word these days, like how a cold in medieval times could kill a person but now was something said to get a day off school. Well, he had medieval levels of regret right now. It was so bad he wondered if a person could perish from this feeling alone. Never getting shot or stabbed, simply dying when he had absorbed a fatal amount of it, when he was lethally wretched with what he had done or failed to do. He had decided to help his school and burned it down. He had decided to help the newspaper and now Urvin was dead. Mugged repeatedly by consequence, he wondered whether he might be cursed, a universal whipping boy. If he'd tried to plant a tree he would have struck a gas pipe. If he'd released a dove, any money said it would have flown straight into the engine of a passing passenger plane.

Nearby gunshots made him jump. Please, god, he couldn't die. Okay, maybe he was useless, terrible, cursed, but what about the list? He had crossed so few things off the list. He wanted to go to a pop-up restaurant, he wanted to recycle, he wanted to wear jeans with holes he had paid for not holes he had made, he wanted to sample fine wine and declare the tasting notes delightful . . . Damn it, what reasons were these? That was the panic talking. None of this would make a shooter lower his gun, it would make him squeeze the trigger.

You are in the VIP room, he told himself. *You are in the VIP room.* Come to think of it, this gutter wasn't that different from the Chicago Pub's VIP room. *Please let him survive this and see Joan again. Please let him be a good son to his parents who were not so bad as all that and needed his help. Please let him not be always so obsessed with number one . . .*

He promised he would not try to help any further. He had learned his lesson. The lesson was that if you believed in things passionately, if you tried your absolute hardest, it was always possible to screw things up more.

Briefly, very briefly, he wondered how the Hollywood movie producer was getting on with his piece of paper saying things were bad.

Life dangled by a thread. He could only hope that it, like this account, was TO BE CONTINUED.

THAT AFTERNOON Cornelius and Stella listened as the wind-up radio spoke of *disturbances* and *unconfirmed reports*. Listened as slowly the language opened to admit *unrest*, conceding little extra details though the picture remained vague. No news was good news, they told themselves. Happiness was the blank page. But lacking hard facts was not a happy restriction. When the radio mentioned *calming shots* and *possible casualties* they put aside their optimism and set out into the streets.

Stella knew instinctively: her son was where the trouble was. Always was that sort of a child. Not so much a troublemaker as involved. Some people passed through life with a whisper, barely touching the sides, while others bumped and clunked their way through the tubes. They took existence literally, feeling every contour, and the world saw this quality in them, was amused and gratified by this display and laid out new bumps accordingly. She knew this because she was the same, aware of every bump.

And Cornelius? He was in blame-Ellis-for-everything mode. A grand and suffering pose, like the man in the myth whose son drove the sun chariot across the sky and lost control, burning the stars and parching the oceans . . .

Before he had complained about constraints. Now he thought this was how things had to be. Chains only hurt if struggled in, that seemed to be his outlook. Whereas the damn newspaper had proved a constant struggle. 'Comfort the afflicted, afflict the comfortable' – wasn't this the phrase, the purpose of the whole enterprise? Only it was no longer clear who the paper comforted and who it afflicted. Mainly it seemed to be afflicting him. So forget it. Forget shining the torch, carrying the flame. He was finished fighting and investigating, finished 'playing footsie with the big ideas' as Fedor put it. He'd take the offer of survival, of living at the lowest level. Let him be a small man with no voice. Let him never write another word if it kept them safe. Let the country sort itself out or collapse trying.

Except he knew cutting out his tongue might change nothing. Expectations of decency, faith in the system, the bottom line generally, had reached such lows even the wildest attacks enjoyed a free pass. He swallowed the humiliations and still felt everything could be taken from him. How was anyone meant to live like this, with existence and oblivion in each other's pockets? The newspaper was a minor and somewhat amateur affair, but while it existed there had been a sense, however slight, that this was a place where people made their own choices. To give it up admitted these perilous elements were too much, that the system was broken – which was exactly when a country needed a press most.

They headed for Independence Square, and they weren't alone. The city which earlier was so hungover and subdued now buzzed with rumour and confusion. Radios burbled vague terror from every window and doorway, but was anyone still listening? Five blocks from the square, cadets informed them they could go no further. *Trouble. Incident. Unrest.* They circled back and tried another route. Same words, same hard faces. Things were under control, said the faces, ignoring the gunfire behind them.

On the fringes of the forbidden zone they saw police questioning the wounded, arresting people who'd been shot. From others they heard stories of carnage. A man with his shoulder darkly seeping spoke of an execution. He drank pomegranate juice brought to him by a mute unblinking boy. With every sip, fluid seeped from the wound. Many dead, he said. He had seen the bodies. At his side the boy stood listening, upright and important in this conversation between adults.

Who had been executed? Did anyone know? 'Cornelius

Dau', said someone, which came as a nasty shock. But hearing the name 'Urvin' was worse, it couldn't be denied with the same certainty, it was far from impossible to believe. Yes, it would be Urvin, wouldn't it? He never did take any crap. Would not kowtow to anyone. That was Urvin.

Searching for Ellis where they could, they noticed how strange and desperate the city had become. Barricades blocked the entrances to Prospect Park where folk once flocked to flirt and colour their tongues on flavoured ices. On dull hooks in the markets of old town, wrinkled cow hearts and silvery goat foetuses promised believers strength or luck or protection from bad spirits. A near-blind crone hawked cobra venom. Good for vision, she said. In a covered tent behind the main post office men and women kneeled before a flame. A worship of light and dark, the same dance that gave print meaning. Ancient rituals rediscovered. A return to witchcraft and superstition. All the extremes rising, even the mythical. Never civilised, the country had regressed. Or perhaps these ways were always secretly there but now made no bones about it.

Abandoning responsibility in favour of paranoia? Madness, muttered Cornelius. The evil eye, the ill-aligned planets, the sacrifice not made? Do be sensible. It was as if people were not satisfied with their despair and wished to insult themselves further, to bury themselves deeper.

The sky deepened its grey. Scuds of cloud above the Newtown hills hinted at rain. Snatches of radio spoke of possible fatalities. Grease smoke hung in the air. After death, dinner. After that, who knew? Night was coming. A storm was gathering. And still no sign of their boy. Only fear filtering through. Fear that he was not all right, that he'd been caught by a crowd-calming bullet and taken it too literally.

In desperation they went to the press.

But others were already there.

AND THE BOY, how was he getting on in the gutter?

Not great. He had known better times. Paralysis and terror were the dominant tasting notes. It looked like this ditch was to be his home from now on because he could not, he would not, move for the life of him.

Darkness stole in early. Though day was not quite ended, the light was merging with the objects like it was closing time. Once again there was this issue of weather: it wasn't doing any killing, no heavy lifting of any sort, but it wasn't exactly helping either. Just hanging around and looking to trip people up. When there was a bad scene it played up to it. Yes, it was not unreasonable to wonder if the weather was in cahoots.

Mistaken dogs called the night to bear witness, too early and too late. Besides them and the gunshots and the occasional cry, the streets were wonderfully quiet. Hard to say how long he lay there, waiting for such a time as it was safe to move. Waiting and waiting, and the time never came.

The gunfire drew closer. He was scared then and lay still to be more like the gloom. Figures approached. He felt his death getting near.

'Over there,' said a voice. 'Someone's in that gutter. I can see their eyes.'

Shadows moved towards him. He could dash further down the alley, but if he ran they might shoot and the alley was too narrow for them to miss. Or he could stay and meet whoever owned the shadows. What to do? His options were unpalatable.

'Who are you?' someone shouted.

Could he be nobody? If he just kept quiet, would they go away?

'Are you a soldier?'

He was no longer within the life he knew but some way

outside it and he could not be sure the rules were still the same. Meaning he wasn't sure what he could say or do that would protect him from a bullet in the head and what would ensure it. They had fallen too deeply and too suddenly into the impossible for there to be any limits.

'Tell us now!'

A torch beam picked him out.

'No!' he cried. 'Don't shoot! I'm Ellis!'

They ran through the streets, he and the other hunted. Some were armed with knives and planks of wood and even one old-fashioned musket that looked as if its firing would be more deadly to the fellow who bore it. They were many times outnumbered and it was whispered that roadblocks and sentry points cordoned the area. What little cover the darkness gave them it also gave their enemies and all agreed they should hide before they ran headlong into trouble. They had a spot in mind. A rumoured safehouse.

Through the jigsaw of roofs and aerials above them a sliver of new moon tagged along. It was a friendlier body, this moon, more open to discussion. With the sun no understanding could be reached. Too close to it and you burned, too far and you froze.

At last the company came to another grubby alley where they tugged and strained at a rust-buckled door. Though Ellis said nothing aloud he was full of low feeling just then. The alley seemed no improvement on the one he had recently abandoned and the door not the least bit moved by their predicament. But the man with the musket wasn't about to die because of some lousy door. He persevered. To everyone's great relief it finally yielded and in they crept.

All was dark. There was in this place a strong and not altogether pleasant odour, of yeast or things long fermented. Something smashed. Ellis heard movement and clattering and oaths.

'Who's that?' a voice hissed.

'Who are we? Who are you?'

'We were here first. We're asking you.'

A candle was lit, revealing a huddle of scared faces already in their spot.

'Are you hiding from the soldiers?'

'No, moron, we're standing in this pitch black storeroom for fun.'

In the stillness and candlelight all parties had occasion to study each other properly. *Oh boy, was this amateur hour*, thought Ellis. It was clear not one of them was a fighter, whether by profession or disposition. Not one of them could even be mistaken for dangerous (though a number of recent law suits suggested the local police did have some talent in this field). There wasn't one face here with the proper composition for crushing skulls. What chance did this sorry bunch of musketeers have? Survival alone was a tall order.

All woe and misery then, except – amongst the new faces he saw Joan. She was sulking beautifully at the back, alone. Ivan or Igor or whoever had been accompanying her must have got lost in the carnage, but she was here with him.

Footsteps.

Heads swivelled to a second door at the other end of the room. Joan's eyes met his and widened, a finger to her lips. *Not a sound.*

A key scraped the lock.

The skulker nearest shoved a chair beneath the handle.

'Open this door, chickaboos!' said a gravelly voice. 'I hear you creeping about. Come on. Quick quick! On the double!'

Each pair of eyes in that room sought every other. They weren't sure who owned this voice or what it intended.

'What do you want?' shouted the man with the musket.

'What do I want? Oh my poor little chicks! What I want is for you to open this door right now! It's a matter of life and death!'

No one doubted it, but they were anxious it was their lives and deaths the voice was talking about.

'How do we know we can trust you?' asked the musketeer.

'Take a deep breath through your noses,' said the voice. 'Do you smell that? Are your eyes burning? That is Grade A Premium Moses Brand Grain Spirit. My spirit.'

No deep breaths were needed to catch the smell described. It was alcohol all right, bottles and jugs of the stuff, piled high in boxes around the room. A quick inspection revealed the words *PREMIUM MOSES* on the side of each container.

'You have locked yourselves in my inventory room,' the voice continued. 'Ordinarily I wouldn't mind, but I have half a dozen Horsemen out front who wish to purchase a dozen of the Grade A, and if you do not open this door I'll be forced to tell them I've run out. They will not be happy about that, these Horsemen, and will most likely want to check for themselves. Now I don't know these men personally, but they say they've just come from an execution and that it went well – that was the phrase they used. This is why I say it is a matter of life and death you open this door right now.'

The musketeer's gun shook in his grip like it was pulling one way in its decision and he the other. Was this a trick? Did the voice talking belong to the protector or the threat?

'Sounds like Moses to me,' said one.

'Yes,' said another. 'I say we open it.'

With grumbles of doom and 'don't say I didn't warn you', the old musketeer caved.

The door opened to reveal a person of serious flamboyance, cigarette in hand, dressing gown of paisley-patterned silk about his paunchy frame. Chasms of deep amusement or cynicism scored his face, in the cleft of the chin, in the middle of the brow, at the upturned corners of the mouth which waited in readiness for drinking, smoking, wit. The room gave an audible sigh – it was indeed the legendary club owner and irrigator known as Moses.

'At last,' he said. 'Thought we were going to die of thirst out here.'

He slippered past and selected several boxes of his stinking brew.

'Give it a minute after I leave,' he said. 'No lights, no sound.'

Moses was alone in the darkened bar when they emerged. He sat at the counter with a glass in front of him and a fresh cigarette coiling smoke.

'Welcome!' he cried, as if they were old friends and not fugitives who'd hidden in his storeroom for fear of execution.

Some folk went forward to shake his hand and discover news of the curfews and killings. Joan and Ellis hung back and took in the sights of this most famous and celebrated institution, the Chicago Pub:

A long room of tattered upholstery and general shabbiness.

An array of primitive phalluses behind the bar.

An ambience that had inspired someone to write *MORE OF A* above the *TOILET* sign.

A sense that any recreational pursuit within these walls would end in blood, sweat, tears, or other bodily fluids, to the delight of all parties.

A generally low expectation for humanity which infused the place with dread and warmth in equal measure.

A thick drape across every window, but not so thick that headlights of passing jeeps did not sometimes slip in, reminding them of the perils of the night outside.

'This is tense,' Ellis whispered to Joan.

'Yes,' she whispered back.

'Shall we kiss again?'

'No.'

No? He wanted to remind her of what they were saying and doing this time last night. Beyond the kisses, whole oceans. Girls were the only thing stranger than war, he thought.

At the bar the mood of their fellow fugitives had lifted as Moses, splashing liquor into a row of chipped and cloudy glasses, regaled them.

'The other day I caught this guy trying to steal the sign off the front of the premises. Caught him yanking at it with a crowbar, right in the act. "What do you think you're doing?" I said. "That's my sign." He turns to me and you know what he says? "You shouldn't leave it here. Someone like me will steal it."'

This Moses had the attitude of one who carried on regardless. Unfazed, whatever the circumstances. He would have probably spoken the same way to Horsemen or cops and done it with such nonchalance they too would have laughed and forgiven him. In this way he was perfectly suited to the times. There were always one or two who got away with outright blasphemy while others were killed for a look.

'Yes,' he went on. 'Every five years or so this country shits its head through its ass and that time is once again upon us. Yes yes! The season of murder and miracles.' His eyes fell on Ellis and Joan at the back. 'Come forward, little chicks!' he shouted. 'We'll wait this curfew out with a drink, shall we? Don't be shy. A touch of the creature will cure you of that.'

'Moses, this booze is awful,' someone muttered.

'Everyone's a critic,' said Moses. His cragged face betrayed no offence. He seemed incapable of registering any emotion purely. *How could you say such a thing? Poor me. More fool you. Anyway of course it's awful.*

'I can't feel my hands,' said someone else.

'Everyone says that too,' said Moses.

'Is there petrol in this?' said a third.

'One more word,' Moses told them, 'and you'll all be out. I don't care if they shoot you. You're terrible customers.' It was not clear if he was joking.

Ellis, who'd already clocked the large wall of photographs behind the bar titled *The Stupid and the Banned*, had his own fears of being chucked out. Moses might recognise him at any minute. It wasn't hard to find the mugs in question. There he was in his oversized hand-me-down jacket, a little nervous, a little confused, as per usual. Of the two of them he was slightly closer to the camera. The flash (that damn flash!) had bleached out his features. He looked like a scared ghost, a spooked spook. And there was Vincent at his side, grinning his big sloppy grin, one hand on his friend's shoulder like this is the dream team baby. They thought they were just about to storm the VIP and pop the Kristal and bone manifold bitches till the break of dawn. Vincent looked so happy. They looked so young. It was perhaps the only photo in existence of the Fabulous Bonzo Brothers. In another universe those same boys got everything they wanted and ignored the haters and drifted into no bad currents and came to no harm. Yes, he could see that other version of the story, where they were living, he didn't know, just living majestically elsewhere. And why shouldn't that other version be the case? Why shouldn't it be their turn for a change? Why, in the great cast of sinkers and swimmers, did they always have to be stones?

'Health!' cried Moses, shoving into Ellis's hand a large glass whose contents suggested anything but. He raised his own glass and knocked it back in one and motioned for the boy to do likewise.

Could Moses be trusted, with his constant leer, with his soft belly spilling from the folds of his gown? Joan was not deliberating. She took the glass offered and downed the alcohol in one. Her eyes misted a bit and she did the back of the arm wipe across the mouth like maybe she didn't want it lingering on the lips but no terrible reaction, no big deal. So Ellis did the same. Took the drink and knocked it back and *what the hell was this?* At once the harsh spirits fugged the sinuses and squinted the eyes to the point of tears. The taste was indeed like petrol and no relation of any grain he knew. Down his throat it burned a trail of fire that might never be undone.

'Strong wine,' he managed to say.

'Between you and me,' Moses whispered, 'I do add a dash of white spirit. Petrol's too expensive.'

Ellis fumbled for a seat on a tall uncomfortable stool, wishing for one of those blood transfusions Western rock stars so enjoy. Joan watched him like he was some sort of cripple. Next to his gasping person she appeared absolutely fine. He supposed he must have been given a stronger dose or something.

He put his head in his hands and rested both on the bar, hoping for the nausea to pass, pleading with his body to produce a little moisture for his ruined mouth. Why was all the water behind his eyes when it needed to be in his throat? Alcohol was a most impractical beverage.

In the background Moses continued his pronouncements.

'"Your ladyship," I said, "I don't care about a little STD *per se*, but I promised my cock to science and I feel like I've let those fellows down."'

People laughed. Even in these circumstances when they were hiding from death, they chuckled at Moses mouthing off. This is one thing to make clear, that although these were hard times and people's lives were often what Ellis would have called a one star rating, there was a persistent undertone no misery had yet managed to erase. In restaurants not boarded up one might see people dancing after hours. The posters of missing persons were brightly painted. State-sponsored holidays provoked celebrations and talk of the future. They told their best jokes at funerals. Their eyes were trained to sieve the tiny specks of better from the present. Joy would be too strong a word, too hokey a suggestion – let's say they had made themselves comfortable amid the gloom.

Those who didn't appreciate their mentality might shrug at Moses, but he was the full expression of that national type: jaunty as hell, with a knowingness too, well aware of the sadness that trailed every plume of mirth.

*

A door opened and the bar fell silent. Someone entered the room and with heavy feet and deep breaths moved amongst them. Ellis, recovering in his slumped position, had visions of Grotz and his white-haired berserker walking through, choosing the next victim eeny meeny mo.

Words were whispered. The voice of Moses spoke. 'All right, everyone, listen up ...'

A dog in the street would have recognised the iron in that voice now. Ellis lifted his head. Moses stood taller than before and no longer laughing. Beside him a slight and goggling fellow tried to catch his breath. He'd run all the way from something bad.

'Huey here's been on a reccy,' Moses announced. 'The cordons are still up in every direction so we'll stay put tonight. Huey will go out again before dawn and update us.'

Gasping Huey pulled Moses close and told more.

'Other things he saw on his travels,' Moses told the room. 'A number of dead, little fighting. It's all soldiers or police out there now ...'

The messenger looked straight at Ellis as if he knew him. Again he poured whispers into the ear of Moses, all the while with those goggling eyes on Ellis.

'He says he got high up in an old office and looked out past the cordon. Some sort of incident at the *Chronicle* ... Says he saw fire.'

Ellis was up and on his feet. 'What about my parents? Did you see them?'

'I was far off,' said Huey, his voice soft and hoarse. 'I couldn't make out nobody clear.'

Heartache wracked him. Guilt stole over once more. His parents had warned him so many times about overstepping the bounds. They'd tried to protect him but he hadn't listened. They had fed him, clothed and schooled him, and he'd repaid this how? By inciting violence, taking up with unscrupulous characters, running away, making brassy statements for which they would suffer. *By generally being a dick.* Not being a dick was something he was specifically trying to work on, yet here they were, the meter still running. Again he thought of Urvin. Of the fly on his face, hopeful for the moisture in his eyes. Of the hole which the bullet left behind. Urvin had died for what? However much it seemed that standing up and throwing it back was the answer, it could not be worth that. He had failed Urvin and he had failed them. Was everyone this short-sighted or only him? All anger was forgotten. All frustration forgiven. He saw his parents with new fragility: the idea of them could shatter. And now when they were in trouble he couldn't help them – he was stuck in a bar drinking liquor.

'I've got to go back,' he said. 'I've got to see if they're all right.'

Moses accepted these declarations with the patience of someone long in the hospitality industry.

'We'll go in the morning,' he said.

'No,' said Ellis. 'Morning might be too late. I have to go right now.' His tone must have been firm, for he felt the eyes in the room reassessing him.

Moses sighed. 'So impatient,' he said to the room. 'Isn't youth awful?'

Ellis recognised the foolishness of his decision. He didn't want to go either, but there was no choice.

'If Huey here can't get through,' Moses added, 'you've got no chance.'

'I don't care.'

'Okay,' said Moses – and that was that, Ellis thought, expecting the publican to return unruffled to his carousing. 'Okay . . . I'll take you.'

'You? How?'

'I'll drive you out.'

'Will that work?'

'No idea,' said Moses, pouring two large glasses of grain spirit. 'But stupidity loves company.'

One glass was presented to a thankful Huey, the other left on the bar.

'I'll go too,' said Joan.

Why should she, who'd hardly said a word to Ellis since he got here, who seemed embarrassed by his presence or her actions previous, want to go with him? Now she was looking at him with something close to interest or respect.

'I'm not running coach parties here,' said Moses.

'And I'm not a tourist,' she said. 'I'm going with him.'

Later, Ellis thought, when there was more time, he would sit down and make sense of the female mind. He understood so little about girls, especially the ones with scars they guarded like treasure.

'Ah!' cried Moses. 'Let it never be said this bar is not a place of romance! All right, so be it.'

With his free hand he lifted the brimming liquor glass from the counter and turned towards the boy.

'I'm actually fine for drink,' said Ellis.

Before he realised Moses's plans, the barman had thrown the noxious liquid in his face and was leading him, impaired and stumbling, apprehensive and adhesive, out to his waiting car. At this time it was not clear why the man had treated him in this manner and Ellis was full of misgiving.

'You'll have to go in the back,' he said to Joan. 'Loverboy will sit up front with me.'

Ellis was lowered into the passenger seat of an old and roomy vehicle – American, he guessed. Its noises were those of an animal unhappy it had been disturbed.

Wiping his eyes, recovering a little of his sight, he watched in the rear view mirror as Moses raised the back seat to reveal a hidden compartment and lifted out two cases of his Grade A Premium.

'Get in,' Moses said to Joan, motioning to the hideaway. They stared at each other a moment and it was uncertain whether Joan would agree to it. She was not known for her meekness, he was not known for his honesty. It seemed they had reached an impasse. Eventually, however, her eyes lowered and she did as directed.

He shut her in and put the booze cases on top, then settled himself in the driver's seat and touched a tangle of coloured charms dangling from the mirror.

'Keep your eyes shut,' he said.

'But why—'

'Don't ask. Don't think. And whatever happens don't say anything. I mean it, both of you. Not a word.'

The following scene takes place entirely in darkness. Put yourself behind Ellis's trembling eyelids, hear the sounds and threats he heard, fear what he feared. Wonder, how he did, if this Moses could be trusted. He had put his life in the hands of a stranger, one whose reputation was dubious at best – a clubber, a boozer, a moonshine bootlegger, a man not known to tell the truth about anything, a man who wore his dressing gown all day long. Truly, Ellis thought, he must care a lot about his poor fragile parents. And it was not just care, not just love, that pushed him on: now he had knowledge of how bad the world could be.

'This is a terrible idea,' Moses muttered as he drove. 'And before you say anything, I know it was my idea. My idea stinks.'

They had gone half a mile or so when Ellis felt the car pull to a stop. His immediate reaction was to look and discover the cause but some kind spirit restrained him. From the front a light shone in, revealing the colour of his inside skin to the eyes behind. He heard Moses winding down his window and voices approaching.

'Hey, it's Moses! You crazy bastard, what are you doing out tonight?'

Preserved fish and overchewed gum on the breath of the man leaning in.

'Don't you know this whole area is on lockdown?'

'Good evening, gents. And god bless our beautiful nation.'

'Yeah, yeah. What are you doing, Moses?'

'I'm on an errand, gentlemen. Regrettable timing, I know, but I can't delay it.'

'What errand? Who's he?' The light shone on Ellis again.

'He's my errand,' said Moses. 'This little maggot broke into my bar this afternoon, drank near a gallon of my best booze and puked on my penises.'

The interrogators snorted. 'Your what?'

'My collection of phalluses. You know, fertility symbols and such.'

'Oh.'

Ellis could feel them looking into the car where he slumped, sticky and still.

'You should let us deal with him,' one of them said.

'That's booze out of our bellies,' said the other.

'I appreciate the offer, gentlemen, and god knows the little shit deserves it . . .'

Was this the moment Moses turned them in? It would be so easy. Behind his comatose expression Ellis was in turmoil, listening with all his brain for what Moses said next.

'. . . but you see, this runt's mother is the hottest piece of widow ass in the city.'

'Yeah?'

'Gentlemen, she has a bumper of charisma, a bosom of extreme panache. The woman is too much.'

'That so?'

'No joke. I want to deliver him personally. You see my thinking? "Madam, I saved your darling son from the riots." "Oh thank you, kind sir. Here are the keys to the monster truck." You follow me? I've got it all planned out. It's going to be a wonderful evening.'

The sentries laughed, but the laughter fell quickly into silence. Something cold and hard prodded Ellis in the shoulder. He didn't need eyes to recognise the barrel of a rifle.

'That right, boy?' said Fishbreath. 'You got a Mother I Like To Fuck?'

Ellis made no answer. He saw the fire they wished to pull him into.

The rifle prodded again, in the ribs and sharp. He nearly flinched.

'He's out for the count,' he heard Moses say.

'Yes,' said Fishbreath. 'Almost too much out for the count.'

Another prod, harder still. Suspicion was growing among the company. The vow of silence he'd sworn no longer seemed sufficient. What to do when silence was not enough but words were surely dangerous? Moses was right, if he tried to speak he'd give himself away or say too much. All roads led to his undoing. Once again he was back in a nasty movie, a straight-to-video slasher. Could he not star in a nicer, classier feature for once? Something with soft indie mumblings and a ukulele soundtrack, that would be the ticket.

The fourth prod was more of a thump, delivered with what must have been the rifle butt. No one could sleep through such a hit. But still he did not move, still he did not know what to do.

'Go easy with him, gents,' said Moses.

'Shut up, Moses,' said Fishbreath, no friendliness in his voice now.

This isn't right, Ellis was thinking. Surely they wouldn't. He was just a kid.

Oh, now you're just a kid, crowed the voices in his head. *That's not what you were saying before.*

He was hit again, the rifle brought down on his skull with force enough to rattle the jaw. This was it. They would kill him unless he showed some sign of life. If he showed too much life they might also kill him. A delicate situation. So he threw himself between silence and words, between nothing and something, into gibberish.

'Oncorauge dobate,' he mumbled. 'Rice aver ness.'

From which dismal corner of his brain he pulled this non-sense he could not say, but it seemed to work, for the sentries laughed and mocked his voice and did not strike him again.

'Yeah, he's pretty gone, isn't he?' said Fishbreath.

'Wipeout,' his colleague agreed.

A pause.

'One last thing, Moses . . . You mind if we search the car?'

Another pause.

'Of course not,' said Moses.

Round the car the footsteps went. Beams of light fell at different angles on Ellis's eyelids. Moses made no sound. The sentries scratched at the undercarriage of the car. Why didn't they wave the travellers through? It seemed they were look-ing for something specific and wouldn't let the car pass until they found it. The boot was opened and closed. Light shone in through a side window. Words were spoken between them.

The footsteps returned. Fishbreath at the window once more.

'Think we might have found something, Moses.'

'We're concerned by this back seat, Moses,' said his colleague.

'Oh yes?' Moses spoke slow and careful.

'Not carrying anything you shouldn't be, are you?'

'Oh no, gents. And endanger my life? I love myself too much for that.'

Every molecule of air had left the car. In this cage on wheels they sat softly stewing. Ellis pictured Joan curled up in the dark, her fine bones folded in on each other, trying not to breathe as she listened to her fate being discussed. He wondered if he should say something else or if that would be all their geese cooked. Before he could decide the first sentry spoke again.

'So you don't know anything about the grain spirit on the back seat?'

'The grain . . .' Ellis could hear the relief in Moses's voice.

'Yeah, two cases.'

'No. No, I don't know anything about that.'

'Thought not. We'll take it off your hands then. Might be

contraband, you see, and we've got a long night ahead of us. What do you think?'

'I think you can never be too careful, gentlemen,' said Moses. 'I think you should get medals for vigilance.'

One of the sentries opened the back door and lifted the booze off the seat. His hands must have been inches from Joan's face.

'Just do me one favour?' Moses added. 'Leave a bottle for me and my lady friend, would you? I need to get that widow *impartial*.'

The sentries laughed.

'Go on then, Moses. Have a drink for us.'

A bottle was chucked onto the back seat, which gave a muffled cry of shock.

'Eh?' said Fishbreath.

'I didn't say anything,' said his colleague.

'God bless our beloved nation!' Moses shouted.

'Okay,' said Fishbreath. He slapped the roof of the car. 'Bon voyage.'

They were through.

IN THE FOOTAGE it is possible to make out a great pyre of books and papers piled up in the street. Though the light is poor and the resolution poorer, the Chronicle *office signage can be glimpsed behind. Fresh-faced police officers drag material out of the premises. This material, since confirmed: old editions and scribbled reporters' notebooks and blank broadside sheets, dictionaries and thesauruses and books on media law and grammatical style. Every combustible scrap of the paper's history is stacked and made ready. Other officers lug case after case of weighty lead type to a waiting van. The whole scene is agog with parasitic activity. A large beast has fallen in the forest and the earwigs and centipedes have come forth to feast.*

An officer puts a match to the pyre. In seconds it is flames.

The video does not show Cornelius and Stella watching from the shadows. It does not describe how Cornelius felt: as if a part of him was on that fire, each curling Chronicle *a record of his time on earth, a memory of a character or story he had added to in some way. It does not tell those things, but perhaps it suggests that certain stories are fading from the world.*

Fire claws the sky and in its brightness draws the night. The officers stand and observe, their tasks completed, a mood of reverence amongst them. More worshippers of the flame, not for its light so much as its powers of purification. Their faces, watching the evil newspapers burn, are handsome with hope.

A comment beneath the video reads simply: 'Where they burn books.'

THEY HEADED FOR the crime scene first. *If it bleeds it leads*, the late Mr Urvin liked to say, and the *Chronicle* was bleeding all right, the *Chronicle* was wounded severely. The last embers of the fire were still smouldering when Moses dropped them off, promising to return at dawn. With a 'Be safe, little chicks!' he was gone.

They could see no people. No police either, and one could not say the place felt more dangerous for their absence.

It was a sort of date, Ellis supposed. The two of them alone with a softly crackling fire and quiet conversation – except the fire was his father's books and papers, the quietness from fear of being heard, their thoughts of death and peril. Like the scientist's cat-in-a-box, his parents were between two states, in both states, living and dead. This was the real problem with life at present: no one knew which side of the divide anyone was on or if there would be time later to say more, to air the feelings beneath the skin. It was exhausting thinking every moment might be the end of a world.

So yes, a sort of late night date, but no sexy business. Night was now officially the time to worry. In the dark they admitted weakness. Death was the only thing touching them, making overtures, at this time. Could they survive? Ellis didn't know. Ask his brain for a solution and it would flourish a list of what was already known or just repeat *I am thinking, I am thinking*. He wondered how his father would have phrased it, not being one to count the nails in the coffin or to mention coffins full stop, but better at pegging words just so. Or how his mother might have put it, not being one to shy away from a blunt comment, but sharper with her perceptions.

*

'Ellis? Thank god!'

For hours Cornelius and Stella had been going in circles between home, office and barricades, not knowing where else to look. Now the two of them nearly squeezed the life out of Ellis again. This time it was his mother who made the crinkling sound. She had a sheaf of paper clutched to her chest.

'Never do that again.'

'Are you crazy?'

'I'm—' Ellis began, but his parents were in full flow.

'Your father and I were worried sick.'

'I mean sure you're all right this time but—'

'Are you all right? What happened to your face?'

'My god, yes, stay still, let me see.'

'I'm fine,' he said.

'Who did this?'

'Who?'

They noticed his companion. His mother extended a hand.

'Stella.'

'Joan. Pleased to meet you.' This with a properness Ellis hadn't seen in her. That expensive English education wasn't wasted after all. She also raised a hand to Cornelius, who nodded briskly.

'Ellis, you didn't tell me you knew any girls,' his mother said.

Christ. That happy reunion was short-lived.

No need to fish out the key for the door, the lock was already smashed in. They lit a couple of candles and took stock.

'Looks like someone's made a bed here,' said Cornelius, examining the old *Chronicle*s stacked beside the press.

Low-key, Ellis and Joan exchanged a look.

'That's weird,' said Ellis.

At first an autopsy of the office seemed all they were going to do, but whether it was Urvin's death or the carnage in the square or the papers destroyed or the fear they'd lost him too, his parents were primed for something. He'd seen the same look in his fellow citizens as they tried to swarm the shooting

Horsemen, a look of 'if you were going to die you might as well do it right'. Now he understood why his mother had the paper. Publish and be damned. People must be told. While they still had heads on their shoulders they were going to fight. Yes, now he saw: this was not going to stop because they stopped. Unchecked, things would only get worse. His mistake was not the shouting out but that he hadn't shouted loud enough. Prodding at the problem only made it angrier – they had to run it through. These scoundrels had mismanaged the world and it must be taken from them. From them and anyone who under the banner of *public need* or *the good of the people* upheld these terrors and controls. Who claimed to make people safer by the liberties they removed and the information they restricted. Who preached hate and division and distrust. Who seemed to particularly infest their little nation, though in fact every country had such types, only the names changed. How had these scumbags, so undeserving of words, come to control their meaning? How had it reached the point where it was illegal to write about slaughter but not to commit it? The arrogance of it! The abuse!

Who were they to save a country? Nobody, but they were going to try. On this they were all in agreement for once. The unsaid was absolutely at a toxic level. Unwritten articles were killing them. There came a point when things couldn't be ignored any more, when they must be given the right words.

Censorship.
Murder.
Revolution.

They say the stronger the story, the easier it is to write – that night the makeshift *Chronicle* team found the opposite was true. How could they lift the telling? How could they provoke, inspire, crack? To detail every gory truth was callous, to not was manipulative. Either way they too were tyrants who told people how to feel and what to do. What gave them that right, what made them the true authors? And would their words, after all that, be read the right way? Meaning and intention were easy guards to slip. One had to watch these words, one had to keep a close eye. Cornelius and Stella had a good wrestle on this stuff – Ellis thought it was like old times for a minute – except his father wasn't looking to tower over her and she wasn't looking to David-and-Goliath him with sharp little stones, so that was one nice thing.

Another problem. The police had taken all the type. They were out of sorts. They had the paper and the press which the officers couldn't move and a few remaining tubes of ink the cops hadn't bothered to destroy, but no means to impress their message. The newspaper was trashed. For a moment they were flummoxed.

Wait—

Amid the devastation: the hell box, safely overlooked in its corner of shame. That dark and greasy bucket of lettertype, those dirty and broken sorts no good to anyone. Only the most adventurous vandal would have thought to look inside, and they'd scarcely have been excited by what they saw – its contents seemed vandalised already. To the untrained eye this collection didn't look like letters at all but pieces of chipped coal or grubby stones of the kind found in vacant city lots. But the night printers knew better. In that bucket was type that might yet be their friends. Thousands of pieces, a universe of meaning waiting to be formed. These crooked letters might still shoot straight.

It wasn't an easy piece to set. The type took an age to sort and many substitute characters were required. Apologies should be made for the punctuation or lack of it – there was simply no time to get the grease off those fiddly commas and full stops. A poor show ... Look where they had ended up, each time more compromised than the last, the technology now at its lowest point. They were running on waste materials. What was next, smoke signals? They were the cartoon coyote flying along in his homemade plane losing piece by piece until there was nothing left. Only a matter of time before they realised there was no plane underneath them. That was the moment they stopped travelling and fell into a canyon a mile deep.

They took it in turns to ink the chases and pull the proofs and hang them from any raised surface or lay them flat across untrodden floor space when hanging was not possible. The final proofs were cracked and patchwork and riddled with mistakes. But the typos in this particular issue were no accident. They were made with the editor's full consent. They sought a higher meaning, through error if need be. Whether people would see it and rise to it, this was the issue now.

Shortly before dawn, with some three or four hundred copies printed, the printing faltered. Every last smear of ink was finished. The tubes lay about exhausted, curled like wicked witches' feet. They would have to pray it was enough.

It was often said that print is dead. Those who said it no doubt knew better than them, but they hoped these naysayers were wrong. For by this act of printing they had handcuffed themselves to the same fate. If no one read them, no one would save them. If print were dead then so were they.

Earlier Ellis had thought the problem with their lives was not knowing how close anyone was to oblivion. But looking at the four of them there he saw this constant leering threat was a part of knowing, it sharpened love and all the rest. It said, *I demand to know your feelings on this woman, this man, this girl – quickly now, and don't even think about bullshitting me, you'll only be bullshitting yourself.* Death was a revealing, even enlivening, presence. To be fought against tooth and nail, absolutely, yet not without its merits. How about that? He looked into the eyes of death and saw love. Things here were never content with one way of telling and had to be both a blessing and curse.

*

The new day broke but remained gloomy. The sky was low and planning something when Moses returned. His arrival came as a shock to Cornelius. Ellis had been so busy setting and printing he'd forgotten to mention this arrangement, and some negotiation was required between publican and editor. Embattled, bedraggled, drained, suspicious, Cornelius at first refused to hand over their batch of *Chronicle*s. But Ellis knew Moses wouldn't betray them. He vouched for the silk nightgown and the granite smile. They were weak and needed all the help they could get. Soon the others would come for them. It might be they would not live to see or do more.

Y3STERDAY this newspaper lost a colleague & friend he was not a terrorist or enemy of this country yet he was killed as 1

perhaps you know him or others like him who lost their lives or liberty because they did not do as others wanted or were simply in the wrong place wrong time

please dont think we are here to give you answers we R just people same as you we do not presume to tell you how 2 think but consider these questions

should a person who never opposed freedom be shot to protect it

will those who did it stop there

is any of this any of what is happening truly what you want

we are not the answer only the question it !s up to you 2 decide
only you must decide right now
or others will decide for you

A TOUR OF this fair city . . .

Rioting in the petrol queues. Crowds rushing the central bank to ransack what they could. Patients fleeing the hospital, drips and all, some pushed along in their beds. Men handing out guns at the bus terminus. Reports of a lion roaming the Boulevard of National Unity and a family of warthogs on the run – the panicking zookeepers had opened the cages before they fled. Armed civilians going door to door, flushing undesirables out of their neighbourhoods. The Minister of the Interior killed in an ambush, entrepreneurs laying out his body in a hut and charging for admittance (at least *they* knew what they wanted). Soldiers deserting their positions at the roadblocks. Young men with guns firing on other young men with guns, all crying, 'Long Live the Revolution!' The presidential Mercedes stopped and searched. Inside, only the driver. On the calf-skin leather seats no ruler sat.

In the *Chronicle* bunker they had to make do with the radio bulletins, ever more desperately insisting everything was fine, that people remember their glorious nation and stay calm. But the state's ability to deceive had left it and at some point it realised. The radio went silent.

That's when they heard shots and cries. That's when, tired as they were, they piled what they could against the door, the odd angles of busted chairs and tables not fed to the fire, the shelves torn brackets and all from the wall.

Something was coming for them. It had woken furious and faceless, lashing out at anything in its reach, but in time it had picked up their scent, it knew the cause of its anger and stalked the streets in search, drawing ever closer to the press. As the country tore apart they saw clearly this thing or spirit that pursued them. Death was its name and it wanted the final word.

In war some manners are weirdly preserved. If one side wears enemy colours to gain a tactical advantage, the deception should be revealed before a bullet is fired. Soldiers who have come to a house to kill consider it polite to knock first. Little social rules and stubs of decency remain.

Now they heard the knocking at the door. They huddled together at the far end of the room while Cornelius tried to comfort them. Some comfort, he shook more than the rest of them. He was trying to be braver than he knew how to be.

The knocking was swapped for thumping and kicking. Still the door held. The attackers outside consulted and regrouped; they tried Plan B. A brick smashed through the one good window, showering the room in glass.

Really? Again with the bricks?

The stowaways heard jubilant voices and coarse entreaties and spied the carnival colours of Grotz and his violent clowns, setting to work on the window with their rifle butts. One got the distinct impression they were trying to communicate something. The way they demolished the property with unnecessary savagery. The way they drew fingers across their necks and pointed at the cowering inhabitants. Yes, something was definitely being expressed . . .

Soon the cracked pane gave way and they came sharking in, casually observing, stepping over the devastation they and others like them had inflicted. A psychopath's dozen, more or less the usual bunch. Ellis noticed Grotz was not wearing his white hat.

'Wow!' said this top goon, looking around. 'So this is *Chronicle* HQ! This is where the magic happens, uh? So exciting to be here. But I think it's our turn to make the news.'

'And you will be it,' said White Hair, staring at Cornelius. 'We will question mark your head and punctuate your face.'

'You see that?' said Grotz. 'Word play.'

Now the top goon issued instructions. To a small soldier in

an oversized blazer: 'Take all the paper and sling it.' To a boy
with a freshly wounded cheek: 'Smash every letter of type in
this place. Use the axe.'

The boy in the blazer grabbed the remaining sheaves of
paper and ran to the window and threw them as far as he could.
They carried a while, as though about to float away with lives
of their own, before they sank into the dirt. The boy climbed
out and ran after, kicking at them, stomping in delight as a
child plays in a puddle. In the back room the other was heard
bringing the axe down

> vigorously and repeatedly
>> scoring the soft lead type
> bruising it beyond recognition
>> s m a s h i n g   i t   t o   s m i t h e r e e n s

'Whatever you're going to do . . .'

Cornelius stopped. Someone else was stepping through
the hole where the window had been, stooping slightly out of
habit. Fedor approached at his own pace, unrushed, the wise
chief inspecting the scene.

'I suppose the latest article was someone else's fault?' he
asked. 'A break-in? An error? A slip of the hand?'

'No.' Cornelius got slowly to his feet. 'That was me.'

'It was us.' Stella, Joan and Ellis were up beside him.

'Look.' White Hair sashayed up to Joan. 'My favourite. The
real *Murder She Wrote*.'

'It was a mistake,' Fedor continued. 'Criminals running loose,
disorder wherever you look . . . For what? You don't even know
what you want. When the dust clears, people will look at each
other and see nothing in common. What will they do then?'

'That's up to them,' said Cornelius.

'Ha!' cried White Hair. 'This man is getting brave!'

The axe fell
> chopping type

'You're speaking for the people now, Cornelius?' Fedor stood directly in front, one hand on Geffen's desk. 'Very good of you, but you give them too much credit. The people are infants, grasping at whatever rattle is waved in front of them.'

'We know what we don't want,' said Stella.

Fedor's mouth darted to a smile and away, lizard-like.

'You're upset about Urvin. Regrettable, I know.'

'Oh yes, Urvin,' said Grotz. 'Nice guy.'

'You killed him!' Ellis shouted.

'That's unfair,' said Grotz. 'I shot him in the head and he did not live.'

This was how they did it, thought Ellis. This was how they wore you down. This was exactly the sort of rotten phrase that needed cutting out. Murder was murder was murder. With this constant obscuring, this phony and dodging language, they created the grey areas where this rot could breed.

'His problem was he was very negative,' said White Hair. 'Next time he will keep his words to himself.'

'And the others?' said Cornelius. 'Did they all deserve it?'

'Unfortunately yes,' said Grotz. 'You cannot make an omelette without shooting *someone*. Though believe me, bloodshed was the last thing in the world we wanted.'

'The last thing in the world,' said White Hair.

'It hasn't been easy for anyone,' said Grotz. 'I lost my best hat in that riot.'

'Riot?' said Cornelius. 'It was a massacre.'

'Once again,' said Fedor, 'you're talking about things you know nothing about. You see an unpleasant event and want power and progress to take the blame. You think because you know one piece of information you understand the situation. They were desperate and dangerous people. In that state you have no loyalty.'

'They did nothing wrong.'

'Their treason was anticipated,' Fedor replied. 'Please, Cornelius, stop. You're a civilian and a coward. You think too highly of peace and worry too much about violence, as all cowards do. These men here . . .'

'We would kill for our country,' said White Hair.

'We would die for our country,' said another.

'We would kill for our country,' said White Hair again.

'But you,' Fedor went on, 'you'd rather kill a country than a person. *That's* crazy.'

Stella shook her head.

'How can you, surrounded by guns and cut-throats, take the high ground?' she asked.

'A dirty time requires dirty men,' Fedor replied. He glanced at Grotz and his gang. 'No offence,' he said.

'None taken,' said Grotz.

The axe

       fell again,   juddering

                      teeth   in skulls.

White Hair was staring at Joan.

'Is he, like, your boyfriend?' he asked, gesturing to Ellis.

Joan made no answer.

'My heart is breaking into little pieces,' White Hair said to Grotz. 'Little pieces of painful glass.'

'I know,' said Grotz. 'These people are very rude.'

The aggressors edged closer. Fedor and Grotz stood a little way in front, bureaucrat and killer side by side. How strange they should be companions, that the one should be associated with the other. Or perhaps it wasn't so strange. They both pursued the same impossible idea, that elusive 'beautiful thing', and would do anything to realise it.

The Horsemen fanned out in a semicircle. Herders, hunters, trappers. Stella looked from one to the other, turning briskly. But they were too quick. Two goons grabbed her arms and dragged her struggling to the wall.

'Don't touch her!' Ellis cried, running at them.

Over his dead body were these cretins going to lay a fing—

A punch floored him. A knee was pressed into the side of his head, pinning him there, setting his face towards the violence unfolding. White Hair made a shimmying move towards Joan and wrapped his arms around her. She cried out and tried to break free but he held fast.

'Do stop struggling,' he said. 'You are threatening to become truly magical.'

Cornelius tried one final appeal. 'Fedor,' he said, 'whatever you think of me, you must see we are not the real enemy in this fight.'

'You talk so much about fighting,' said Fedor, brushing back his hair and rolling up his shirtsleeves. 'Yet you are so far from it. It's time to bring you closer.'

Recognising his cue, Grotz stepped forward.

'Hope you don't mind,' he told Cornelius, 'but I'm going to use a knife. Out of respect for Mr you know, Urvin. Getting shot in the head was his thing, a thing we did together. I don't want to cheapen that.'

'What a beautiful gesture,' said White Hair.

'It's just how I am,' said Grotz.

Ellis thought it was a shame Grotz and Dr Peabody had never met. They'd have got on famously. Whereas he, he felt he had met Grotz plenty. If death would spare him any more of Grotz it might not be such a hardship.

From a sheath on his belt the Horseman pulled a blade that could have carved a cow in two. A machete for hacking and disjointing. He advanced, knife raised, smiling his lazy smile. Only his flaring nostrils announced his intent. Cornelius, eyes on the blade, edged away behind the desks.

Ellis watched helplessly. In the corner of his vision he saw his mother struggling and Joan being slow-danced by the white-haired brute. He couldn't move. He could do nothing to help them. If he were to die here and now, what would happen to them? No, he thought. He could not die. What he was saying should not be said.

The knifeman lunged, testing. Cornelius leaped back just quick enough.

Again the two men circled, locked in this silent contest. None of the Horsemen tried to intervene, Grotz was enjoying it too much to be interrupted. He was happy to stalk his prey and take his time with it. The psychology of the victim was clearly part of the sport, for his smile widened when Cornelius in panic did something unexpected, and when Cornelius's behaviour was predictable he sought to shake things up by showing the whites of his eyes and stomping his feet as if about to rush at him. Then he'd laugh and look at his victim almost with affection, so great was his relish of the fear he inspired.

Cornelius, backing away, scoured the room for something to use as a weapon. He snatched at a paperweight on Urvin's desk. Grotz grinned and quickened his movements and drew close, swinging again. But Cornelius sidestepped the attempt and with the glass weight caught him hard on the jaw. Grotz, momentarily stunned, tried sluggishly to raise the blade again but his target was too close for him to wield it so he made a grab for Cornelius who darted out of his reach. But the move only evaded capture a moment – Fedor now grabbed Cornelius by the neck.

'Leave him to me,' he said.

'I thought we were friends!' Grotz shouted, clutching his jaw.

'I've got it,' said Fedor.

Yes, thought Ellis, if anyone was going to kill his old man it would be Fedor. They went way back.

But Cornelius was not done fighting yet. Thrashing out, he caught Fedor with an elbow and swivelled to get him in a lock of his own. In the thicket of arms each man struggled for a grip on the other, trying to gain the advantage. At some point in the tussle Fedor got a hand free and pulled a knife. But the arm attached to the hand was not free – Cornelius held it as firm as he could, resisting – and Fedor could only force the blade closer, increment by increment, to the tender temples, the soft and crucial eyes.

'No!' Stella screamed.

Closer and closer came the blade. Cornelius, seeing he had to act, kneed Fedor in the groin. In the split second this bought he angled his head sideways and bit hard at the hand with the knife. Fedor cried out and dropped the weapon. A small victory, though in general the editor was flagging. One foolish lunge and Fedor had him in a chokehold. A forearm pushed against the narrow of his throat.

The taste of defeat rose up in Ellis, as if all the poisonous words of the last few weeks were in his gut, seeping their toxins, disagreeing with him. They were all so very tired, so very unwell. He saw his father slowing down. Was he trying to absorb these attacks just long enough to get his strength back, to let Fedor exhaust himself? Bad idea. His attacker didn't tire. Sensing Cornelius weaken, Fedor found new strength and squeezed harder. Ellis could only watch his father slowly drain of life while Fedor with his free hand fished for the blade. All four of them were pinned, floored, finished. At the side of his vision he saw White Hair on top of Joan, wrestling with her jeans, eager for what came next.

'Stop,' Ellis whispered. 'Please.'

'When you say "stop",' said the boy pinning his head with a knee, 'what exactly do you mean?'

His vision was blurring.

Why was this boy doing this? Was there a why?

He tried to picture the young man's face, he tried to see him as a boy like himself, like Vincent. Vincent crushing his skull. Vincent watching it happen. Vincent leaning over Joan. Vincent doing nothing to stop it. They were all Vincent, every face.

'Do you want to kill me?' he whispered. Dumb as it sounded, he hoped he could appeal to him on some human level.

His attacker thought about it.

'Okay,' he said.

The floorboards bowed beneath. That was his head being pressed into the boards. On the other side of the room, White Hair was still wrestling with Joan's clothes. In her eyes Ellis saw nothing, nothing at all. His mother he couldn't see for all the goons. In the corner Fedor had his father choked half to death. Ellis thought again of that officer's house, the lousy wallpaper he undoubtedly possessed.

The good news was the struggle was over.

The bad news was they would soon die because of it.

    Something sweet about giving up.

    No breath, no weight, no form.

He felt so ... what was the word?

    At least

        at least he had that one moment

    with her

        that one moment

    with them all

        on the same page

  but look now

    death in the corners

        darkening everything

and still

      no

        god damn

            light

    the world

    the word

    blacked out

He █████████

  tried to ████

    now this other one stood over ███████

      both looking down

    like ██████ angels

Then a strange thing. The two grunts disappeared from his dwindling vision. His head stopped being crushed into the floor. And the gunshots, they might have been before or after, he couldn't rightly say.

The next face he saw over him belonged to a soldier he didn't recognise. The man wore no tracksuit or pointy white hat. Stella's face appeared alongside.

'Ellis, can you hear me? Are you OK?'

'Ellis?' Joan was at his side too. She knelt and stroked his face. In her concern she was radiant.

He managed a croak. Slowly the world was returning. Air was filtering back into the lungs. His arms ached madly. With great delicacy he extracted his head from the floorboards. *Ah, the neck was even worse. Many regions reporting damages.* He moved weakly, useless as a tortoise on its back. He had to get to his feet and see what was going on.

His mother and the soldier helped him up.

There was his father, scuffed and bloodied, a great purplish welt coming up on one eye, but alive. They had all survived! *Please let him not be dreaming or on the other side of death.* No, his body hurt too much to be dead. It must be over, nothing else could explain it. It was beyond his comprehension, it exceeded the limits of his experience: they were free at last! Breathing deeper, he fancied he could smell freedom in the air itself, infusing every one of them with its sharp potential.

But the mess it had made . . .

Grotz and two of his men lay dead. White Hair sat up against a wall, bleeding from a hole in his throat that did not look mendable. Four other Horsemen slouched under guard. Fedor was nowhere to be seen.

The new soldiers massed about the press, alert, attentive, their uniforms crisp and correct, their guns new and slick. These were not civilians who had picked up arms this morning.

A man who appeared to be their leader approached.

'Mr Dau?'

Cornelius found his voice.

'Yes?'

'As the captain of this regiment, I want to thank you for your help.'

'What regiment?'

'You and your family should go home. Let us finish up here.'

'We can rest later,' said Cornelius. 'First we need to tell the world about this. The violent acts, the casual slaughter, how those murderers brought it upon themselves . . . I can give a full report.'

'Absolutely,' said the captain, 'I'd like to hear it. But later. When we establish control we'll have plenty of time for that, god willing.'

'God willing?' Cornelius echoed dumbly.

'Go home now,' said the captain. 'Get some rest.'

Outside the sky was bruised to blackness. Faint darts of rain struck the paving stones and were swallowed. Beyond, the streets were in uproar. The fighting was in its final moments and utter confusion reigned: reports of gunfire from the centre suggested some were still butchering each other, while here the battle was over and soldiers exchanged cigarettes with their enemies. Others slumped dead or dying. Civilians pushed through the melee with wounds or weapons of their own or searched desperately for loved ones. Some way off a disreputable publican raised an arm in greeting. Ellis and Joan lifted their arms in reply.

Directly in front two soldiers dragged a prisoner towards a jeep. His head hung low. He stumbled. Fedor's hair had fallen forward to reveal the beginning of a bald patch.

'Hey!' Stella called to the soldiers.

The soldiers stopped and looked at her.

'You won't shoot him, will you?'

The soldiers looked at one another, confused.

'Please,' she said, 'try him in a court of law.'

'Sure,' said the first. 'We'll make sure he gets a fair trial.'

'Then we'll shoot him,' said the other.

They laughed and led Fedor away.

Peals of thunder. Rain growing heavier. Overhead some large bird circled, native or escaped. With his mother supporting, Ellis moved slowly forward. All the times he'd tried to shrug her off were forgotten – in this moment he was unspeakably grateful.

As they stood bracing themselves, a miracle occurred.

The lights came back on.

Every streetlamp as far as the eye could see, blazing in the speckled gloom. In the press and the houses too, bulbs burning bright and true. Power at last! Beautiful, electric light! In that moment every citizen there felt the twinge of worship, the fervour of those ancient civilizations that presented the sun with bleeding hearts or tried to catch it in nets and nooses, that sang hymns to the god who appeared at dawn or threw chariots and horses into the sea in case that fiery deity, travelling the length of the heavens each day, had worn his out.

Music started. Real music, not the love-your-country radio crap. It sang, it carried. Dogs cocked their ears towards it. Soon the Internet and phone lines would be back up and they would be a country in the world again. A small, insignificant country, but in the world all the same. The news would spread. People in foreign lands would talk of their problems over coffee shop counters; at dinner parties they'd mention *massacre* and wring their hands. *A troubled state. A teething nation. A beautiful ancient place full of modern ruins. One could only hope the worst was behind them* . . . Wasn't that odd? To think of people in other countries discussing their problems, predicting their habits and behaviour like they were populations of foxes or pigeons.

Ellis saw the city clearly: the ruined buildings and dusty streets, the bullet holes and peeling propaganda, the vendors who even now nosed out of their premises motioning for passers-by to snag an empty bargain. Spray-painted on a wall he read *YOUNG HAVE COURAGE 2 FIGHT* and knew, without knowing what the vision meant, these words would soon be erased. Light filled the distant windows and spires downtown, yet the mountains and storm clouds behind remained dark, darker even than before. For the shadows had also deepened with the illumination, as if the beams contained both states, dark and light, and shone them equally and without bias.

Scattered around was a sea of paper, the sheets which the young soldier had thrown out. Some of it crumpled and muddied by jackboots, some of it purest white. And all unmarked by print or words of any kind. Again Ellis thought of Urvin, he heard the words of the dead man calling forward.

Happiness writes white.

He wanted to believe this was it, that the pages needed no alteration, no words, because the struggle was over, the lights back on, the tyrants defeated. There was just one small problem, one nagging doubt . . . He wasn't sure there ever came a time when nothing more needed to be said, when words ceased to be important. A white page in this world was a sign of something forbidden or not yet spoken. Each sheet at his feet was a war waiting to be fought; he had only to look up to see a hundred stories crying out to be written.

So don't look up, whispered his backing band.

Someone cranked the music and people began to dance. Not all – some were still weeping or searching or wounded – only those who had survived unscathed. They twirled and shook and called for it to be cranked louder. An open bottle did the rounds. With a ragged cry a rouged-up woman stormed into the centre of the dance, hitching her skirt and stomping her heels. Others joined the swirl and the party spread across the street, trampling the last white sheets.

He wanted to save them. The sheets of paper, that is. He wanted to rush out and push away the revellers and gather what he could before it was too late. It drove him crazy seeing all those sheets ruined. But he was so tired and sore and bashed about he could only watch as the people danced. He didn't know if they were dancing to forget the chaos or celebrate it or if they thought they were free now or what. He was getting a little sick of this freedom stuff, truth be told: it felt like another idea people threw themselves at without consideration.

Time to go home. Sleep, he knew, would not be possible. Not yet. First he must write his own account. An account of events as they had unfolded, to be added to all the other accounts, the great churn of stories changing and proliferating minute by minute: the grainy videos, the arrowed and circled photographs, the trembling testimonies and convenient explanations, the hearsays and official fictions. Some would contest his account, saying they had heard no mention of a newspaper at the eleventh hour or a fight to the death. They might dispute that the Daus had saved the day. The trolls and Peabody types, or some larger body, might say, 'But this isn't true, is it?' They might point out coincidences and exaggerations that suggested the story was false. They might offer contrasting accounts that said Grotz died some hours earlier in fighting on the other side of town, or that he was still alive – or even accounts that placed one Ellis Dau among the young bucks on the stage of execution. All of which he would deny fiercely, giving the old two-fingered salute wherever necessary, and saying he knew what he knew, that his version alone was the truth. Whatever mistakes he might have made in the past, whatever events he wished had happened differently or not at all, he stood by the acts now described. Yet even as he was saying these things he would know it wouldn't make a difference. 'Everyone wishes they were stronger,' they'd tell him. 'You're not the only one. People cannot bear very much reality at the best of times.'

Here were the headlines that could not be contested. Here was what remained of the news. They were alive, in so far as they were not dead. They were free, in so far as they were not in gaol. They had hope, and whether it was true or false was not a distinction hope bothered to make. They had each other, which was all that could be known or trusted in the universe.

Were they happy? That was too strong a word, too hokey a suggestion, but there were specks of better to be sifted and sieved ... Were they beaten? No, Ellis didn't think so. The lights were once more flashing on the routers. There was always more to say, more to tell. More to challenge. More to not accept. He was still a small body against the rest, too small to do it alone, but with Joan and his parents big shadows could be conjured on the walls. If only, if only there were some way they could be safe too ... It seemed a great cosmic error that silently swallowing all manner of crap was considered best practice for an untroubled life. He refused to accept it, even if he were only a small body against the rest.

And what was the rest?

Bunk and slander, rumour and conjecture, error and misinformation, unknowns and unmentionables. It was the flower and the hand that plucked, it was the spider in the storeroom and the fly in the condemned man's eyes, it was ten thousand years of this and it would be ten thousand more. It was the dance, the endless dance which in its glee and mayhem trampled all else underfoot. It was the wild revellers who turned and turned, and the others with their eyes glued to the ground as if nothing could hurt them so long as they did not look up. It was the grey grey sky, the watchful soldiers beneath, and always waiting, always present, the blank page.

Acknowledgements

I am extremely grateful to the following:
Anya von Bremzen for her suggestions and Soviet contacts
David Trilling, Anna Lelik, and all the journalists at *kloop.kg*
Etienne and Alya, my tenement hosts
Mick Clayton, letterpress compositor at the St Bride Foundation, Fleet Street
The peerless agenting talents of Sue Armstrong
My fantastic editor Sophie Buchan, and all the W and Enners
My mother, for her brilliance and support
Laura, as always.